THE BATTLE OF EDEN SPRINGS

Note for Librarians: A cataloguing record for this book is available from Library
and Archives Canada at www.collectionscanada.ca/amicus/index-e.html

Printed in Victoria, BC, Canada.

ISBN: 978-1-4251-5575-9

*We at Trafford believe that it is the responsibility of us all, as both individuals
and corporations, to make choices that are environmentally and socially sound.
You, in turn, are supporting this responsible conduct each time you purchase a
Trafford book, or make use of our publishing services. To find out how you are
helping, please visit www.trafford.com/responsiblepublishing.html*

*Our mission is to efficiently provide the world's finest, most comprehensive
book publishing service, enabling every author to experience success.
To find out how to publish your book, your way, and have it available
worldwide, visit us online at www.trafford.com/10510*

Trafford PUBLISHING™ www.trafford.com

North America & international
toll-free: 1 888 232 4444 (USA & Canada)
phone: 250 383 6864 ♦ fax: 250 383 6804 ♦ email: info@trafford.com

The United Kingdom & Europe
phone: +44 (0)1865 722 113 ♦ local rate: 0845 230 9601
facsimile: +44 (0)1865 722 868 ♦ email: info.uk@trafford.com

10 9 8 7 6 5 4

This book is dedicated with love to
Phyllis for enthusiastic encouragement,
Jim, Jr. for steadfast support,
Mary Beth for tireless efforts to spin straw into gold.

Acknowledgment

With particular thanks to Mary Beth for many long hours spent critiquing, editing, and suggesting improvements to the draft for this book. Her literary talents and creativity helped to transform an engineer's factual presentation into a much more colorful and imaginative tale, and for this I am most grateful.

Edward L Housman, Attorney At Law
Compton Building, Suite 1
615 Fourth Street Eden Springs, West Virginia
Phone 1893

1952

	M	T	W	T	F	S	Su		M	T	W	T	F	S	Su
Jan		1	2	3	4	5	6	Feb					1	2	3
	7	8	9	10	11	12	13		4	5	6	7	8	9	10
	14	15	16	17	18	19	20		11	12	13	14	15	16	17
	21	22	23	24	25	26	27		18	19	20	21	22	23	24
	28	29	30	31					25	26	27	28	29		
Mar					1	2		Apr		1	2	3	4	5	6
	3	4	5	6	7	8	9		7	8	9	10	11	12	13
	10	11	12	13	14	15	16		14	15	16	17	18	19	20
	17	18	19	20	21	22	23		21	22	23	24	25	26	27
	24	25	26	27	28	29	30		28	29	30				
	31														
May				1	2	3	4	Jun							1
	5	6	7	8	9	10	11		2	3	4	5	6	7	8
	12	13	14	15	16	17	18		9	10	11	12	13	14	15
	19	20	21	22	23	24	25		16	17	18	19	20	21	22
	26	27	28	29	30	31			23	24	25	26	27	28	29
									30						

Jul		*1*	*2*	*3*	*4*	**5**	**6**
	7	8	9	10	11	12	13
	14	15	16	17	18	19	20
	21	22	23	24	25	26	27
	28	29	30	31			

Aug					*1*	**2**	**3**
	4	5	6	7	8	9	10
	11	12	13	14	15	16	17
	18	19	20	21	22	23	24
	25	26	27	28	29	30	31

Sep	1	2	3	4	5	6	7
	8	9	10	11	12	13	14
	15	16	17	18	19	20	21
	22	23	24	25	26	27	28
	29	30					

Oct			1	2	3	4	5
	6	7	8	9	10	11	12
	13	14	15	16	17	18	19
	20	21	22	23	24	25	26
	27	28	29	30	31		

Nov					1	2	
	3	4	5	6	7	8	9
	10	11	12	13	14	15	16
	17	18	19	20	21	22	23
	24	25	26	27	28	29	30

Dec	1	2	3	4	5	6	7
	8	9	10	11	12	13	14
	15	16	17	18	19	20	21
	22	23	24	25	26	27	28
	29	30	31				

Contents

Prologue

"WATCH THE mule on that slope, boys! There's patches of ice under the snow," Eleazar called out in his deep voice, breaking the stillness of the winter day. After a pause to catch his breath, he added, "We don't want Nell to break a leg, and have to put her down out here."

His four sons worked in pairs to locate the battle victims lying frozen on the ground in contorted positions, and carry them across the field to the wagon.

"Set them up there in the back quickly now, so we can haul this load off, and come back to get the rest of them out of the snow. Going to take us about four trips to cart them all away. It's warming up and it'll thaw out before long. We need to finish this job before sundown, if we're to stay ahead of the foxes and the buzzards."

As soon as a half dozen bodies were piled on the wagon, the two oldest sons drove the mule carefully down the slope and off across the field in the direction of Chimney Rock. Within the hour, they were back with an empty wagon, and the men continued their work. The sun was getting low in the southwest sky by the time the last of twenty-two lifeless soldiers in blue and gray uniforms had been placed in the wagon. The sloping hillside, which had earlier seemed more like Armageddon than Eden, now lay empty and still, covered by a white winter blanket.

"You boys have done well today," Eleazar commended his sons. "But we've more to do before we lose the sunlight. Let's follow the wagon back toward Chestnut Ridge, and finish the Lord's work, so we can get home."

By the time the sun had dipped to rest on the southwest horizon behind them, the five men had arrived at the base of Chestnut Ridge, and moved the last of the corpses into its final resting place.

"Only two things left for us to do," Eleazar intoned. "First we'll offer up a prayer for these dead soldiers." Eleazar's voice grew louder and deeper, as though speaking from the pulpit of a country church, "Lord, we commend these poor boys, Reb and Yank alike, to You. Forgive their manifold sins, and receive their souls into Your eternal kingdom. And preserve their mortal remains here, away from those who sent them off to die in battle, until the resurrection to come. Amen."

"Boys, you know what to do now," Eleazar commanded. "First, move Nell and the wagon back a piece."

While the youngest boy drove the mule and wagon away, the three older sons worked together with experienced hands at the face of the cliff, completing their appointed tasks. "We're finished, Pa," the oldest called out, as they walked back toward the wagon. "It's ready for you."

Eleazar came forward holding a match to perform the final act, and then retreated quickly to stand with the four boys. Less than a minute later, everything was over, and the quiet of winter returned to the valley again. "We're done now. We gave them the best resting place we could, and now we can go home and get the chill from our bones by the fire."

It was a cold, rough ride for father and sons back across the frozen field in the wind blown wagon to the home-place on the knoll. Snow was falling again by the time the young men took the mule back to the barn.

Their father went directly to the house and walked back to the bedroom where his infant son lay sleeping. Lifting young Gideon from the crib, Eleazar held him in his arms close to his body and whispered, "Our fields have now been cleared of the desecration of their war. Preserve this land in peace when I'm gone."

Life returned to normal for the Buchanan family, as winter passed and the new green growth of spring healed the scars of battle left on the valley. The Confederacy yielded grudgingly to the strength of the Union, and three years later, Lee surrendered at Appomattox.

After the war's end, Eleazar and his older sons lived out their lives in peace, and their role on the battlefield that cold winter day remained a family secret carried with them to their graves. Only Gideon remained of the five sons, left behind to carry out the charge given to him in the cradle by his father.

Chapter 1

"I HAD A pretty good idea of what we were going to have for dinner again tonight," Doug commented between bites, looking across the oval kitchen table toward his father. "We must eat more pinto beans than any family in West Virginia."

"That's a mighty big claim, son," Ed laughed. "I don't think we have 'em more than six days a week, and I'm sure there must be others who also enjoy them on Sunday. But since you seem to want to try something different, maybe tomorrow we can change the menu to feature black eyed peas.

"You know, the Lord works in mysterious ways. Maybe He provides us with beans, just like He provided manna to Moses and the Israelites wandering in the wilderness. And they lived on that stuff for forty years. I believe the scriptures say it tasted like wafers, made with honey."

"I think I'll order the manna tomorrow," Doug replied. "It must have tasted a lot like vanilla wafers or graham crackers, and right now either of them sounds like a nice change from these things."

"Well, if we're as blessed as the Israelites, we'll only have to eat 'em for thirty-nine more years," Ed laughed, leaning back in his chair, enjoying his own humor

Meals had become much simpler for the Housman men in the four years since Louise had died in Charleston following a prolonged illness. In the period following their move to the small town of Eden Springs, Ed and Doug had learned to prepare a number of simple dishes, but often resorted to meals that required little more effort than a quick purchase at the grocery store to be warmed on the stove. When pressed for time, there was always the reliable loaf of bread and jar of peanut butter on the shelf. Mealtime routines were just a minor part of the changes in their lives that soon followed.

The relocation to Eden Springs had been driven by the opportunity for Ed to purchase the law practice of a retired friend, John Crawford, and his desire to make a new start away from the red brick bungalow and well manicured yard filled with memories of Louise. "Every brick and board in this house shows her touch," Ed had once commented. But leaving behind the home where they had set up housekeeping after the wedding in 1934, the only home Doug had ever known, was not without sadness.

Life following the move was different for both of them. The familiar old city neighborhood in Charleston and established circle of friends had been replaced by a small town environment and new acquaintances. The move had required Ed to put in long hours in order to get his arms around Crawford's law practice, and Doug to work hard trying to make new friends within the small community, and at nearby Tyler High School.

Ed had made the transition the more easily of the two. Capable and self-confident in his work, and projecting a friendly and helpful personality, he had been quick to win over people in the community. The busy daily schedule helped to take his mind off the sadness and depression he had coped with following Louise's death. "I don't know how we got along before you came to town," one of the elderly Patterson sisters once commented, after Ed had driven them to the grocery store for their weekly purchases.

Doug had taken longer to adjust following the move. Possibly it was because of an inherent shyness, or an adolescent lack of self-confidence, compounded by being somewhat small for his age. But his determination to win acceptance had paid off, and after a year of school activities and sports, he was well liked by most of his classmates in the tenth grade. Making new friends among the boys had not been difficult, but winning popularity with the girls had proven to be much more challenging.

"You remember Mother told us we could never get along without a woman in the house," Doug commented as he cleared the table and began washing the dishes in the sink. "And she was usually right." His mother had been gone long enough that both could speak of her without feeling the crushing sadness of the years immediately following her death.

"You think that one of us needs to get married and bring home a woman to cook and clean? I bet there are a lot of pretty girls in your class at school, and maybe one of them would have you if you asked. Around here, there are girls who are ready to marry and settle down at sixteen."

"I can think of two in my class that would suit me fine," Doug observed, as he dried the dishes and stacked them in the cupboard. "Either Vickie Vicelli or Janice Gilmore. But there are a couple of major problems: every boy in the tenth grade class has a crush on them, and neither of them would have me on a bet. I'm afraid it's all up to you."

"I believe you may be selling yourself a little short, and you're certainly putting a lot of pressure on a forty-four year-old small town lawyer. But I perform some of my best work under pressure, and I'll see what I can do. Maybe I'll run a classified ad in the Madison County Post: 'Ageing lawyer with teenage son seeks matrimony with beautiful, wealthy lady who like to cook and clean.' Maybe an eligible woman who looks like Lana Turner and cooks like Betty Crocker will come to town for a vacation at Eden Springs Resort."

"Right, Dad. Eden Springs attracts all the beautiful young actresses wanting to get away from Hollywood."

Both knew that the regular clientele at Eden Springs Resort was predominantly elderly people who returned year after year for a quiet vacation at the nineteenth century mineral springs spa, where home-style meals, nature walks, dips in the mineral springs pool, rocking chairs on the porch, and croquet on the lawn were the most exciting attractions.

"There's a basketball game tonight at the high school," Doug reminded his father as he folded the dish towel and hung it on the rack to dry. "We're playing the Monroe High Hilltoppers.

Some of my friends on the junior varsity team are taking their girlfriends, and we're all going to sit together. The Titans are going to need all of the home court noise they can get from us, because the Hilltoppers are the best team in the district."

"I'd enjoy seeing a good high school basketball game tonight myself," Ed commented, "but I brought work home from the office again. You have a good time."

Doug walked the familiar half mile route from his house to school an hour later and entered the noisy gymnasium, where students and their families had already started to fill the bleachers. The gym also doubled as the school auditorium, and the backboard on one end swung down on a hinged mounting bracket just in front of the stage. Standing near the door, Doug saw his JV teammates and their girl friends sitting behind the scorer's table, halfway up toward the top of the stands. Doug worked his way around the crowded gym floor, climbing up through the bleachers to join them.

His friends spotted him coming, and Mike Rhodes called out, "Dawg, about time you got here. We've been saving a seat for you."

The very first day when Doug Housman had been introduced at Tyler High, Mike had hung the nickname "Dawg House" on him, and the "Dawg" part had stuck. Doug had accepted the new nickname in a good natured way, realizing it was part of his initiation to the new school, and soon after, he and Mike had become best friends.

Sitting beside Mike was his steady girlfriend, Virginia "Ginny" Johnson. Both had short, curly brown hair, were slim and athletic, and had a good sense of humor and an easy going attitude. Mike's dad joked that they were so similar he thought they could pass for brother and sister, except that Ginny was much better looking. A teacher had matched Mike with Ginny as part of a sixth grade dance program, and they had been a couple ever since.

Freddie Palmer and Shirley Martin sat next to them. They also were a steady couple, but polar opposites in looks and personalities. Freddie had dark hair and a dark complexion, and was the tallest and heaviest boy in the group. He was the one always keeping things stirred up with his wise cracks. Freddie

struggled with geometry, Latin, English, and just about everything else, and worked hard to maintain a "C" average. Shirley,
the top student in the tenth grade, had blond hair, and was tall
and slender. Opposites had obviously attracted, and no one
would ever confuse them as blood kin.

Rounding out the group were Ronnie Myers, the best natural
athlete and the most competitive boy in the tenth grade, and
his girlfriend, Barbara Ann Stevens. Wayne Miller, the youngest and quietest boy in the group, and Barbara Ann's identical twin sister, Mary Pat Stevens, sat on the bleacher below
them. The twins were bright, pretty, and almost impossible to
tell apart, except for a small chicken pox scar on Barbara Ann's
hand. Their similar looks had caused problems on more than
one occasion, including the night at a Christmas party back in
December, when Ronnie had ambushed Mary Pat under the
mistletoe and thoroughly smudged her lipstick before she
could convince him that he had the wrong twin.

Doug spotted Vickie Vicelli and Janice Gilmore sitting together a few rows higher in the bleachers, laughing and talking with a group of boys nearby. Vickie looked striking in a red
skirt and white sweater, the school colors, her long blonde hair
pulled back in a pony tail with a red scarf. Without thinking,
Doug stood for a few seconds staring at her. He was startled
when she suddenly turned her head, and their eyes met. An
amused look came across her face, and she started to laugh,
maintaining eye contact until he looked away. He could feel
his face turning a shade of red that almost matched the color of
his hair, and he self-consciously slumped into the vacant seat
beside Mike.

"Thanks for saving me a seat," Doug exclaimed. "It looks like
the whole town's here again tonight."

"Yeah, Eden Springs pretty much shuts down for a home
football or basketball game," Mike commented. "It's that way
with a lot of the small towns in West Virginia. Even the mayor's
here tonight."

Doug looked down toward the floor of the gym and watched
the twelve juniors and seniors on the varsity going through
warm up drills. He considered most of the boys to be likeable
schoolmates, and two of them to be really good friends. Len

Hacker, a senior who had moved to Eden Springs a year after Doug, was the only boy on the team that he really disliked. Len was a natural in all sports, and a standout on both the varsity football and basketball teams, but was also known to have a quick temper and an aggressive attitude, particularly toward younger boys at school. Doug knew that none of his friends wanted any part of Len, and that all of them tried to avoid him whenever possible.

He recalled an earlier encounter with Len when the JV and varsity football teams had finished practice and were using the shower room together. When he was blinded by soap in his eyes, and tried to step under a shower to rinse it out, Len had yelled at him, "Get the hell out of the way," punching him hard in the stomach, knocking him back against the wall. Remembering the incident made Doug feel ashamed, knowing that he had chickened out of a fight just because he did not think he could win.

The referee's whistle sounded for the opening jump ball, and almost immediately, the Hilltoppers took control of the game. It was obvious that the Titans were completely overmatched against the taller and quicker visiting team, and all of the home crowd cheering would not help. By half time, Monroe had built an overwhelming lead and put their second and third string players on the floor. The Tyler fans in the bleachers had experienced similar blow-outs during games earlier in the season, and resigned themselves to another loss, settling back to make the best of things.

During a referee's time out, the senior cheerleaders dressed in white sweaters and red pleated skirts, came dashing out on the floor waving pompoms. This triggered the boys in the stands, and they began their noisy chant, "Do the Skyrocket!" The girls obliged, forming a line down the center of the floor. As the cheerleaders and crowd screamed, "Goooooooooo, Titans," the girls spun around quickly, causing their skirts to flare out and flash their bare legs and white satin tights. Afterwards, raucous yells and whistles echoed off the rafters of the gym. "That cheer never fails to arouse my school spirit," Mike cracked.

A look of mock reproach came over Ginny's face, as she punched him in the ribs with her elbow. "And you never fail to disgust me."

The score at the end of the game was Monroe 44-Tyler 20. Walking down through the bleachers, Mike turned to Doug and commented, "I think our JV team could have scored more points than that. The varsity really stunk it up again. They were throwing up bricks all night."

"Yeah, that's right," Doug answered, trying to keep a straight face. "If our JV team scrimmaged the varsity, we'd smoke 'em. We'd put you on Len Hacker, and you could take him to the basket all night long, one on one."

The crowd quickly cleared from the gym and dispersed down the brick walk in front of the school. Mike, Freddie, Ronnie, and Wayne wandered away from the school grounds holding hands with their girlfriends, meandering slowly along the concrete sidewalk in the dim light of the widely spaced street lights.

"See you in class tomorrow, Dawg," Mike called out to Doug, who was striding ahead by himself. "Oh yeah, there's something I meant to ask you. Can you ride over to Old Man Buchanan's place with me after school? We ought to get his permission before we camp on his land Saturday. I've got my dad's pickup truck lined up. Freddie's riding along, too."

"I can go with you anytime after school," Doug called back. "Come on over to the house and blow the horn when you're ready."

Doug found that his dad was still up when he arriving back at the house, seated in his favorite chair in the living room, looking over some paperwork from the office. "Don't forget, I've got a Scout meeting tomorrow night," Doug said "By the way, five of us are planning another camping trip this Saturday out on the Buchanan farm north of town, up on top of Chestnut Ridge."

"You can have all of the winter camping for both of us. I'll take sunburn over frostbite every time. I'll never understand why you boys want to sleep out in the open on the ground when the temperature drops below freezing like it will Saturday night. Can't see how that could be any fun. And you come back with a bad head cold every time you go."

Ed stood and slipped his papers into his leather briefcase, picking up a book from the adjacent table. "I'm heading upstairs to bed now. Think I'll read a little of my new Perry Mason paperback before I turn in."

"See you in the morning," Doug called out, heading to the re-frigerator for a glass of milk. He found himself thinking about his friends hanging out down at Gil's Drive-In, wondering what it would be like to be there, sitting in a booth with a pretty girl, listening to some good music on the juke box.

Chapter 2

DOUG HEARD several blasts from a car horn shortly after he got home from school, sending him scurrying down the steps two at a time and out to the street. Climbing into the cab of the black '49 Ford pickup truck, he found barely enough room beside Mike and Freddie to squeeze in and pull the door shut.

"Y'all ready to go?" Mike inquired, and without waiting for an answer, shifted the truck into gear and pulled away from the curb. After driving five miles north from town, Mike turned east onto a rutted gravel road leading up a slight grade for another half mile to the Buchanan home. A row of wood poles meandering beside the road supported looping electrical power lines mounted above a telephone wire, all running toward the house.

The gravel road ended in a large circular driveway fronting an imposing Greek style antebellum brick mansion with stately white columns. Everyone in the area knew the house by the name Roseanna. According to local history, Marcus Buchanan had built the once-magnificent home sometime after the Revolutionary War and named it in honor of his beautiful wife. Since that time, the house had deteriorated for many years from bad weather and lack of care. Damaged wood could be seen near the capitals and bases of the tall white columns, paint peeled from the imposing front pediment, tiles were missing from the roof, and untended shrubs and weeds grew in the yard, clear indicators that the family members living there could no longer maintain the property.

Mike stopped the truck in front, and the three boys climbed out. As they started toward the house, Mike commented, "This place looks like something out of one of those Edgar Allen Poe stories we studied in English Lit. The old man, Gideon, and his wife, Hester, must be over ninety years old, and their twin sons, Daniel and Jonah, in their fifties. Freddie, it would scare the living hell out of you to be out here alone on a dark night, when they might be roaming around."

"Yeah, sure," Freddie responded, sarcastically. "Nothing bothers y'all, does it? You're both totally fearless, aren't you? I haven't forgotten the camping trip last year where you two heard something moving around in the brush late one night, and claimed it was a bear. I thought I was going to have to clean your drawers out in the creek."

The boys climbed the cracked concrete steps leading up on the porch to the wide front door with its dirty glass panes. Doug rapped sharply several times with the massive brass knocker. After a few minutes, the door opened, and a large shaggy-haired man with a beard, wearing worn, stained coveralls, stood looking at them. They recognized him as one of the twins.

Doug broke the silence. "Would it be all right with y'all if we camp up on Chestnut Ridge behind your house this Saturday, like we did back in November?" The man continued to stare at them with no expression, and then slowly nodded. Without uttering a word, he turned back into the dark interior of the house and shut the door behind him.

"Well, he sure doesn't go in for a lot of small talk," Freddie remarked, as they walked back to the truck. "I wonder which of the sons that was. My dad said that either their mother was too old to have children, or something went wrong when she gave birth, because both of them have always acted strange. But I guess you have to give them some credit. They've been taking care of their elderly ma and pa, and running this place for a long time.

"Dad said there's a nephew of the old man named Julian Grant who moved here from Bluefield over a year ago. He drives out here from time to time to keep an eye on things. Dad thinks he figures to inherit the property some day down the road. This farm, with the house and all of the land, is worth a lot of money."

"I'm not sure the locals want any more Grants around here," Mike commented. "General Ulysses S. Grant didn't make a lot of friends when he came through here near the end of the Civil War. I've heard my grandfather call him Useless S. Grunt. Do you suppose Julian could be one of his descendents? Grant's a pretty uncommon name in these parts."

The boys returned to the truck, squeezed in, and started back to town in high spirits. Mike turned on the radio and found a station playing the top hits for February from the Saturday Night Hit Parade. When the current number one song came on, he cranked up the volume, and all three chimed in with Kay Starr on *Wheel of Fortune*, Freddie badly off key. Mike couldn't stand it for long, switching off the radio, and complaining, "Frederick, you couldn't carry a tune in a bucket."

The three boys were approaching the outskirts of town when Doug glanced at Mike and inquired, "You ever bother looking at the fuel gage on this truck? I don't think the needle is supposed to be sitting on 'E.'"

Mike wheeled into a nearby Gulf station and paid the owner to pump a dollar's worth of regular into the tank. "I'm glad you noticed that. My old man told me he'll skin me alive if I bring his truck home on empty one more time."

"Who cares," Freddie mumbled. "All I want is to get out of this truck and stretch out. Your two big butts take up all the room." Even Freddie couldn't suppress a grin, fully aware that he was bigger, wider, and forty pounds heavier than either of his friends. "Anyway, we got the permission we need for the camping trip, and all we need to do now is get our things together."

During the following week, Doug spent his afternoons after school rummaging through the attic and basement, digging out gear stowed haphazardly after the previous outing.

"Someone might think you're getting ready for an African safari," Ed joked, as he watched Doug digging through a large cardboard box. "You boys really seem to live by the Scout motto, 'Be prepared.'"

"I guess so," Doug replied, continuing to build a pile of things to pack. "You don't want any surprises after you've backpacked in and set up camp, like finding out that you came off without a roll of toilet paper."

The five boys met behind the Eden Springs Methodist Church the following Saturday morning, each carrying a full canvas knapsack, rolled sleeping bag, and other camping gear, attached to an aluminum pack frame. Slipping their arms through the canvas straps and hitching the packs on their shoulders, they walked down the driveway to the two lane state highway, and started north toward the Buchanan farm. The six mile hike usually took a couple of hours, and they planned to arrive in time to set up camp and have lunch at noon.

The conversation switched to their favorite topic when Freddie remarked, "I was checking out the girls' gym class yesterday. They were all running around in shorts, and a lot of them have great legs. Did you know that Ginny and Vickie can do a back flip on a mat, just like they do off the low board at the swimming pool?"

Mike turned to Doug with a quizzical expression. "I know Ginny. In fact, I know her pretty well. But that other girl? I can't figure out who she is. Do you know anything about her, Dawg?"

Doug answered with a straight face, "Vickie! That name does sound familiar, but for the life of me, I can't picture her, either. Maybe she's that stocky girl who lifts weights, or the new girl in class who never shaves her legs. Sorry, I can't figure out who she is."

"Don't beat yourself up too bad about that, Dawg," Freddie chimed in. "She hasn't figured out who you are either. Or for that matter, what you are."

Freddie's put-down got a laugh from everyone, but a weak smile from Doug. He had never revealed how sensitive he was about being left out of the tenth grade dating scene at school, and he was not about to show his feelings now.

"I owe you one, Frederick," Doug said, making a motion with his index finger as though chalking a blackboard. "You might want to look around to see where I am before you go out on that overhang up on top of Chimney Rock."

On arrival at the farm, the boys veered away from the gravel road leading up to the Buchanan home. Following the path beside a split-rail fence for a half mile, they arrived at Stony Creek, passing an old saw mill with flume and water wheel on a field-stone foundation. Picking up a trail along the creek bank, they followed it up the side of the ridge toward the top. All five were out of breath by the time they reached the top, glad to slip off their packs at the clearing where they would camp for the night. "You can really see a long way from up here on the ridge," Freddie observed.

"You can get a lot better look from the top of Chimney Rock a little further up," Mike replied. "We'll go up there in a little while and check it out. Dawg said he's going to walk behind you to make sure you don't fall."

"No way he's walking behind me the rest of the way," Freddie laughed. "Dawg holds a grudge."

After a quick lunch, the boys continued up the spine of the ridge in single file. The trail became narrower approaching the top, and the drop off below it much steeper. A short distance from the spectacular boulders forming Chimney Rock, Mike stopped and said, "You should be able to make out Roseanna soon. We're almost directly behind the house, about a half mile away."

Ronnie, wiry, agile, and quicker to take a risk than the others, scrambled down the steep slope below the trail to look around and knelt beneath a large rock outcropping. Suddenly he called out excitedly, "Hey, come down here and take a look at what I've found!"

The others worked their way down the slope to the spot where he was crouched beside a dark slit in the bank. "I'm almost positive this is an opening to a cave. You can feel the cool air. Dad told me there's caves all through this hillside. He said that one of the old timers told him about a huge cave with an entrance somewhere down at the foot of the cliff below us. According to what my old man heard, the cave was closed off by a rock slide back during the Civil War."

Doug picked up several rocks and began tossing them into the hole. The first made a faint clattering noise as it landed, but the next two tossed further inside returned no sound. "I bet this opens onto a deep shaft," he commented. "Maybe this cave connects to the big one down below. I'd like to come back here with a flashlight and look inside."

"I've got a better idea," Ronnie exclaimed. "Tomorrow morning let's go down to the bottom of the ridge and walk back over to the base of the cliff below us. We've never explored there before. Maybe we can find some sign of the old cave entrance."

Continuing to the top of Chimney Rock, Wayne called out, "Check out the view! I can see Roseanna, and a lot of old farm buildings closer this way."

The boys had been climbing around on the rocks for hours, when Mike said, "I think it's time to head back to camp and start thinking about dinner. I'm starved."

"Y'all go on ahead," Doug yelled back. "Freddie and I are going to walk out on that ledge and see who can spit further over the side. If he doesn't show up again, we can draw straws to see who gets his paperback copy of I, The Jury, the one with all the good pages dog-eared."

When the sun dipped below the ridgeline that evening, the temperature began to drop quickly. All five boys dug out their jackets and slipped them on. Doug noticed that Freddie glanced from time to time beyond the light of the campfire into the darkness, and he sensed an opportunity for payback.

"We didn't see any sign of old Gideon and Hester when the three of us stopped at their house earlier this week," he remarked. "We just saw that one son. He looked big and strong as a gorilla. I bet both of 'em will be up here prowling around tonight, after we're asleep."

"Shut up, Dawg," Freddie replied nervously. "Try to find something else to talk about that makes some sense."

When it was time to turn in, the boys placed several large logs on the fire, and crawled into their sleeping bags, still wearing heavy jackets. All knew it would be a long, cold night ahead, with little or no sleep. "Would somebody get up and bring me another blanket?" Mike asked plaintively, sliding deeper into his sleeping bag.

The next morning, the boys broke camp, hiked back down the ridge, and walked along the foot of the cliff below Chimney Rock. Boulders and smaller stones covered much of the ground, making it difficult to picture where a rock slide might have sealed a cave entrance ninety years earlier.

Spotting a crevasse in the face of the cliff, Ronnie worked his way through the gap, and found himself standing in an open space surrounded by vertical limestone walls. The other boys standing outside heard his muffled voice call out, "It looks like someone's been working in here. There's some big rocks pried out of the way, and a couple of logs have been hauled in to prop up a slab jutting out of the bank."

The words were hardly of his mouth when a loud, deep voice called out from across the field, "Y'all get away from there! You'll get hurt." Looking back toward the house in the distance, the boys could see two burly, bearded men standing less than a hundred yards away, staring in their direction

Ronnie scrambled back out from the crevasse, as Mike muttered, "Well, now we know they can talk. I don't think they're fooling around with us. It's time to scram." The boys quickly walked back in the direction they had come, glancing back over their shoulders.

Hiking back along the highway toward town, Ronnie said, "It looks to me like they're using logs as props to prevent a rock fall, just like coal miners do when they're working in a shaft. But I can't figure out why in the world those two are taking the risk of getting hurt when there's nothing worth digging up out there."

They were halfway back to town when they were joined by a stranger, a small cross breed stray without a collar. The young male beagle and terrier mix appeared to have been dropped beside the road by its owner. It happily trotted along beside them, the way lost dogs usually latch onto the first person passing by. The outline of the dog's ribs showed through his dirty brown and white coat, which was covered with burrs and Spanish needles.

"I don't believe that dog's had anything to eat for days," Doug commented. "Looks like he's starving. I've got some food left in my pack, and I'm going to stop and dig it out, if y'all will hold up for just a minute."

"You're making a big mistake," Wayne cautioned him. "My sister started feeding a stray female that came to our house a year ago, and that dog's still there, living with us like part of the family. My old man had to pay the vet to have her spayed and get her a rabies shot."

Doug slipped off his pack frame and dug a half dozen slices of bread out of his canvas pack. As he tossed each slice, the dog would catch it the air, chomp on it a couple of times, and down it in a single swallow. "He goes after food just like Freddie does in the cafeteria, only he's got better table manners," Mike observed. Freddie responded with his middle finger.

Doug found two franks after he ran out of bread, and threw them to the stray. The dog ate them even more quickly and then jumped up on Doug's leg, begging for more. "Sorry, boy, but that's all I have," Doug said, patting him on the head.

"You've done it now," Wayne remarked. "He's going to follow you home."

The stray was still beside Doug when they reached the outskirts of town. It remained with him as he separated from the group and headed up the street toward his house.

"I'm going to take a hot shower when I get in, and then hit the rack for a few hours," he called out. "I didn't get any sleep last night. Hey, which one of you wants to take this fine animal home?"

"Don't say I didn't warn you, Dawg," Wayne yelled back. "Like the Katzenjammer Kids say in the comics, 'you brought it on yourself.' Let us know what you name him."

When Doug got home, he looked down at the sad and forlorn looking stray, sitting on its haunches, watching him intently. "You think I'm a soft touch, don't you, boy?" Doug said aloud. "I probably should have my head examined for feeding you and letting you follow me."

Inside the house, he opened a can of corned beef hash, and filled an empty Maxwell House can with water. Carrying them outside, he watched the dog quickly gobble the hash, and then began lapping up the water, wagging its tail for the first time. "You've just adopted me, haven't you boy?" Doug exclaimed.

Sitting on the steps pulling burrs and ticks off the stray, he was still busily at work when his dad drove up.

"What did you bring home with you this time?" Ed asked. "Looks to me like a two year-old feist of dubious ancestry."

"What a relief to hear that," Doug replied. "I was afraid he was just a plain ol' mutt."

"What are you planning to do with him?"

"He looked like he really needed a meal, so I gave it to him," Doug replied. "Is it OK if he stays around here for a while? I thought we could name him Ed, Jr., and maybe call him Junior, or JR for short."

"You can keep him if you want, and anything you want to call him is fine with me. Personally, I don't care if you name him Edward Housman, Jr., or Harry Truman. But once you adopt him, you're going to have to take care of him, and pay for his rabies shot, dog tag, and vet bills out of your allowance. And you're going to be responsible for housebreaking him and turning him into a civilized member of the family. Welcome to the world of parenting."

Chapter 3

"I RAN INTO Laura Jackson at the courthouse today, and she told me something interesting," Ed remarked, as his son concentrated on geometry homework across the kitchen table, with JR at his feet. "She was talking to her brother in Charleston last week, and he told her there's a rumor circulating that geologists discovered a seam of coal somewhere in our area about this time last year. Nothing ever came out in the newspapers around here, which makes you doubt that the story is true. If it were, you would expect to read about it on the front page."

"Who did you say you ran into?" Doug asked, trying to hide a grin. Doug had heard his dad speak of Laura before, and knew that he found her to be not only intelligent and well informed, but also very attractive. During the past two years, Ed had worked with her on contracts and deeds for several pieces of property. Since taking over her late husband's real estate business, Laura kept a close eye on commercial developments, and she knew a great deal about what was going on in the area.

"What do you suppose a big coal deposit would mean to the people living around here?" Doug inquired, laying down his pencil and scratching JR between the ears.

"I'm not sure, son. Eden Springs is best known today as a tourist destination because of the mineral springs, and the overall natural beauty. Both of the furniture factories south of town are far enough out not to pose a problem for the town. There's a tremendous contrast between this area and the coal fields. In that part of the state, 'Coal is King.' It brings in the jobs and the money, but it can also permanently change the countryside, and unfortunately, it's often not for the better. I would personally hate to see this area mined for coal. Anyway, I plan to make a phone call to a friend back in Charleston and see if I can learn anything more about the rumor."

As his dad walked out of the room, Doug put aside any concerns about the impact of coal mining and returned to his geometry homework, until JR began pawing at the front door. While Doug waited in the doorway, JR carefully checked out every tree in the yard before selecting one, and then trotted back to the house with his tail wagging. "It doesn't take a whole lot to entertain you, does it, boy?" Doug commented, as he closed the door behind them, and they went upstairs to bed.

The next morning, Doug overslept. Wolfing down his breakfast, he ran out of the house, and headed off to school, on the double. He arrived out of breath and climbed the steps to the front entrance, passing the cornerstone engraved with the founding date, 1902. As he rushed down the hallway, he passed students clustered in groups, talking and waiting for the opening bell to ring before entering their classrooms. Doug noticed from the corner of his eye that Vickie was standing next to Ginny and Shirley, but he made an effort not to look toward them. He felt no desire to recreate the embarrassing moment earlier in the week when she'd caught him gawking at her before the basketball game.

Mike spotted Doug in the hallway just outside the room where they would have their first period Latin class, greeting him with his best Bugs Bunny imitation. "What's up, Dawg?"

"Too early to say," Doug replied. Then, trying to get a rise out of Mike, he added, "I've heard that Mrs. Wilson's going to give us a pop quiz today. Hope you know everything about Caesar's last campaign in the Punic Wars."

"Not a problem," Mike said. "I know everything there is to know about ol' Julius. Just wish he would have spoken English. I'm more worried about our JV basketball team practice this afternoon. Coming down the ridge the other day, I turned my ankle, and it still hurts to walk on it. It might slow me down in making my patented Bob Cousy-type drives to the basket for lay-ups."

"Yeah, that truly would be a huge loss to the team," Doug replied. Mike was a good athlete and one of the best players on the JV squad, but it was an unwritten rule among the boys that you never acknowledged a friend's skill, particularly when he was around.

The two boys went into the classroom, finding their usual seats near the back of the room in the space they called "the sanctuary." Doug had learned that in Mrs. Wilson's Latin class, you didn't want to sit in an exposed seat up front, where you were sure to be called on for answers. He had observed that Thelma Wilson was all business in teaching, and that one way or the other, you would know a lot about the now-dead language of the Roman Empire before she gave you a passing grade. Math and science came easily to Doug, but Latin was a real struggle. Fortunately for him and everyone else in the class, except Latin whiz kid Shirley Martin, Mrs. Wilson did not pass out a quiz, and the day was off to a fine start.

The bell rang for lunch period at 11:30, and Doug joined other students walking down the steps to the school cafeteria in the basement. Several of the girls ahead of him were giggling together, possibly talking about the boy in front of them who had obviously not yet discovered Lifebuoy or Arrid. Doug could hear the animated sounds of many voices speaking at once as he entered the room.

The cafeteria had the aroma of freshly cooked vegetable soup, blended with the sour, musky odor of old woven rawhide leather chair seats. Doug filed through the food line, setting a bowl of vegetable soup, small bottle of milk, and a Spam sandwich on his tray. He walked over to a long wooden table in the corner of the room and joined his usual lunch-time group of friends.

"Hey, Dawg," Freddie greeted him as he sat down. "I've been thinking some more about that lost cave on the Buchanan place. If anyone knows anything, it would be Mr. Barry. He's always telling us in his American history class about researching old records at the library and court house to learn more about this area. He's a big local history expert, and he says he's going to write a book someday."

"Good idea for once, Frederick," Doug replied. "Let's talk to him after school today, before we go to basketball practice." Their conversation continued for the next half hour until the bell rang. As students noisily filed out of the cafeteria, Doug turned to Mike, "Why don't you stick around with Freddie and me after fifth period class, and we'll see if we can catch up with Mr. Barry."

The boys located Sam Barry in his classroom after school, clearing books from his cluttered desktop, and placing student homework papers in his worn briefcase. He looked up as Doug, Mike, and Freddie approached, and Doug said, "Mr. Barry, we have something we'd like to talk to you about, if you're not busy."

"Boys, I'm always busy, or at least I try to give that impression. But I certainly have all the time in the world for the three brightest history students here at school. Fire away with your questions!"

Although Sam Barry was a demanding teacher, he was well liked by his students because of his sense of humor, fairness, and ability to relate to teenagers. His remark brought a grin to the boys' faces, knowing they were barely average in their scores.

Doug led off. "Last weekend while we were camping on Chestnut Ridge, we were looking around near the bottom of the cliff below Chimney Rock. Ronnie Myer's dad has heard there's a cave somewhere in that hillside and that there used to be an entrance where people could go inside. According to what we're told, the entrance was closed up by a rock slide a long time ago. We wondered if you might know anything about it."

"Have a seat for a few minutes," Sam invited the three boys. "You've brought up a very interesting subject, and I'll be glad to share with you what I know about it. Almost everyone who has lived here for very long has probably heard about that famous lost cave. I've kept an eye open for any information I can find, but I've never come across any written records or photographs

to verify the existence of such a cave, or what might have happened to cover up an entrance, if there ever was one."

He settled back into his chair behind the desk and continued,
"I don't know whether you know it or not, but almost all of the
farm land in the valley between Pine Ridge and Chestnut Ridge,
just this side of Abner Gap, has been in the Buchanan family
since this area was settled, some time after the Revolutionary
War. You may be aware that during the Civil War, a company
of Confederate troops engaged a much larger Union force right
in that same valley. It was in bitterly cold weather during the
winter of 1862, and the skirmish came to be known as the Battle
of Eden Springs.

"One of my hobbies is investigating that military encounter,
trying to learn what actually took place. I've looked over documents and photographs at the court house, the town library, and
in a number of old family homes in these parts. I've also taken
a number of trips to Charleston, Richmond, and Washington to
go through Civil War archives. And I correspond regularly with
history teachers and professors at area schools and universities
who also study the Civil War.

"Now, getting back to your question, although there's no
concrete evidence, I believe that there may be a cave below
Chimney Rock, and I'm basing my opinion on stories repeated
by several of the old-timers around here. I think that whatever
occurred to bury the entrance may have coincided with the
Battle of Eden Springs. I've even wondered if something like
misdirected cannon fire might have triggered a rockslide. It's
an intriguing mystery, isn't it, boys?"

"It sure is," Mike said, with growing interest. "You make
me think there really is a cave out there." Glancing at Doug
and Freddie, he continued, "We had an encounter with the
Buchanan twins while we were exploring that area, and as soon
as they saw us snooping around, they ran us off."

"Maybe they were concerned that you would get hurt. And
just possibly, it might have been something more. This cave
mystery deserves some good detectives, and I think you all
should help investigate it further. Let me know if you learn anything more. But be careful about going out on the Buchanans'
property without permission. I wouldn't want to see any of

you get hurt out there, or have to come downtown to the jail and bail you out, if Sheriff Daniels arrests you for trespassing." With a wink, Sam stood and resumed clearing his desk.

The three boys quietly left the room and started toward the gym, anticipating that Coach James would run their legs off at practice to get them in shape for the upcoming game with Allegheny High. Their expectations soon became reality. For the next two hours Coach proceeded to put them through the hardest workout of the season. Everyone on the JV team was completely out of gas by the time the whistle blew to end practice.

"I think ol' Jesse was trying to kill us today," Mike commented in a low voice, careful that Coach wouldn't overhear him using the nickname Tyler students had hung on him when he first joined the school faculty. "I'm about to drop over. And those two new guys that smoke are hurting a lot worse than any of us."

Doug was relieved to see that the varsity had finished practice earlier and was already gone by the time the JV squad got to the locker room. He had not looked forward to encountering Len Hacker there again. He and his teammates stepped under the hot showers and did not come out until the water started to run cold. Going back to their lockers, they toweled off, dressed, and wearily headed for home.

Doug noticed that his dad's car was not parked in the usual spot in the driveway when he arrived, tired and stiff. Walking around to the backyard, he unclipped JR's collar from the chain attached to the clothes line and went inside the empty house with the dog trotting behind at his heels.

Accustomed to starting dinner when his dad was late, Doug walked into the kitchen toward the refrigerator, looking for leftovers that could be warmed over. Then he caught sight of Ed's handwritten note on the table: "Don't fix anything for me tonight. I'm meeting Laura for dinner. See you around 9:00."

"Well, that simplifies things," Doug commented aloud to JR. Taking a loaf of bread and a jar of peanut butter out of the cabinet and a quart of milk from the refrigerator, he continued the one-sided conversation, "This'll be another of my nutritious and well balanced meals tonight. Bet you're ready to eat, too." Opening a can of Red Heart dog food, he emptied it onto a plate on the floor and watched as the dog quickly wolfed it down. "Emily Post might say your table manners need a little work, boy," Doug observed, patting him on the head. "How about some dinner music?" Turning on the radio nearby, he heard the familiar voice of Patty Page singing the *Tennessee Waltz*.

"This is the first time he's taken Laura out to dinner, or anywhere else, for that matter. I wonder what finally brought this about? You probably know, but you're not going to tell me, are you, boy?"

Chapter 4

As ED turned his '51 Ford sedan into the parking lot of the Stafford Steakhouse, he recognized Laura's '52 white Olds station wagon. Upon entering, he could see her seated near the back of the room watching for him. Running her own real estate business and dealing with a wide spectrum of clients had given her a quiet confidence interacting with people. It was apparent that she was quite at ease waiting alone until his arrival. As he approached her table, she extended her hand to greet him. He asked, "Have I kept you waiting long?"

Laura flashed a pretty, wide smile, and replied, "No, I've only been here a short time. I was showing a house to a client earlier this afternoon, so this has worked out well for me. Have you had a busy day?"

Sitting down and glancing across the table, Ed found her as striking as the first time he had encountered her walking past him at the court house. "No, it's been a fairly quiet day, and an uncommonly pleasant one. But having dinner with you tonight is definitely the frosting on the cake." He thought he could detect a momentary blush pass across her face.

"Are you Irish, Ed?" Laura inquired, looking straight at him with wide eyes. "You definitely have a gift for the blarney. I believe you could sell a lot of over-priced real estate to little old ladies if you came to work for me."

"Sorry, but I'm going to have to decline the job offer. You see,

I already make a great living shuffling papers and handling all of the legal mumbo jumbo down at the court house." They were still engaged in light conversation when the waiter approached their table and took drink and dinner orders, red wine, to be followed by the filet mignon specialty of the house.

While waiting for their meals, Ed asked, "I'm curious to know whether you've heard anything more from your brother about that alleged coal discovery around here. I'm asking because I just called an old college friend that practices law in Charleston, with several mining companies as clients, and he knows nothing about any mining activity or interest in our area. I'm positive he wasn't holding anything back from me because of business confidentiality. If there's any truth to that rumor you told me about earlier, everything's certainly being kept hush-hush."

"I did talk with my brother again," Laura answered, as the waiter refilled her glass. "He told me he'd heard that story from a friend during a dinner conversation at his Elks Club. The person he was with happens to be a sales manager for a large company selling electrical equipment throughout the coal fields. The only reason the subject came up was that my brother had mentioned earlier that I have a real estate business in this area.

"He hasn't talked with his friend again since that evening, so he was unable to provide any more information. It looks like there's no way for us to find out whether there's any truth to the rumor, or whether it's as incredible as Frank Scully's sightings of those flying saucers.

"But there's something I have discovered that may only be an interesting coincidence. Someone with plenty of money is now trying to buy up undeveloped agricultural land in the valley between Abner Gap and town. The biggest single tract of that land is, of course, the 2500 acre Buchanan farm. I keep wondering why anyone would be interested in purchasing extensive acreage in that area at this time. You certainly couldn't justify the cost of buying the land for commercial farming or timber, although there is a lot of old growth timber on the Buchanan property. It makes you stop and wonder, doesn't it?"

"It certainly does," Ed answered. "It wouldn't be hard to connect the dots between the rumor of a coal discovery in our area and the report of someone wanting to purchase large tracts of land north of town. If anyone is up to something big, they're going to have a hard time keeping a lid on it. Between the two of us with all of our contacts, we should be able to find out what's going on before long."

The dinner conversation returned to an enjoyable discussion of everyday activities, as the waiter returned to remove their empty plates and bring them coffee and pecan pie for dessert. "You're going to force me to do a lot of walking tomorrow to make up for eating like this tonight," Laura remarked.

"I wanted to feed you really well. You're shrinking away to nothing but skin and bone, and I just can't stand by and watch a pretty woman starve to death." He tried to hold a straight face as she started to laugh.

They walked together to her car, and he opened the door for her to slip behind the wheel. She stood facing him with her hand on his arm and said in a soft voice, "That was the best meal I've had in a long time. Thanks for a wonderful evening." She hesitated for a moment, as if waiting to see what he would do.

Looking at her brought back a flood of emotion that Ed had not experienced since Louise had died four years ago. He wanted to reach out for her, but something held him back, preventing him from acting on his feelings. The opportunity was quickly lost, as she got into her car and shut the door. "I had a great time, too," he called out lamely, inwardly kicking himself as she drove away.

At home, Ed was greeted by Doug from the living room sofa, "Well, how did your first date with Laura go? Do JR and I need to start coming along to chaperone you two kids?"

"We had an outstanding dinner and a great time," Ed responded, as he hung his coat in the hall closet. "I'd like to give you all a full report of all the romantic activity, but it might be too much for a boy of your tender years and his young dog to hear." As he went up the steps, he found himself reliving what had occurred just before Laura drove off, thinking, I'm as backward around an attractive female as my sixteen year-old son, with a lot less time to fix the problem.

Chapter 5

Ed WALKED into his office the next day and saw that his legal assistant and right hand, Carolyn Carson, was already on the job. He could smell the aroma of freshly perked coffee and see her sorting through the incoming mail at her desk in the next room. He quickly realized after taking over the law practice that the most valuable asset was Carolyn, a capable and pleasant woman twelve years his senior. She had worked for the previous attorney, John Crawford, since the day he had hung out his shingle, and through experience and on-the-job training, could handle much of the day to day business without direction.

"Good morning, Ed," she greeted him. "I've just updated your calendar for the day. You have a meeting this morning with Robert Simpson and his wife. They're good country folks who've owned a farm four miles north of town for many years. When you have time, I can tell you what they want to discuss."

"Thanks, Carolyn. Let me grab a quick cup of coffee to get my motor running, and you can fill me in right now."

In colorful language, Carolyn painted a picture of the Simpsons as frugal farmers who still lived as though "the great depression" had never ended, watching every dime they spent. "Some of their neighbors comment that everything they own is held together with baling wire and jar rings," she related with a laugh. "Out of the blue, they've received an offer to purchase their farm, and they're in a real quandary as to what they should do."

When Robert and Ethel Simpson arrived, Ed invited them into his office, closing the door behind them. Robert produced a letter, saying, "Mr. Housman, three weeks ago we received this registered letter from an out of town man we've never dealt with before, wanting to buy us out, all of our hundred and ten acre farm including the house. He offered us almost twice what we thought our place was worth. We never even thought about selling and moving, but we're not getting any younger, and we don't have any children to help out, or take over the farm down the road. We're not getting rich farming and may never get another offer this good. If we sold the farm and moved into town, I could probably find a job in a garage doing engine repair work or something. What we need is some sound advice about what to do."

Robert passed the letter across the desk to Ed. The bold letterhead read *Copperfield Enterprises*, with a Beckley address. The letter detailed an offer to purchase the Simpson property for a lump sum amount, with a thirty-day cutoff for acceptance. It was signed "William P. Thorpe, Jr., Vice President."

Ed studied the letter closely before returning it to Robert. "Mr. and Mrs. Simpson, the decision whether to accept or reject this offer is ultimately going to be yours. You need to take enough time to become fully informed and consider the sale of your farm from all angles. If I were you, I wouldn't be stampeded into acting too quickly. There are a number of ways I believe I can help you. One is to identify some of the pros and cons of selling which you might otherwise overlook. Others are to investigate the validity of this offer, represent you to protect your interests in any negotiations and sale, and see that all legal requirements are handled properly. If you decide you want to use my services, I'll need to borrow this letter to get started."

Ethel, who had been sitting quietly until now, suddenly became animated. "If we decide to sell, maybe I could finally have a nice modern kitchen and bathroom, just like my sister in Roanoke has," she interjected. "Sarah has an electric stove, and a new Frigidaire with a big freezer compartment," she added, looking plaintively at her husband.

Robert glanced at his wife as they stood and prepared to

leave. "We definitely want your help, Mr. Housman. To tell you the truth, we haven't slept very well since we got that letter, and I almost wish we'd never gotten it. You can hold on to it as long as you need it."

Ed reviewed the letter from Copperfield Enterprises a second time as soon as Robert and Ethel departed. Ethel's touching dream of a nicer home ran through his mind again and again, as he worked throughout the remainder of the day.

Stopping at the local florist on the way home, he told the owner, "I'd like to place two orders, each for a dozen red roses to be delivered on the fourteenth." He filled out two small cards, slipped each into a matching envelope, and handed them back to the florist. The first was to Carolyn: "Happy Valentines Day to my favorite legal assistant." The second was to Laura: "Happy Valentines Day from a secret admirer." Continuing homeward, he found himself in the pleasurably nervous state of anticipation that he'd nearly forgotten. He hoped that Laura's reaction to the flowers would confirm his hunch about her feelings toward him.

Doug was walking up to the front door coming home from basketball practice just as Ed pulled into the driveway. Rolling down the window, he called out, "Let's go down to Gil's and get a hamburger and a milkshake. I don't think either of us feels like eating leftovers or sandwiches again tonight." Doug veered over to the car and climbed in, ready for his favorite meal.

As they walked through the door at Gil's, they found themselves surrounded by teenagers sitting in booths and on the stools at the counter, talking and listening to songs playing on the brightly lit Wurlitzer in the corner. Glancing around the room, Doug did not see any close friends among the group. Both ordered their usual when the young waitress came to the table. "Got anything special on for tonight?" Ed asked. "Maybe a dog obedience class?"

"Nothing I'd call special," Doug replied between bites. "And JR hasn't enrolled anywhere I know of. I do have some geometry homework to do, and I brought home a Latin reading assignment to look over, but that shouldn't take me the whole evening." Anything happen at your office that you need to tell me about?"

Ed tried to keep from smiling at the sincere manner with which Doug had made the inquiry. Since Louise's death, the two had developed a different relationship that sometimes seemed more like best friends than father and son, and it worked well for them. For two people who had left familiar settings and old friends behind, and were starting over again in a new town, life could be lonely at times. Moving to Eden Springs had tightened the bond between them. "No, nothing I need to get off my chest right now. Did you get enough to eat?" Doug only smiled and patted his non-existent belly as they made their way to the car.

On the way home, Doug told his dad about something that had taken place near the end of the school day. "Mike bought Ginny a Valentine and a heart-shaped box of chocolates yesterday, and put them in her locker after she went home this afternoon, which was no big deal. But I found out later that he and Freddie set me up. They brought in a mushy Valentine, wrote some kind of note on it and signed my name, and then stuck it Vickie Vicelli's locker. She's been out sick a couple of days, but I expect she'll be back in school on Friday, and I know she's going to find it. The whole thing makes me awfully uncomfortable about running into her at school that morning. I'd hate to have the prettiest girl in our class think I'm completely goofy."

"I believe she'll figure it out pretty quickly, don't you?" Ed replied. "Who knows; she may be flattered by the card and start paying some attention to you. Remember that 'faint hearts never win fair ladies.'"

"You're really making me start to feel a lot better, Dad," Doug said, as he rolled his eyes. "Maybe I'll decide to show up at school on Friday after all. If I can just get a few more pointers like that from you, I'll probably become the next Humphrey Bogart."

"I promise to keep working with you. Tomorrow's the big Valentine gift day for most of us, but it looks like your excitement won't come until the following morning, which gives me a little more time for your lessons."

When Ed entered the office the next day Carolyn was holding a dozen red roses that had just been delivered. "Ed, thanks for remembering me on Valentine's day. Frank used to send me flowers on special occasions, and this means a lot to me. On holidays like this, I still miss him so much."

"I share that feeling, Carolyn. I still think about Louise every day, and she's been gone four years now. Staying busy helps, but at times likes Valentines Day, the memories come back when I'm least expecting them, and I start feeling sad and depressed. We both know what that's like."

Carolyn swallowed a lump in her throat, and quickly changed the subject. "I got a call from Clarence Henderson just before I left the office yesterday. He and his wife Hazel have received an unsolicited offer from Copperfield Enterprises to purchase their farm, which borders the smaller Simpson place. The Hendersons and the Simpsons are long-standing neighbors and very close friends. Clarence and his wife have talked with the Simpsons, and they know that the Simpsons have retained you as their attorney. Since the Hendersons are facing the same decision, they want to meet with you now."

Laura's comment a few days earlier flashed through Ed's mind: "Someone with plenty of money is interested in purchasing land between Abner Gap and town." Collecting his thoughts, he replied, "Please go ahead and set up an appointment with the Hendersons. I plan to get started on this by making a few phone calls before I meet with them."

His first phone call was to Laura, who quickly asked with easy mischief, "Is this my Valentine secret admirer? The red roses are beautiful! Thank you so much!"

"You're very welcome. I'm glad that you knew that the roses were from me. I imagine that getting flowers from men on Valentines Day is old hat to you, and you probably have to make a list to keep the names straight." There was a brief pause in the conversation as Ed waited for her reply.

Laura was at a momentary loss for words. Only an hour earlier the florist had delivered an elaborate arrangement of cut flowers from Dan Wohlford, a man she had met at a party the previous summer. Although they had gone out together on several occasions and hit it off, Laura felt no exclusive attachment toward Dan, or any other man.

"I've received flowers before, but never any as pretty as these," she replied. "And I don't get enough to bother writing down names."

"It's good to hear you like the roses. I hope you'll enjoy them for a few days on your desk. I hate to change the subject, but I'm trying to get more information about the person or people trying to buy up land out north of town. Without giving out any client-confidential details, I can tell you that I'm now being contacted by some of the land owners directly involved."

"I'd really prefer to stick with the discussion of secret admirers who send me flowers," Laura replied. "But as for the more mundane subject of someone trying to buy up all of the land out toward Abner Gap, I'm afraid I don't have any new information to share with you. Whoever the buyers are, they're not going through my agency, or any other local real estate firm as far as I can tell. Sorry I can't offer more help."

"Please keep your ear to the ground, and let me know if you find out anything else."

"I promise, you'll be the first to know. Ed, I've got to run. I'm already five minutes late for an appointment to show a new home to a prospective buyer. If you like, we can talk more about land acquisitions later, or better still, get back to the subject of secret admirers. Bye now!"

Ed phoned Copperfield Enterprises in Beckley shortly after Laura got off the line. When a woman on the other end answered, he said, "This is Ed Housman in Eden Springs. May I please speak to Mr. William Thorpe, Jr.?"

"I'm sorry, but Mr. Thorpe is out the office," the woman answered. "He should be back within the next few days. May he return your call then?"

Ed left his phone number, and afterward spoke to Carolyn. "I'll bet you that William P. Thorpe, Jr., is there right now, having his secretary screen his calls. By the time he gets around to calling back, I doubt that I'll have to explain who I am. Undoubtedly, he'll do some homework, and know I'm representing two local land owners considering his offers."

Ed's third phone call was to Phillip Wine in Beckley. Phil was a classmate and fraternity brother from law school days at Washington and Lee, who had practiced law in Beckley for many years. After catching up on the news with Phil, he inquired, "Can you tell me anything about Copperfield Enterprises headquartered in your home town?" Phil's reply confirmed Ed's worst fears.

"I can certainly help you with that, Ed. Copperfield Enterprises is nothing but a front for Barker Mining. Both companies are owned by a very wealthy and politically powerful coal magnate, Robert Copperfield Barker. Copperfield Enterprises was set up to facilitate business negotiations with people who may be familiar with the reputation of Barker Mining for taking coal without much regard to land reclamation. In certain parts of the coal fields where his mining operations have caused the worst damage, the locals call him 'Copperhead,'" and some feel that's an insult to the snakes.

"Barker Mining has been actively searching for new coal deposits in this end of the state for years. Possibly they've made a find in your region, and they're trying to secure ownership of the land and the mineral rights to underlying coal before word gets out and the price of the property skyrockets. That's about all I can tell you."

"Thanks for giving me that information, Phil," Ed responded. "That's exactly what I needed to know." Before closing, he added, "Good talking to you again. Take care of yourself, and let's plan to get together and have a beer at the next class reunion."

Phil's words returned to Ed throughout the day, and when the pale February light faded to dusk, he was still mulling over their implication. When he first entered law school, he had wondered whether someday there would be conflicts between client interests and his own set of values. At that time, he had pictured these situations as matters of black and white, with easy solutions. All you would need to do is refuse to take on such clients.

But now looking at the Simpson and Henderson scenarios, everything seemed to be a muddy gray. The financially strapped families were being offered once in a lifetime opportunities to sell their farms, but with a consequence that the land might be permanently spoiled. Refusing to represent the Simpsons and Hendersons would not be likely to change the outcome, and might only result in the families being victimized by a shrewd buyer. Ed left the office, briefcase in hand, hoping that the cold night air might help him sort out his jumbled thoughts, but there were no easy answers.

Chapter 6

"DARN! I forgot to wind the alarm clock. Here we go again!" Doug exclaimed to JR as he jumped out of bed on Friday morning. He threw on the same clothes he had dropped on the chair the night before, skipped breakfast, and rushed out the door on the run. Jogging all the way to school, he arrived in time to follow the last students straggling into the building. The sound of the bell echoed through the corridor as he stepped inside, announcing the start of the school day, forcing the boys and girls off toward their first period classes.

Glancing across the hall, Doug saw that Vickie was back in school, standing by her open locker with two friends, holding a card in one hand and her books in the other. The three girls looked his way, all laughing. "I'll get you for this, Mike," he said under his breath, as he walked past them and into the classroom, looking for his seat near the back. As he went by Mike's desk, he delivered a sharp, glancing blow to Mike's upper arm, causing him to flinch.

"Dawg, that really hurt!" Mike exclaimed, rubbing his arm and laughing. "What was that all about?" Mrs. Wilson scowled at them, and they both settled a little deeper into their seats, trying to avoid attention from her during the daily Latin translation question and answer session.

"What did you write on that Valentine?" Doug whispered.

"Vickie was showing it to two other girls, and they were all about to crack a rib laughing at me when I came in."

"You have a funny way of showing gratitude, Dawg," Mike replied in a barely audible voice. "She definitely knows now that you're a member of her fan club. Who knows what you could get out of this? You ought to be thanking me, not slugging me on the arm like that. " Both boys continued to avoid eye contact with Mrs. Wilson, and mercifully the period was soon over without either being called on for answers.

Ronnie caught up with them after class and wasted no time telling them what was on his mind. "I'm still looking for my pocket knife, the bone-handle Case XX I always carry with me, and I can't find it anywhere. I know that I had it in my pocket two weeks ago when we were climbing around at the foot of Chimney Rock, but I don't recall seeing it again since then. That was my grandpa's favorite knife, the one he used to carve whimmydiddles, sling shots, and walking sticks. He gave it to me a month before he died, and it means a lot to me. I wonder if y'all would be willing to go back there with me this Saturday to look around and see if it's lying somewhere on the ground."

"I don't know whether I want to go out there again," Doug replied. "I'm kind of gun-shy about going back after we just got rousted out by those two gorillas, and taking a chance on running into them again. If we did, we couldn't go up the road near their house, or they'd see us coming. We'd probably have to stay on the highway another half mile, and cut back through the trees to stay out of sight. I don't know how fast those two men can move, but I know both of you are faster than me, and I sure wouldn't want to be the one they run down."

"Don't act like a chicken, Dawg," Ronnie retorted. "You're starting to sound like Freddie. I really need you and Mike to help me out. Are you both good for this weekend? We can bike out there, look for my knife, and be back home by early afternoon. I promise, I'll do something for you next time to pay you back."

Doug and Mike reluctantly agreed to meet at Ronnie's house and bike out to the farm early Saturday morning. "I don't think we want anyone else along on this expedition, if we're trying sneak in and get back out of there without being seen,"

Doug remarked. "I'll clip a flashlight on my belt, in case we need some light back in that crevasse where you were climbing around last time. You're going to owe us big time for this one, Ronald."

Saturday morning turned out to be cloudy, cold, and windy, as the boys started north up the highway toward Chestnut Ridge on their bikes. Their heavy jackets, toboggans, and gloves helped to break the chill, and within a short time they felt almost uncomfortably warm, pedaling quickly along the road into a slight headwind. Less than an hour later, they'd passed the farm and arrived at the timber covered base of Chestnut Ridge. "Let's leave our bikes here close to the highway, hidden out of sight behind this stand of rhododendron," Doug suggested.

The three boys started on foot, single file, walking at a fast pace along the tree line in the direction of Chimney Rock. "So far, so good," Doug remarked in a low voice. "No one can see us. But we need to push it. It's starting to look like snow."

By the time they arrived at the base of Chimney Rock, snow flakes were starting to swirl. "I don't think we'll have to worry about seeing those two Buchanan men today," Mike commented, as the three began to search the ground along the path where they had walked during their recent camping trip.

Ronnie retraced his earlier route along the foot of the cliff to the crevasse in the rock and carefully stepped through the opening into the interior space surrounded by vertical stone walls. Searching along the ground inside, he suddenly called out, "I found it! It was back in here lying on the ground. I guess it must have fallen out of my pocket when I was bending over. Both blades are a little rusty, but that's all that's wrong with it."

Doug and Mike moved toward the crevasse to join him. Suddenly something caught Mike's eye, and he exclaimed in surprise, "Come look at this. There's a big pile of road apples over here in the dirt. And you can see tracks made by horse shoes all around us. Why would someone bring a horse out here?"

Ronnie called back to him, "I think I know. There's a big pole lying on the ground in here with a piece of rope tied to the end. I can see brown horse hair tangled in the other end of the rope. It looks like someone might have been using the pole as a lever to move rocks out of the way. They probably used the horse for pulling on the end of it."

Before Doug and Mike had time to reply, they heard Ronnie's excited voice echo from the crevasse again, "Come in here quick! Someone's opened a hole back in here under the rock slab. Dawg, I need to borrow your flashlight a minute."

Doug and Mike scrambled through the crevasse and crawled beneath the overhanging slab on hands and knees to join him. Ronnie took the flashlight from Doug and directed the beam of light inside the opening. Suddenly he whistled loudly enough to make the other two boys' ears ring. "Man, oh, man! You aren't going to believe this! I'm looking into a cave the size of that big one I saw last summer in Luray. I'm positive this hole wasn't open when we were exploring around here during our camping trip. Someone must have pried the rocks out of the way since then."

"Let's have a look, Ronnie," Doug requested. Holding the flashlight as far back in the hole as he could reach, he stuck his face close to the edge and peered inside, detecting the unmistakable smell of damp cave rock and dirt. The flashlight beam was not bright enough to light the ceiling or the back of the chamber. Redirecting the beam downward, Doug observed, "I can see the floor of the cave. It looks fairly flat in the front toward us."

Then something in the faint light caught his attention. "What in the world is that? I can barely make out something on the ground that looks like a couple of rows of wooden crates. It's too dim inside to tell much, but they appear to be a pretty good size, almost as big as caskets. Take a look, Mike, and tell me what you think." As Doug drew his arm back from the hole, he accidentally rapped the flashlight against the rock, and the light went out. "Crap," he exclaimed. "My flashlight just went out, and I can't get it to come back on. I must have busted the filament in the bulb!"

"Good job," Mike muttered in irritation. "Now we can't see a thing in there. Give me your flashlight for a minute, and let me see if I can get it back on again." Mike tried removing and replacing the batteries and bulb without success. "No way any of us are going to get this thing back on out here without a new bulb," he concluded. "Dawg had to go and bang it on a rock, and now it's deader than a hammer."

"I think we'd better be heading out of here," Ronnie said. "The snow's really starting to come down now, and if it starts to stick, we'll have to bike five miles back to town on a slick road."

The three boys moved back outside through the crevasse in the rock, with snow now turning their toboggans a wintry white. Looking toward the farm they were surprised to see two men in clear view feeding livestock off in the distance.

Crouching back close to the ground, Mike commented, "That was close. I don't think they saw us, but we'd better lie low until they leave."

The boys sat on the ground for almost an hour, repeatedly brushing the snowflakes from their clothing, shivering in the cold air, while the two men went about their farm chores. Finally, the men finished taking care of the livestock and walked away from them, disappearing across the field.

"Let's get out of here now," Mike pleaded. "My butt's frozen solid from sitting here waiting for them to clear out."

The three boys stiffly stood and jogged through the blowing snow back to the tree line, where they were no longer in sight of the house. They continued on, walking at a fast pace along a trail at the base of the ridge, until they got back to the rhododendron thicket where they had hidden their bicycles earlier. After brushing off their bikes with gloved hands, they headed back toward town, riding single file on the shoulder of the highway.

The snow had now begun to stick, making it difficult to detect icy spots on the pavement. As the three descended a hill and went into a sharp curve, they were totally unprepared for a patch of black ice lying under white cover. When Ronnie applied his brakes, his rear wheel lost traction, sending him and the bike flat down to the pavement, skidding across the road into a ditch on the other side.

Doug and Mike braked carefully to a stop, and ran back to check on Ronnie. "Are you hurt bad?" Mike called out in concern.

"I think I'm OK," Ronnie grimaced. "I've skinned up my leg pretty bad, and torn my pants all to hell, but I don't think I broke anything. It could have been worse."

Using Mike's less-than-clean handkerchief, they wiped the

blood and dirt off Ronnie's leg, then remounted their bikes and cautiously continued on their way.

When they arrived back in town, Ronnie said appreciatively, "Thanks for going with me today. I'm sure glad to have my knife back. I'm going home now to clean my leg up, and put some iodine on it where I took the skin off. It's been a pretty exciting day, hasn't?"

"We had a lot more excitement than we needed," Mike replied. "But I'm glad you got your knife back, and that you weren't hurt bad when you hit that ice and wrecked on your bike." The boys separated and pedaled off into the swirling snow, heading toward their homes.

Riding his bike up the driveway, Doug jumped off and rolled it toward the garage. The instant he lifted the overhead door, JR bounded up from his scatter rug on the concrete floor to greet him, jumping up on him with his tail wagging. As he dried the melting snow off the bike with a rag, JR continued to give him a frisky welcome home. "Take it easy, boy," Doug gently reprimanded him. "You're going to tear my jacket."

When he stepped into the house with JR following on his heels, Ed called out to him, "You're either a little late for lunch or a little early for dinner, son. Where in the world have you been all this time? I was starting to get worried. It's been snowing for over an hour."

"Let me make a sandwich and grab an orange drink, and I'll fill you in on everything," Doug replied. He proceeded to relate what the three boys had seen, while Ed listened closely. "You won't believe the size of that cave we were looking in," he exclaimed. "I was the only one that got a look at the wood crates."

"I'm glad you boys got back safely. But the next time, I want to sign off on any adventures where you and your friends plan to go trespassing on other people's property, and end up biking five miles on a highway in the snow."

After a short hesitation, Ed added, "I'm amazed you boys saw where the Buchanans have located that old cave below Chimney Rock! Who'd have thought that they'd be able to clear out a hole where you can actually look inside."

"And who'd have ever thought they would use a work horse

to move rocks out of the way," Doug chimed in.

"I can't imagine what you were looking at before your flashlight went out. Why in the world would anyone store a bunch of wooden crates on the floor of a cave? And why do you suppose the family has been working so hard to get inside? It's all very curious."

"I don't have any idea what's going on out there," Doug answered. Putting his arm around the dog's neck, he added, "Maybe we could take our fine hound out there and let him go in that hole and sniff around. You'd find out what's inside and come back out and tell us everything, wouldn't you, JR?"

Chapter 7

CAROLYN RECEIVED the expected phone call late Monday morning, informing Ed, "Mr. Thorpe with Copperfield Enterprises is on the line for you."

After they exchanged greetings, Ed explained, "Mr. Thorpe, I'm an attorney representing the Robert Simpson and Clarence Henderson families. Both have received offers from your company to purchase their property. Neither had considered putting his farm on the market before receiving your letter. I'm trying to assist them as they consider the offers and the pros and cons of selling their property. It would be helpful if you could tell me about Copperfield Enterprises, and why your company is interested in buying these properties."

Thorpe replied, "Copperfield Enterprises is a holding company for an investor who speculates in businesses and real estate in West Virginia. The owner thinks that real estate in the area north of Eden Springs is a good investment, based on the general long term growth potential. Since the end of the war, the population across the entire country has been exploding, and we're both familiar with that old cliché about land, 'they're not making any more of it'."

Ed quickly realized that his inquiry was going nowhere, and that he was unlikely to obtain any truthful or helpful information. "Mr. Thorpe, the Simpsons and Hendersons are going to need more than thirty days to decide whether or not to sell their farms. This is the biggest decision of their lives."

"Mr. Housman, unfortunately our business situation does not permit us to give you and your clients more time. You have thirty days, as stipulated in the letters. After that, our offers will be off the table. I hope to hear from you soon with their acceptance."

Ed hung up the phone and spoke to Carolyn. "William Thorpe knows he's in the driver's seat, and he isn't about to negotiate an extension or anything else. He's well aware that the Simpsons and Hendersons have never seen this kind of money in their lifetimes, and he knows that neither couple can expect to have an offer for their property like this again. He's dangling a very enticing carrot in front of them."

Glancing at his schedule for the day, he continued, "Please see if the Simpsons and Hendersons can meet with me briefly after lunch. Normally, I wouldn't want to see both couples together, but obviously, they've already been talking with each other about this matter."

The Simpsons and Hendersons showed up that afternoon a few minutes ahead of the scheduled time. Ed opened the conversation, "I wanted to give you some new information about the offers to purchase your farms. First, Copperfield Enterprises has denied my request for an extension of the thirty-day offer period. Second, we now know quite a bit more about Copperfield and have some insight as to why the company may have such an urgent interested in buying your properties.

"I've recently discovered that Copperfield Enterprises is a subsidiary of Barker Mining, which is owned by a powerful businessman named Robert Copperfield Barker. I've heard rumors of a major coal discovery in the valley where you all live, and I think that Barker may now be trying to buy up land out that way in order to develop a coal mining operation. You should consider what I've just said to be personal conjecture, but also realize that it's based on the best information we have at this time."

There was a moment of complete silence after Ed finished before Clarence responded. "I'm surprised that Barker Mining may be speculating on a coal seam out our way. I've got family living in the coal fields near Nitro, and I've heard them talk about Barker Mining for years. My sister's house has cracks in the walls and foundation that were caused by Barker crews blasting too close to their home. She and her husband were never able to collect for the damage. My brother-in-law calls the company owner 'Copperhead.' I never had any idea where he got that until you just told us Barker's middle name is Copperfield."

Robert glanced toward the Hendersons and replied, "I hear what you're saying, Clarence, but we don't know they'd do the same kind of damage to the land around here. The price they're offering for our farms would buy a lot of property just as good as what we have, and we'd have money left over in the bank to help us out in the years ahead. I think we ought to look at this from all sides, just like Mr. Housman told us, before we go making our decisions."

As the Simpsons and Hendersons left the office, Ed closed the door behind them and sat back down at his desk with a cold cup of coffee, trying to decide what he should do next. The thought of a strip mining operation near Abner gap seemed almost incomprehensible, and yet what other real motive could Barker Mining have for buying land up that way at such inflated prices.

As he was preparing to wrap up things for the day, the phone rang, and Carolyn told him that Dr. Jannsen was holding on the line. He knew the doctor, a man twenty-five years his senior, from a visit the previous year after Doug had sprained an ankle during football practice. When Ed picked up the phone, he heard a voice with a distinctive accent say, "Mr. Housman, this is Arnold Jannsen. I wonder if I could drop by your office before work tomorrow and speak with you for a few minutes? Would you be available if I were to come over around 7:30?"

"Certainly. I'll be right here, and it would be a pleasure to have you drop in. I'll be looking for you first thing tomorrow morning."

As Carolyn passed his desk, Ed glanced up and remarked, "Dr. Jannsen's coming by before work in the morning, but I have no idea what it's all about. I'm a little curious, since I haven't had any dealings with him for quite some time. I suppose I'll just have to wait to find out."

Carolyn had not yet arrived when Dr. Jannsen showed up the next morning. Ed met him at the door, saying, "Good to see you again, Dr Jannsen. Let's go in my office where we can sit down and talk. And please call me Ed."

"Thanks, Ed," Dr. Jannsen replied. "And I'd like it if you'd call me Arnold. We don't seem to run into each other very often, considering that this is such a small town. I believe my grand-daughter goes to high school with your son. Anyway, let me get right to the purpose of my visit, so I don't tie you up long."

Dr. Jannsen took a seat and began to talk. "Please treat what I am about to tell you as confidential. For well over thirty-five years, I've provided medical care for Gideon and Hester Buchanan, and also for their twin sons, Daniel and Jonah. The parents are now over ninety years old, and the sons are past fifty. You're probably aware that the family lives in an old man-sion up on the knoll, on land that spreads from the top of Pine Ridge across the valley up past the top of Chestnut Ridge, and all the way north to Abner Gap. Gideon's father, Eleazar, lived during the Civil War. He was a very religious man and a strong willed pacifist throughout his life. He adamantly refused to co-operate with either the Union or the Confederacy during the war, making it even more ironic that the Battle of Eden Springs was actually fought on his land. Gideon was just an infant at that time.

"The family still lives a pretty primitive life today. About thirty years ago, the REA ran electric power out to their place, and a little later, the Madison County Telephone Company put in a phone line on the same poles. The house has running water pumped from a well, and indoor plumbing connected to an old septic tank, but other than lights, water, and indoor plumbing, there've been few improvements and very little maintenance to the home. The house is still heated in the winter time by a couple of woodstoves, and fireplaces in a few of the rooms.

"The Buchanans don't have a lot of money coming in. They do have small checking and savings accounts at the Farmers and Merchants Bank in town. The bank also handles their tax returns. But Gideon and Hester are a classic example of farm owners who are land-poor. Although they own property that is worth a considerable fortune, they have very little in the way of disposable income and savings. The two sons run the farm, and that generates just enough money for them all to live on.

Tony Vicelli, my-son-law, who owns the Fresh Harvest Market, buys some of the meat and produce for his store from them. In turn, he makes a special trip out to their house once a week to deliver groceries."

Arnold paused to catch his breath, and then continued, "I realized that the family needed domestic help about fifteen years ago, so I arranged for Myrtle Spencer, a widow who lives alone nearby, to come in and keep house for them during the day. The crux of the matter is this: the elder Buchanans are in declining health and cannot expect to live a great deal longer. Hester has congestive heart failure, and Gideon is crippled with severe arthritis. The sons are still in good health, but are so backward, and act so strange from living out there alone all of their lives, that many people around here think they are simple minded.

"You may be wondering why I'm telling you all of this, so I'll get to the point now and tell you where you fit in. John Crawford, the attorney who retired and sold you his practice, did some legal work for the Buchanans and drew up their current will about five years ago."

"I knew that John handled their will, but I've had no contact with the Buchanans since I moved here," Ed commented.

"Ed, Gideon's will leaves the place to the two sons after he and Hester are gone. The executor is Julian Grant, Gideon's nephew who moved here last year from Bluefield. For years, Julian's been trying to get Gideon to revise the will to make him the next heir in line for the farm after the sons are gone. Things have changed recently, and Gideon senses that his nephew's now trying to gain control of the estate. Recently, Julian came by the house and insisted that Gideon authorize him to find a buyer for the property. He promised to help find a home where all four could move into town. Gideon doesn't want to sell and he's determined that he, Hester, and their sons will all finish out their lives under the roof of that old house. When I told him you'd taken over John Crawford's practice, he requested that I arrange for you meet with him and give him your advice. Are you interested in taking Gideon on as a client?"

"I would definitely like to talk with him. What's the next move?"

"I anticipated your answer. Can we plan to meet with them at their home late Friday afternoon? I need to go back out there

and see how Hester is responding to some new medicine I prescribed for her, while you're talking with Gideon."

"I'll join you at their home at 4:00," Ed replied. "I want to see
if there's a copy of their will filed in my office, and try to famil-
iarize myself with it before I go out there. I'm looking forward
to meeting the family and getting a look inside that old mansion. Thanks for coming by to discuss this, and for setting up
the meeting."

Ed settled into the routine workload with Carolyn after Dr.
Jannsen left the office. One particularly complex case took most
of their morning, and they were still working together when the
phone rang just before lunch. When he picked up the receiver,
Ed was surprised to find that the caller was William Thorpe, his
tone sounding surprisingly warm and friendly, quite unlike the
terse voice Ed remembered from the previous conversation.

"Mr. Housman, this is William Thorpe again. I had the pleasure of speaking with you on the phone a few days ago. I'll be
driving through your area tomorrow, and I'd like to have lunch
with you. Could you meet me at the Eden Springs Resort dining room at noon? I have a private matter I'd like to discuss
with you."

"Does this possibly pertain to your offers to purchase the Simpson
and Henderson properties that we discussed on the phone?"

"No, this involves something entirely different. I don't mean
to sound mysterious, but I'd like to defer discussing the purpose of our meeting until we can talk face to face."

After agreeing to the proposed meeting, Ed spoke to Carolyn.
"Mr. Thorpe must have gotten out of the bed on a different side
this morning. He was most pleasant speaking to me. I'm having lunch with him tomorrow, and he made it sound like we're
two old school buddies getting together for a reunion."

"One thing about this business," Carolyn observed. "You
never know hour to hour what's going to happen next, particularly when dealing with people like Thorpe."

Ed returned to his work, and was still at his desk after Carolyn
departed. It was later than usual when he finally rolled into the
driveway and walked up to the house. He ran into Doug as he
came through the front door.

"You're late, and your dinner's cold. The next time I want to sign off on any adventure where you're going to tie me up in the kitchen like this."

Ed couldn't suppress a laugh. "What's that all about?"

"Let's just say that the chickens have come home to roost," Doug replied, grinning.

After hanging his coat in the closet, Ed joined Doug in the kitchen and said, "I have a real adventure to offer you. How would you like to go out to the Buchanan home with me Friday afternoon after school? You'll get to walk in through the front door and meet the family like a gentleman, and not have to sneak around out in back of the house like a chicken thief, the way you and your friends apparently did the last time you were there."

"Sounds like fun to me. What time will we leave?" As he warmed his dad's dinner, Doug added, "I hope the two sons didn't catch sight of us when Mike, Ronnie, and I were out there on that snowy day, trespassing on their property. You probably haven't seen them up close yet, but they're both huge. I wouldn't want either of them holding any grudge against me."

Chapter 8

E D STOPPED by the diner on the way to work the next morning and picked up a half dozen warm doughnuts. He stopped at Carolyn's desk, leaving three of them wrapped in a napkin beside her typewriter, then went back to his office. Sitting down with a cup of black coffee, he impulsively dialed the number for Jackson Realty and asked for Laura. When she picked up, he said, "Good morning, Sunshine. I thought I'd give you a call before you get out and start showing property to clients this morning."

"Good morning, Ed, and good timing. I was just killing a few minutes before an early appointment to show several houses to a new family moving into town. What's up?"

"That's probably enough time for me to tell you several things I've learned about the real estate activity north of town. I'll fill you in quickly, so I don't hold you up. A law school classmate told me that one of the buyers, Copperfield Enterprises, is nothing but a business front for Barker Mining. After finding that out, I talked with a Copperfield vice-president named Thorpe, and I put him on the spot by asking why his company is so interested in buying up farms in this area. Without missing a beat, he told me that they're simply speculating on land around here because of the post-war baby boom and population explosion everywhere. That's such an absurd answer that it could probably win first prize at a liar's convention. Does any of this surprise you?"

"I certainly knew nothing about a connection between Copperfield Enterprises and Barker Mining until you just told me, but it all starts to make sense now. I have some new information to share, too. I've learned that a sales contract just closed with the owner of several other sizeable tracts of land in that same area. From what you tell me, I'd bet my life that the buyer is an agent for Copperfield and Barker."

"I hadn't heard about that. But here's one other thing, and I've saved the best for last. Thorpe called me back yesterday, talking like he's my new best friend, and told me he's driving down from Beckley and wants me to meet him for lunch today. He's very mysterious about why he wants to get together, and what he wants to discuss with me. He said it has nothing to do with the purchase of land around here. Would you care to take a guess?"

"Ed, I have no idea. But it does seem very curious that he's so anxious to meet with you right now, but won't tell you what it's all about. I'd like to be a fly on the wall when you're talking to him. Give me a call back later with a full report of everything that goes on."

"You'll be the first to hear," Ed promised. After the conversation ended, he returned to his work, and he was still engrossed much later when Carolyn approached him.

"Are you aware of the time?" she inquired. "You're going to be late for your luncheon appointment with Mr. Thorpe." Grabbing his coat, he dashed out of the office.

The parking lot held only a few cars when Ed pulled up in front of Eden Springs Resort. There was one that Ed had not seen previously around town, a shiny new dark blue Buick sedan. The hostess recognized him as he entered, informing him, "Mr. Housman, a gentleman is seated at the table across the room waiting for you." Walking toward the table, Ed observed a tall middle-aged man in a dark blue business suit, staring at him through gold framed glasses.

The man stood as Ed approached, extending his hand and introducing himself. "I'm William Thorpe, and I believe that you must be Edward Housman." It became obvious that he was very self-assured and held strong opinions, as dining conversation covered the spectrum from the current state of the national economy to Southern Conference sports. Thorpe was obviously a big fan of the West Virginia Mountaineers basketball team.

"The 'eers had another great season under Coach Brown," he announced. "Red works the boys a lot more on offense than Coach Patton did, and you can tell the difference by the way the team's been putting points on the board for the last two years. Anytime you go 24-4 for the season like they just did, you're doing something right. When Vandy football coach Henry Sanders said back in the '30's, 'winning isn't everything, it's the only thing', he may have been joking, but I've always thought he had it exactly right. Winning is the only thing that counts, as far as I'm concerned."

A waitress approached their table during the meal to refill their water glasses. She was obviously very young, new to the job, and anxious to please the customers. As she poured from a large pitcher, the ice suddenly shifted, and water splashed on the linen table cloth beside Thorpe's glass.

"Watch what you're doing," he reprimanded her sharply. Observing her leave the table on the verge of tears, he glanced at Ed and said, "I don't know why these places can't hire competent help." Then he changed the subject, his irritation falling away as if nothing had just happened.

When they had finished their meal, and the dishes had been cleared from the table, Thorpe offered Ed a cigar, then pushed his chair back and lit one himself. He began, "Mr. Housman, or Ed, if I may call you by your first name now that we've gotten better acquainted, I'm going to get right to the point without beating around the bush as to why I asked you to join me for lunch today.

"Copperfield Enterprises is investing heavily in real estate in this area, as you're aware. We expect to develop certain parcels of land we've purchased for different purposes, and we need the full time services of an attorney with the right skills, experience, and political contacts to protect our interests, and help us realize a good return on our sizable investment. In looking for the right attorney, we've done some research, and we believe you're the person who exactly fits the bill for us. We've checked around, and our study indicates that attorneys in private practice in towns the size of Eden Springs have an annual income in this range."

Thorpe pulled a business card and pen from his pocket, scribbling a figure on the back of the card. Looking at the amount, Ed could see the round number was somewhat more than the current yearly income from his business. Then Thorpe continued, "If you come to work for us, we are prepared to immediately sign a contract that will pay you this amount per year." Looking directly at Ed, he took the pen and wrote "2 x" in front of the first number. "How do you feel about the salary, Ed? There are other benefits as well, but I thought the salary might be most important to you. I know that you have a son who'll be going off to school in a couple of years, and having enough money for a child's college expenses is very important to a parent."

"I must confess, I'm totally taken aback by your offer," Ed replied. "I never dreamed that this was the matter you wanted to discuss with me today. If I were to accept the job, specifically what would you expect me to provide in the way of legal services? I'm sure you're already aware that I have very little training and no experience in corporate law. Practicing law in a small town like this makes you more a legal jack of all trades."

"Your lack of training and experience in corporate law is not a problem for my company. Your duties would vary widely, depending on the needs of our businesses. Using your own words, you would be a legal jack of all trades for us, taking direction from me personally, and functioning as my right hand man. The attributes we are looking for beyond legal competence are total loyalty to the company, and the ability to be very discreet in conducting our business, much of which is extremely confidential."

"I take your offer as a professional and personal compliment. I certainly won't pretend that I make nearly the money now that your company is prepared to pay me. On the other hand, I do own my business, and I've always enjoyed the independence that goes along with being my own boss."

Looking steadily at Ed and speaking in a voice that seemed to have lost some of its earlier warmth, Thorpe responded, "Mr. Housman, I'm reminded of a famous quotation from Shakespeare that goes, 'There is a tide in the affairs of men which taken at the flood leads on to fortune.' Your personal tide of opportunity is running very high as we speak. I really believe it would be in your best interest to accept my offer. Go home and think about what I've just laid out before you. In the game of life, you probably get only one chance like this to join the winning team. I assure you, life is much more pleasant for the winners. I'll need to hear from you very soon."

"I appreciate your driving down today to offer me this position," Ed replied. "I'll give it serious consideration and get back to you with my decision just as soon as possible."

When Ed got back to his office, he found that Carolyn was gone for the afternoon, leaving him without the benefit of her valued advice. Remembering Laura's request for an update following the meeting, he dialed her number, and heard her pick up the phone. "I'm back from lunch with William Thorpe. Do you want to hear what just happened? You may want to sit down before I fill you in."

Ed related everything that had been discussed at lunch. "I'm still not sure what to make of Thorpe's employment pitch. He's offered me an annual salary which guarantees me more money than I expected to earn in my career if I 'join the winning team.' But he also implied that I only get one chance to join, and if I don't, life may not be as pleasant."

"Ed, you can't be thinking seriously about going to work for Copperfield and Barker for any amount of money," Laura said. "You're the very one who told me about their reputation for exploiting the land and the people of West Virginia. I know it's said that everyone has his or her price, but I've come to know you well enough to be certain Thorpe and Barker couldn't buy you. I don't think anyone could buy you. You'll have to refuse the offer, or you won't be able to live with yourself."

"I guess just seeing the large salary figure he marked on his business card had me carried away at the time. Looking back, I suppose that I should've told Thorpe no on the spot, but somehow, it seemed that I ought to at least consider his offer. I'll call him in the morning, and tell him that I've decided to decline. Now I suppose I'll have to worry about the unpleasant part of not joining his team."

"Maybe you're reading too much into what he said about life being better if you join the winning team. Maybe the unpleasant consequence of declining the offer is only a figment of your imagination. If I thought otherwise, I'd be more worried than you. But you've definitely made the right decision, and it's the only one you could live with. I think you'll sleep better tonight. Please let me know what he says."

"Laura, before you hang up, there's something I want to say," Ed interjected. "Thanks for telling me you don't think I'd sell out to the highest bidder. Hearing that you respect my integrity means a lot to me. I'll call you again soon, and let you know how Thorpe reacts."

Ed reported the events of the day to Doug when he got home that evening, including Laura's comments. "She paid you a nice compliment, Dad, and I think she steered you right," Doug said. "You told me about Barker Mining earlier. I don't think you'd be happy working for a company with their reputation for any amount of money. We may not be rich, but we're getting along just fine right now."

Despite what Laura and Doug had said, Ed couldn't help but continue to mull the pros and cons of Thorpe's offer throughout the evening. The prospects of a secure college fund for Doug's education, a new home for both of them on a large tract of land, and other possible benefits stayed in the back of his mind until he finally dropped off to sleep.

Ed called Copperfield Enterprises late the following morning, feeling a nervous anticipation about the conversation to come. When the secretary got Thorpe on the line, he said, "Mr. Thorpe, I've had enough time to consider the position with Copperfield Enterprises you discussed with me yesterday, and while I appreciate the confidence you demonstrated by offering me the job, I've made a decision to decline."

William Thorpe responded in a flat voice, as though he had anticipated Ed's answer, "I'm sorry you've made your decision to refuse the offer of professional employment with Copperfield Enterprises, Mr. Housman. I truly regret that you've decided to reject such a generous offer with so little serious consideration. I believe it would have been in both our best interests if you had decided to accept and come to work with us. But since your mind is obviously made up, I don't see any need to pursue this any further." Thorpe hung up without further comment, giving Ed no time to say goodbye.

Ed smiled wryly as he hung up the phone. He had the feeling of a player whose coach has not just pulled him from the starting lineup, but has also booted him off the team, telling him to clear out his locker and turn in his equipment. I'll be on the other side of the ball from the Copperfield team from now on, he thought

Chapter 9

ALL IN all, Friday was a good day at school for Doug. Mrs. Wilson was out sick, and the substitute teacher quickly gave up trying to conduct her Latin class according to the lesson plan, instead allowing the students use the period as a study hall. Geometry class went even better, as Mr. Powell returned test papers from the previous day. Doug's mark of 100 tied Shirley Martin's for the highest score in the class.

"You must have copied off Shirley's paper, Dawg," Mike said. "I wish I'd gotten a few answers from her, and then maybe Old Man Powell wouldn't have bled all over my paper. Did you ever see so many red marks?"

"I can't help it if I'm another Einstein in the field of math and science," Doug replied, enjoying the moment. "I got a look at Vickie's test paper when they were passing them out just now, and she missed a bunch of problems, too. Maybe she'll ask me to start helping her with her homework after this."

At lunch time, Doug sat down at a corner table with Mike and Freddie and said, "I need for y'all to cover for me at basketball practice after school today. Tell Coach I had to miss practice because I had a doctor's appointment. That's not a total lie, since I'm going with my dad to see some people, and Dr. Jannsen will be there. The next time you have to miss a practice, I'll do the same thing for you."

"We've got you covered, Dawg," Mike promised. "But Jesse may have to cancel practice today, since the star of the JV squad won't be there to demonstrate ball handling and shooting technique."

As he stood to leave, Doug noticed Vickie in a blue sweater sitting at a table beside stocky, dark-haired Len Hacker. The two were looking at each other, talking and laughing, the mutual attraction very obvious. It puzzled him that the prettiest girl in the tenth grade was sitting there making eyes at the most obnoxious senior. It doesn't look like she's got her mind on finding a geometry tutor, Doug thought. Len couldn't pass eighth grade math, unless the teacher graded his exam on a curve.

Doug had just gotten in from school when his dad pulled up in front of the house. Ed slid over to let him take the wheel of the car, as he often did since Doug had gotten his driver's license. "Dr. Jannsen's going to meet us out there," he said, as Doug turned the car around and headed north.

Driving up the long gravel road to the house, they saw that Dr. Jannsen was waiting for them in the driveway, sitting in his black Buick, with the motor running and the heater on. After exchanging greetings, Ed said, "I hope we haven't kept you waiting long. Carolyn and I looked all through our office file cabinets, but we couldn't find a trace of the Buchanans' will anywhere. Maybe Gideon keeps a copy somewhere, possibly here at the house, or more likely at the bank."

They climbed the steps leading up to the front porch, where they encountered the two sons waiting for them by the door. "How are your ma and pa doing today?" Dr Jannsen inquired in a friendly voice.

"Bout the same," the one standing on the left answered, holding the front door open for them.

Dr. Jannsen introduced Ed and Doug to the sons, Daniel and Jonah. The five men then entered the house through a foyer, which opened onto a spectacularly ornate central room with high ceilings and dark wood paneling. Doug found the inside of the house to be as cold as the porch outside. Heavy drapes at the tall windows and dirty glass panes blocked most of the light, making the interior dark even in daylight. At one side of the room, a curved staircase with walnut railings led to the second floor, but stacked cardboard boxes blocked the steps. It looked as though no one had gone upstairs for weeks, or possibly months. The dark wood furniture appeared to have been brought in soon after the house was built, many, many years earlier. The only signs of modern improvement were exposed electrical wires running from switches on the wall to overhead lights.

As they walked through the cold, dark hallway toward the back of the house, Doug noticed the peeling paint on the walls and warped boards in the floor. But the thing that struck him the most was the damp, musty smell, one that you might expect in an old store room where doors and windows are never opened.

A tall, thin woman entered the hallway ahead of them through a side door. Her gray hair was pulled straight back in a bun, and she was wearing an apron over a faded blue house dress and heavy gray sweater.

Dr. Jannsen greeted her with smile. "Good afternoon, Myrtle. I'd like you to meet Mr. Housman and his son Doug." Speaking to Ed and Doug, he said, "This is Myrtle Spencer. She's the housekeeper for the family."

"Pleased to meet you," Myrtle muttered in a raspy voice with a country accent. She then quickly scurried ahead of them down the dark hallway, the heels of her worn work shoes creating a tapping echo along the corridor, until she passed through a doorway on the other end and disappeared from sight.

The two sons led Dr. Jannsen, Ed, and Doug back to a large bedroom, where they saw a frail, white-haired lady with dark eyes, lying in bed propped up on pillows, a crocheted comforter pulled up around her. The room was somewhat brighter and much warmer than the rest of the house, and it was obvious why. Old lace curtains had been pulled back from the dirt-spotted glass window to let in the sunlight, and a hot pot-bellied stove in front of the adjacent brick fireplace made the nearby part of the room uncomfortably hot.

A tall, bespectacled old man with sparse white hair and a straggly beard sat in a straight-back chair at her bedside. He took a carved wood cane from beside the bed, using it to push himself slowly to his feet as they came in the room.

Dr. Jannsen spoke, "Mr. and Mrs. Buchanan, I'd like to introduce Mr. Edward Housman and his son, Douglas. As I told you the last time I was here, Mr. Housman is the attorney who's taken over Mr. Crawford's practice. He's here to discuss changes to your will, at your request."

Gideon Buchanan smiled, holding out his hand, and speaking in a low, quavering voice, "Hester and I are privileged to meet you and your boy, Mr. Housman. We appreciate your coming all the way out here to talk with us." Hester looked at them and nodded her head. "Could you and I go into the library to talk, Mr. Housman, while Dr. Jannsen attends to my wife? Your son can go back in the front room with my boys, while we're conducting our business." Gideon motioned for Ed to follow him, as he hobbled out of the bedroom into the hallway.

Doug returned to the front room, following Daniel and Jonah. Having seen how age had impacted the Buchanan family, the two sons no longer seemed so ominous and threatening to him, despite their size. Rather, they seemed almost pathetic, overwhelmed by the circumstances of their family. It appeared to Doug that they were fully aware of the failing health of their mother and father, with no idea of what to do, and were relieved that Dr. Jannsen and Ed Housman were now in their home to help. One of the twins dug into the pocket of his coveralls, pulled out an apple, and offered it to him. Doug hesitated, then reached out to take the apple. "Thanks," he said, unable to distinguish between the two men.

The second son looked at him closely and spoke, "I saw you before." The remark was unsettling to Doug. He was unsure whether the man was talking about the time he was standing at the front door asking for permission to camp, or possibly the time he and his friends were discovered snooping around the family property below Chimney Rock.

"I let you camp up on the ridge," the man continued. "I'm Daniel, and this here is Jonah. You can tell me by where I cut my finger tip off with an axe." Daniel held up his left hand to show where the last joint of his index finger was missing.

"I'm Doug Housman," Doug reminded them. "My dad's a lawyer. He's here to help your father."

"We know that," Daniel said. "You got your coat on. Let's go out to the barn. We'll show you the new calf born yesterday."

On the walk to the barn, Doug wanted to ask the men about the reopened cave entrance that he and his friends had recently discovered out at the foot of Chimney Rock. But he realized that if he asked, he would tip off the two men that the three had been back on their property, trespassing.

When they reached the barn, Jonah opened the door and led Doug to a stall where a day-old calf stood nursing its brown and white Guernsey mother. "They're milk cows," Daniel commented. "We got some beef cattle over in the other field." The two men led Doug around the pens, proudly showing off their livestock.

Entering one of the sheds, Jonah lifted the cover of a sturdy wooden bin and filled a metal pail with cracked corn. Doug followed the men through a gate into a fenced pen containing a large number of chickens and a few ducks. Jonah handed the pail to Doug, gesturing for him to scatter the grain on the ground. The men smiled broadly as the flock rushed in to compete noisily for the grain. There was a crippled duck that seemed to be their pet, and judging by its size, it obviously received special attention at feeding time. By the time the Daniel and Jonah had finished showing him around the barns and pens, Doug's opinion of the twins had undergone a complete change. He sensed that the two were as attached to the lame duck as he had become to JR.

Ed and Dr. Jannsen had finished their business with Gideon and Hester, and were sitting in front of the house in the Buick talking while waiting for Doug to return. As he approached, Ed got out of the car and walked over to his Ford. Doug looked back at Daniel and Jonah, raising his arm to wave goodbye as he climbed into the seat beside his father. Standing on the porch in the twilight, the sons reminded him of two forlorn old hunting dogs. "Hope I wasn't late getting back from walking around the farm," he said apologetically to his dad, as Ed headed back down the unpaved road toward the highway.

Ed turned off the radio to talk. "I'll tell you what just went on back there, but you must keep this to yourself. Gideon has lost trust in his nephew, Julian Grant, who's the executor of his will. Gideon is well aware that his wife is failing, and he realizes that he may not have too much longer himself. He's requested that I draft a revised will and act as executor.

"Gideon wants to be sure his sons inherit the home, farm, and all other assets after he and Hester are gone. And he wants

Roseanna to be restored as soon as money is available, and the farm to be preserved intact as a Civil War memorial park after the sons are deceased. Gideon plans to cut Julian out of his will, and leave him very little except for family belongings which are worth almost nothing. Gideon is a bright man, and he's well aware that his nephew will be very upset when he learns of these plans. He expressed a concern that Julian may try to do something to prevent them from being carried out."

Doug looked closely at his father and asked, "What do you think Julian could do to stop him?"

Ed replied, "If anything happened to Gideon before a new will could be executed, the current will would stay in effect, and Julian would remain as executor. To make matters worse, Gideon is confused as to whether he's ever given Julian power of attorney in the event he's incapacitated. If he's done so, this could give his nephew the opportunity to have him declared mentally incompetent, and sell the farm against his wishes. Julian seems to have earned a reputation for being shrewd and vindictive. Dr. Jannsen knows Julian, and he thinks Gideon's concerns are valid."

"What will you do next?"

"Gideon has given me his key and written authorization to enter his strong box at the bank in order to get the existing will. He wants me to revise it, and to prepare a letter granting me power of attorney, according to his instructions today. He feels a strong sense of urgency about getting this done."

Doug settled back in his seat, mulling over what his dad had just said, trying to visualize what kind of man Julian must be in order to scheme against a helpless relative.

Ed and Doug stopped by Gil's when they reached town, buying burgers and fries to go. Back at the house, they ate their meal in the kitchen, and afterward, Doug fed JR a can of Red Heart, which disappeared almost as quickly as it hit the dog dish. Then he and his dad moved into more comfortable chairs in the living room. "Might as well relax for now," Ed said. "Nothing more I can do for Gideon until Monday." Looking over at Doug, he inquired, "Have you and your friends got anything planned for tomorrow?"

"Nothing special. Some of my buddies and I will probably

have a pickup basketball game tomorrow afternoon over on the court beside the church. Usually about six of us show up, and we choose up sides and play three-on-three. There's a new kid from Bristol who's here for the rest of the school year, and I invited him to join us. Tomorrow night, I may go over to the canteen. There's always a group of kids from school that hang out there on Saturday night to shoot pool, play ping pong, dance to the juke box, and all the usual stuff. What about you?"

"It seems strange for me to be back in the dating scene at my age, but I'm going to ask Laura to go out to dinner and take in a movie with me tomorrow night," Ed said. "*War of the Worlds* is playing downtown at the Lyric, and I've had a thing for science fiction since I was your age."

Picking up the phone he dialed Laura's number, and when she answered the phone in her low voice, he said, "This is Ed, again. I wondered if you'd like to go out tomorrow night for dinner and a movie."

Laura hesitated for a few moments, unsure of how to answer. She felt it unnecessary to mention that earlier in the day she had accepted a similar dinner invitation from Dan Wohlford. Collecting her thoughts, she replied, "Ed, normally I would love to go out with you, but I've already made plans for tomorrow. I really wish you'd called me earlier. Could we try it another time?"

"Certainly," Ed replied, trying to conceal his disappointment. "I'll call you further ahead the next time. Hope you have a good evening. Bye, now."

Chapter 10

E D WAS waiting at the front door when the bank opened on a rainy Monday morning. He spoke to the manager, Hiram Underwood, explaining the purpose of his visit. After displaying the key and hand scribbled authorization from Gideon, he followed Hiram back to the vault, signed the safe deposit record book, and together they opened the door to the strong box.

The box was filled to the top with old documents, most of which had darkened from white to tan with age. Two stood out as more recent additions, due to the light color of the paper on which they were printed. The first was the original will, created by John Crawford in 1947, and signed by Gideon, Hester, and witnesses. The second was a carbon copy of a letter, written by an attorney in Bluefield in January of 1952, signed by Gideon, assigning power of attorney to Julian Grant. Ed took the two documents and slipped them into his coat pocket, before closing and locking the strong box.

"May I look at your safe deposit record book again to see who's been in the family strong box lately?" Ed asked. It took only a quick glance to find the two most recent previous entries: January 21, 1952 - Julian Grant, Executor for Gideon Buchanan (written in neat cursive), and on the line above that, Gideon Buchanan - June 14, 1947 (entered in an almost illegible scrawl).

As the two men walked to the front of the bank, Ed said, "I need to talk to Gideon about one of these documents, and see what he may be able to tell me. If I may use your phone, I'll call my office, and leave word with Carolyn where I'm going."

Heading out of town, Ed's windshield wipers provided the hypnotic background rhythm of a metronome in the steady rain. Heavy clouds overhead combined with the dark, wet asphalt pavement to make the road difficult to see, and he soon turned on his headlights.

There was no traffic in sight for almost two miles, until he noticed an approaching vehicle through his rear view mirror. The straight stretch of highway turned into a roller coaster of hills and curves as it crossed over a low ridge, causing him to decelerate below the fifty mile an hour speed limit. He observed the vehicle behind him continuing to close the distance separating them, until it was almost up to his rear bumper. Even with the rain streaming down the back window, he was now able see that it was a dark colored panel truck, most likely a late model Ford, running without headlights. It appeared that two men were sitting in the cab.

Approaching a sharp left turn in the highway, the truck suddenly pulled into the left lane and started to come around him. Ed concentrated on keeping his car centered in the right lane while going into the curve side by side with the truck. Feeling apprehension for the first time, he wondered what could possess any driver to make him try to pass on such a dangerous stretch of road. The answer was soon apparent, as the truck pulled just ahead of his car, then turned back onto the right lane. "Look out, you damn fool!" Ed shouted. "You're going to wreck us."

Trying to avoid a collision, Ed hit his brakes and steered to the right, both right wheels rolling off the pavement onto the shoulder, spewing dirt and gravel up behind the car. As the truck continued to crowd further into his lane, he had no choice but to veer completely off the road and into the underbrush of the adjacent field. Just as he left the road, he glanced over at the truck cab and saw an expressionless, broad-faced man in a ball cap staring back at him.

Reacting without thinking, Ed pumped his brakes as hard as the wet ground permitted without locking the wheels, steering through the brush to the right to miss one large tree, and then back to the left to avoid another. Skidding through the undergrowth, he finally brought the car under control, and stopped at the edge of a deep, rocky ravine. "Thank you, Sweet Jesus!" he fervently said aloud.

Stepping out of the car to stand in the heavy rain, Ed checked it over quickly. The tires, radiator, and oil pan appeared to be intact. Except for mud caked on the wheels and underneath the fenders, and deep scratches in the maroon paint on the front and both sides, there appeared to be no major damage.

Slipping back behind the wheel, soaking wet, he put the car in reverse, and carefully drove through the mud and briars, maneuvering around several large trees, back to the shoulder of the highway. He could see no trace of the truck in either direction as he stared intently up and down the road. Carefully pulling onto the pavement, he turned the car around and headed back toward town, driving at a much lower speed than he had while going the other way only a short time ago.

Ed drove straight to his office, where Carolyn saw him enter, dripping wet, and exclaimed, "Good Lord, Ed, you look like a drowned rat! What in the world happened to you? Let me give you a towel to dry off."

"I'd appreciate that towel, Carolyn. I keep a clean suit in the closet, and I'll change, as soon as I dry off, and wipe up some of the mud that I'm tracking all over your clean floor."

Slipping out of his wet jacket, he continued, "A couple of men in a truck just ran me off the road on the way out to the Buchanan place. There's no doubt in my mind that they were deliberately trying to wreck me, and they almost did. I could've been hurt pretty bad if someone up there hadn't been looking out for me. As soon as I can get changed into dry clothes, I'm going to report this to the state police and sheriff."

Ed cleaned up, then made phone calls to the state police headquarters and the sheriff's department. Officials at each agency took down the sketchy information he was able to provide. Ed had realized before making the calls that the limited information would be unlikely to lead to an arrest, but he still felt better after hanging up. And if he were to encounter the two men again, he was certain that he would be able to recognize the tough looking one who had coldly stared him in the eye while his partner forced him off the road. "I may not get back to the office today," he told Carolyn, as he went out the door. "I'm going to take my car to the garage and get it checked out to be sure it's safe to drive."

Ed decided not to keep anything back from Doug when he got home from school, relating everything that had happened earlier in the day. However, he did not mention how close he had come to a deep ravine, or how serious it would have been if he had skidded over the edge. "I didn't wreck the car, and that's all that really matters," Ed said in a reassuring tone.

"I've been worrying about what's going to happen to the Buchanans," Doug said apprehensively. "Now I'm a lot more concerned about what might happen to you. You don't have any idea who those two men are who ran you off the road, or whether they're still somewhere around."

"You're right. But hopefully they've left the area, and we won't see any more of them around here. I feel safer knowing that the law enforcement people across this end of the state are on the lookout for them now."

"Dad, please be careful," Doug pleaded. "The state police and sheriff may not be anywhere near if you run into them again. Have you thought about carrying your .22 target pistol in the car?"

"You're not allowed to do that in this state, and I certainly hope that won't ever be necessary. We don't want to start having gunfights here on Main Street like the one at the OK Corral. Anyway, tomorrow it's supposed to be sunny, and I won't have to drive in the rain when I go back out to Roseanna."

When Ed got a phone call after dinner, he was glad to hear Laura on the line. "I called your office late this afternoon, and Carolyn told me you were out. She was pretty close-mouthed when I asked her about your whereabouts. All she'd tell me was that you had some sort of an accident while you were driving up the highway north of town today. What happened?"

At first Ed only told her that he had run off the road in the rain, midway between town and the Buchanan farm. Laura pressed for more details, and she soon extracted the same information Ed had shared earlier with Carolyn and Doug.

"Good Lord, Ed," Laura exclaimed. "You could have been

killed. And you were going to keep everything from me except for some big lie about how you just ran off the road because of the rain. What should I do with you? I'm not sure I can ever believe anything else you tell me after this."

"We haven't been around each other that much up 'til now. But if you'll take the time to get to know me better, you'll come to realize that I'm usually completely truthful. I promise that you'll get straight answers out of me from here on."

"You're going to have to earn my trust, now. But more importantly, what can I do for you? Would you like to use my other company car until yours is out of the shop?"

"Thanks for your offer, but I already have something lined up with the dealer. There's really nothing I need. But just hearing that you're concerned about me means a lot. I promise I'll let you know if anything new develops, but I don't expect it to. I certainly hope I've seen the last of those two men."

"Me too," Laura said softly. "I'm thankful you weren't hurt today. It could have been so much more serious. You take care of yourself, Ed, and I mean that from the bottom of my heart. Bye now."

Chapter 11

E D PICKED up the loaner car on Wednesday morning and headed off toward Chestnut Ridge. On the way, he slowed at the sharp curve where he had been forced off the road the previous day, seeing the muddy tire tracks running through the low scrub brush between the trees. In bright daylight, it seemed impossible that he could have brought his car from highway speed to a stop without hitting a tree, or turning the car over. Wilbur Shaw couldn't have handled his Indianapolis 500 race car much better than that, he thought.

He drove up the long gravel drive, mud spraying from small puddles in the road, leaving his car near the foot of the porch steps. One of the sons met him at the door, leading him into the library, where Gideon was sitting on a black leather couch in front of a fire. Gideon nodded to him with a cordial smile and extended his hand.

Ed began, "Mr. Buchanan, I went into your strong box yesterday, and I found your existing will, which I have with me today. But one reason for my visit is this copy of a second document. You were concerned that you might have signed a power of attorney for your nephew, Julian, sometime in the past, and apparently you did so just last month. You must have authorized your nephew to open your strong box. I can only assume that he has the original document in his possession."

Gideon stared at the power of attorney bearing his signature, deep in thought, trying hard to recall what he had done a month earlier. Growing agitated, he looked up at Ed and replied, "Mr. Housman, I recall signing a paper for Julian last month, because he said the bank needed it for their records. And I did loan him the key to my strong box, because he told me that he needed to look over my will. But I can assure you that I never intended, under any circumstance, to give him the legal authority to make decisions on my behalf. What must we do now to straighten this out?"

"I'll go to work now to draft a revised will and new power of attorney, as we discussed the last time we met. But there's something very important that you should know. Your property may be a great deal more valuable today than it was only a few years ago. I've heard rumors that coal was discovered in this area last year, and I have first hand knowledge that a mining company is trying to buy up all of the land adjoining your farm, offering inflated prices for quick sales.

"Your 2500-acre farm is obviously the centerpiece required for a mining operation in this area. Without your land, I don't believe mining would be economically feasible in this valley. We need to move quickly to protect your interests and preserve your property. Please do not, under any circumstances, sign any more papers, or have any further business contacts with your nephew, unless I'm present to advise you."

"I will be most guarded in how I handle myself in the presence of my nephew, Mr. Housman," Gideon assured him. "I realize that he is even more devious than I had thought, and that he may be acting contrary to my wishes."

As he prepared to leave, Ed sensed something moving on the far side of the room. From the corner of his eye, he glimpsed Myrtle Spencer standing in the shadows of the hallway, just outside the other door. She disappeared, without making a sound.

Ed looked at Gideon and asked, "Do you have a problem with your housekeeper trying to eavesdrop on your conversations? It appears Myrtle may have been trying to overhear what we were talking about just now. I don't know how much she may have heard, but I'd prefer that she not know anything about what we're trying to do."

"Myrtle has worked for us for many years and can be trusted, I assure you, Mr. Housman. She's almost like a member of our family. If she did hear anything, I'm quite sure that she'll keep it to herself."

"I'll get back to you just as soon as I have the new papers for you to sign," Ed said as he departed, leaving Gideon sitting alone in the room.

When he arrived back at the office, Carolyn caught up with him before he could take off his coat. "You had a call from Robert Simpson earlier. He told me there's no need for you to call him back. He just wanted to make you're aware that he and his wife are giving very careful consideration to accepting the offer from Copperfield Enterprises. He also mentioned that he thought the Hendersons were starting to think along the same lines. He seemed very apologetic, as if he thought you might be disappointed in them if they decide to go ahead and sell."

"I don't want either family to think I'm trying to steer them. Regardless of what they do, it won't change my opinion of them. But privately, I'd hate to see that beautiful area north of town developed for a coal mining operation. Can you imagine the changes it would make around here? It would be a blow to the pristine beauty of this entire region."

Ed spent the afternoon drafting a revision to Gideon and Hester Buchanan's will and a new power of attorney for Carolyn to type the following day, leaving them on her desk. When he arrived at the house, JR began barking from the backyard, a sign that Doug had not yet gotten in to feed him. I believe for once I beat him getting home, Ed thought.

He was correct. With no basketball practice, Doug usually would have been home well before his father. However, he, Mike, and Ronnie had decided to go by Sam Barry's office after school, anxious to inform him about what they had discovered at the foot of Chimney Rock during their recent search for Ronnie's knife.

Standing in the doorway, Doug spoke up, "Mr. Barry, your detectives are here with something important to report back to you about the lost cave on the Buchanan farm. Do you have time to talk to us?"

Sam looked up with interest, "Well, you've certainly piqued

my curiosity with that remark. Come in and tell me what this visit's all about." The three boys joined Sam, excitedly taking turns talking about what they had recently discovered, including what Doug had glimpsed just before the flashlight went out.

Sam responded, "You boys have no idea how fascinated I am with the report you've just given me. We should try to get permission from the family to go back out there and look around some more. Mr. Housman, I wish you hadn't broken your flashlight until you all got a better look inside the cave. I'm extremely curious about the objects you saw on the floor, those two rows of wooden crates that looked as big as caskets. All of you come over here and have a seat, and let me share a few things I know."

The three boys settled into chairs across the desk from Sam, and he continued. "I told you earlier that researching the Battle of Eden Springs has been a hobby of mine for years. From the work I've done and information I've been able to gather, I believe there were probably twenty-two men killed in that encounter, ten Confederate and twelve Union soldiers. The identities of many of the soldiers can be determined from Civil War documents archived in Richmond and Washington, showing troops listed as missing in action after military engagements.

"But one important piece of the puzzle is still a mystery: What happened to the bodies? When Union and Confederate scouts returned a short time later in the dead of winter to reconnoiter the area, they couldn't find a trace of the victims, on the field or buried in makeshift graves. Digging so many graves in the frozen ground would have been extremely difficult and time consuming. It was as though someone had taken all the victims from where they fell, and carried them off. And if anyone knew what actually happened to the bodies, he kept it a secret throughout his lifetime onto his death bed."

"I don't follow you, Mr. Barry," Ronnie exclaimed. "What does that have to do with the lost cave?"

Sam replied, "I'm not sure, myself. If the bodies had been moved into an open cave, then the scouts would have certainly discovered them, unless the cave entrance was sealed by something like a rock slide shortly afterwards. And if the cave was sealed very soon after the battle, there'd have been no time

for someone to make twenty-two caskets, and place the bodies inside. Still, it seems more than curious that our friend Mr.
Housman, who got the best look inside the cave, used the word
"caskets" to describe what he saw.

"Since you've been acting as the detectives in this investigation, and have had some contact with the family before now, do
you think you could get permission for us to go on their land
again this Saturday? It would be good if the sons could accom-
pany us, so they'd know that we're not up to any harm."

"I can call their house tonight and ask, Mr. Barry," Doug
replied. "I saw a wall phone, and I met the two sons, Daniel
and Jonah, when I was out there a few days ago with my dad
and Dr. Jannsen. I thought about asking them what they're doing out around the cave, but I didn't want to tip them off that
Mike, Ronnie, and I'd been trespassing on their land earlier.
Truthfully, I was kind of afraid of them until this last visit, but
after I spent some time around them, I believe they're more
normal and much gentler than most people think. I'll come by
your office when I get to school tomorrow and let you know
what they say."

"That sounds good, Doug. Assuming that we'll be able to get
their permission, we need to start rounding up some things to
take along. It might be good to have several flashlights with
extra batteries and bulbs, and maybe even a lantern. Let's ten-
tatively plan to meet at 9:00 Saturday morning in the school
parking lot."

After leaving the office, the boys headed off toward home.
On the way, Doug filled Mike and Ronnie in on what he had
seen during his recent visit to the farm. But as his dad had in-
structed, he avoided disclosing the reason for calling on Gideon
Buchanan that day.

"What do you think the odds are that the sons will let us
come out Saturday and look at that cave?" Ronnie asked.
"When we were on our camping trip, they didn't want us anywhere around there."

"I believe it'll be different this time," Doug replied. "I think
they now see Dr. Jannsen and Dad, and maybe even me, as
their friends."

Chapter 12

DOUG GREETED his dad when he arrived home, then told him about the discussion he and his friends had with Sam Barry at school. "If you don't mind, Dad," he said, "I'd like to make a phone call to the Buchanans before dinner, and get permission to go out to their farm this weekend."

Doug dialed the Buchanan home, and discovered that the deep voice on the other end belonged to Jonah. "This Saturday morning, my friends and I would like to come out and look around on your land near the foot of Chimney Rock. We're hoping to find some sign of an old cave. Would that be OK?" After waiting for a few seconds and receiving no answer, he repeated the request, and almost immediately heard the sound of the receiver being dropped, dangling on the cord against the wall.

A few minutes later, Jonah came back on the line. "Daniel says it'll be alright if you come on. He'd told me that he didn't want anyone messing around out there, but he changed his mind when I told him it was you. We'll show you around."

"Thanks. We'll see you Saturday morning." Hanging up the phone, Doug remarked, "That went better than I expected. The sons just gave us permission to come, and it sounds like we'll get to see everything. They don't know that we've already had a quick look around, and have seen where they've uncovered the entrance to that cave."

"I'm sure you're in for some excitement Saturday," Ed responded.

While clearing the table, Ed inquired, "With basketball season over, what do you and your friends have planned for this coming Friday night? I've decided to ask Laura again if she'd like to go the movies. Last week she told me she'd already made other plans, and what I gathered was that someone else beat me to the punch in asking her out. I've heard that she's seeing quite a bit of Dan Wohlford, a newcomer to town who works for the paper company."

"Got some new competition in town now, Dad?" Doug joked. "I think you'd better get on the phone with Laura. This is Wednesday, and my buddies tell me that their girl friends don't like being asked out at the last minute." Putting the dishes in the cupboard, he added, "I'll probably go out to the canteen Friday evening and hang out with my friends. It's as much fun as anything, and except for the cost of soft drinks and snacks, it's free entertainment."

"I think I'll take your advice," Ed said. He picked up the phone, and dialing her number, heard her familiar soft voice.

"Laura, this is Ed. Would you like to go out with me Friday evening to take in *War of the Worlds* at the Lyric? I thought we could stop by the diner to grab a bite, and still make it over to the theater in time to catch the first feature."

"How could I possibly refuse an invitation for an exciting evening like that," Laura replied. "I've been a big science fiction fan for years, and my friends say that this movie is one of the best they've seen."

"Can I take that as a yes?"

"That's definitely a yes. I guess getting you to throw in the big box of popcorn will require some negotiating. What time do you want to pick me up?"

"You don't have to negotiate to get the popcorn. I'll even buy you a Milky Way to go with it. I'll plan to come by your apartment and pick you up at 5:30, if you can be ready then. That'll give us plenty of time. Unless, of course, I have to come in the parlor and meet your father before he'll let me take you out."

"You won't have to go through that drill," Laura laughed. "My folks live in Parkersburg. Besides, they pushed me out of the nest years ago. See you Friday after work."

Ed spent much of the next day making final changes to the will and power of attorney for the Buchanans. It was nearly closing time when Carolyn had finished revising both documents on her Underwood. As he slipped the completed papers into his brief-case, and started toward the door, he called back to her, "Hope you have a good weekend. I'll see you on Monday morning."

An hour later, Ed pulled up in front of Laura's apartment and rang the doorbell. When she appeared, she was wearing a blue sweater and skirt, which emphasized her trim figure and set off her long auburn hair. "I knew that you'd be wearing something pretty tonight, but I wasn't expecting for you to look so much like a young Hollywood star. I feel like I'm escorting Arlene Dahl to a movie premier."

"Thanks, Ed," she replied, slipping on a jacket. "I told you earlier, you really have an Irishman's gift for the blarney. But don't think all these nice compliments are going to get you off the hook after offering me the big box of popcorn and candy bar. Promises are promises."

Seated at the diner, they lingered over dinner and coffee for almost an hour in pleasant conversation, getting to know more about each other. They exchanged stories of their lives growing up, their families and friends, coping with the loss of spouses, coming to Eden Springs, and their careers. "Tell me more about your son," Laura said. "What's it like, holding down a respon-sible job, and raising a teenage boy as a single parent?"

"Doug's never given me any problems growing up, either before Louise died or since. Sometimes he shows some typical teenage lapses in judgment, but nothing serious. Being left on his own without a mother at a fairly young age has made him pretty independent. He's coped with her death, picked up the pieces, and gone on with his life remarkably well. I think that Louise must look down on him and feel proud. I know I do. But I should warn you, he tends to be somewhat shy around adults he hasn't yet gotten to know. And apparently he has a reputa-tion at school for being bashful around pretty girls. I'm afraid you fall into both of those categories. But on the plus side, he has red hair like you, only more toward carrot red than your shade of auburn. It would be nice if you could get to know him.

I believe you'd hit it off."

"I'd like to meet him, Ed. My brother has a teenage son about the same age as Doug, and we have a lot of fun doing things together when he comes here to visit. How about the three of us planning to play some tennis? Doug could bring a date for mixed doubles."

"I think that's a great idea, assuming he could get up enough nerve to ask someone," Ed replied. Glancing at his watch, he added, "The time has really gotten away from us while we've been talking. We better get over to the Lyric, or we'll miss the previews and cartoon."

Sitting together in the dark theater away from other movie-goers, Ed and Laura were soon completely engrossed in *War of the Worlds*. The movie became more suspenseful as it went on. Alien flying saucers, with cobra heads emitting the deadly chattering of angry rattlesnakes, slowly searched through destroyed buildings for surviving Earth people. As the climax approached, the theater became deathly still, and Laura reached out to Ed. He took her hand, and was still holding it when the movie ended and the lights came on. "Those aliens were pretty scary," Laura said. "I'm glad I was sitting next to you. I didn't eat much of my popcorn after the flying saucers attacked and started destroying our cities."

"You can take it home with you," Ed said, laughing. "Movie theater popcorn is still good, even when it's cold."

At Laura's front door, she turned to say goodnight, and Ed didn't hesitate. Putting his arms around her waist, he pulled her close and held her. She lifted her face, and they shared a long kiss. He was still caught in that moment all the way home.

Fortunately, when he got there, Doug was still out with his friends, and he was spared the usual friendly interrogation of how the evening had gone. When Doug finally got home and called out to see if he was still up, Ed pretended to be asleep.

Doug overslept the next morning, rolling out of bed in high gear. He pulled on old clothes, grabbed his flashlight from the top of the dresser, and ran out the door. After walking double-time along the familiar path to school, he found that Mike and Ronnie had arrived earlier, and were sitting with Sam Barry in his green Chevy sedan. Each had brought along a flashlight

with fresh batteries. Doug climbed into the front seat beside
Sam, and they quickly pulled out and headed north up the
highway in the direction of Abner Gap.

When they reached the driveway at Roseanna, they caught
sight of the two sons walking out toward their car, one of them
carrying a battered kerosene lantern. Doug determined which
of the two men was Daniel by checking for the axe-shortened
index finger, and he introduced Sam, Mike, and Ronnie to the
sons by name.

Daniel turned to Jonah, grinning, "He knows how to tell
which of us is which, now."

"Can we walk back toward the foot of Chimney Rock with
you now?" Sam inquired. Daniel nodded, and the six started
out together walking in single file, following Jonah's long
strides.

After hiking along the worn foot path leading from the back
of the house, past the barns and fenced pastures, and across
a wide field, they arrived at the vertical face of the cliff. The
massive boulders of Chimney Rock towered high above them,
framed against a blue sky as they looked up. Turning left, they
followed the path along the base of the cliff for a short distance
until they reached a vertical seam in the rock. Doug recognized
that it was the same crevasse that he, Ronnie, and Mike had
explored earlier.

Daniel and Jonah motioned for Sam and the three boys to
follow them, as they stepped through the gap into the interior space surrounded by high rock walls. Walking toward an
overhanging slab braced by logs, the two men stepped aside,
so Sam and the three boys could see. Doug, Ronnie, and Mike
were surprised to find that more rocks had been pried back
from under the slab, and the small hole they had observed earlier was now a cave entrance large enough for a man to crawl
through on hands and knees.

"May we take a look?" Sam asked, unable to keep the excitement from his voice. He and Doug crawled under the slab to
the edge of the hole, holding their flashlights inside. With the
beams from two lights, they could see the front of the cave,
with a flat floor near the entrance which appeared to slope
steeply downward further to the back, and a ceiling towering

overhead. "This looks more like a cavern than a cave," Sam exclaimed. "It's huge! I'm sure that we're finally getting to look inside the lost cave that people around here have talked about for ninety years."

Doug moved closer to Sam and whispered, "I can get a lot better look today, but the last time we were here, I'm positive that I saw wooden crates lined up on the floor of the cave. They're gone now."

Sam turned to Daniel and asked, "Have you all been inside?"

"We've looked around in the front, but we haven't gone far back."

"Could you take me inside the cave with you today?"

"Yes, but you'll have to be careful going in and coming back out. Getting on and off the ladder's a little treacherous."

"Did you find anything when you first went inside? Has anything been moved?"

Daniel glanced nervously at Jonah, and then back at Sam, shaking his head.

Sam turned to the three boys. "I'm sorry I can't let you to go in the cave with us. I don't have your parent's permission, and it sounds like getting inside and coming back out may be dangerous. But I promise, I'll tell you about everything we see."

Daniel struck a wood match to light the kerosene lantern, while Jonah walked behind the rock slab and returned carrying a crude wooden ladder, made of two long poles with nailed board rungs. The two men slipped the ladder through the opening and rested it on the floor of the cave. First Daniel, carrying the lantern, then Jonah, and finally Sam, carrying a flashlight, backed through the opening. Carefully placing their feet on the rungs, they climbed down to the floor of the cave below.

As Sam had observed from outside, the cavernous room was wide, with a high ceiling overhead, and a flat dirt and rock floor in the front, which dropped off dangerously further to the back. He spotted footprints in the dirt that the men had made earlier, but he saw no other signs of previous human entry or activity. As the three men talked, their voices echoed repeatedly from the stone walls of the cave chamber, making it difficult to understand each other.

After exploring the room for some time, Daniel spoke up, "I

didn't fill the lantern all the way up, and the kerosene's getting low. We better think about getting out of here." Just as they were turning to leave, something small and shiny reflected in the light of Sam's flashlight, and he stooped to pick it up, slipping it into his pocket. The three men followed each other up the ladder and emerged from the cave, squinting in the bright daylight, brushing the dirt from their clothes.

"It would take a group of experienced cavers with the right equipment to explore that chamber thoroughly," Sam commented. "But if you two will kindly permit us to come back again, I'd like to take some photographs the next time."

The group returned on the same path to the house, where Sam and the Buchanans washed up at a long-handled pump over a board-covered rainwater cistern. "We appreciate your showing us around," Sam said, wiping his hands with his handkerchief. "You must have done a lot of hard and dangerous work to open that cave entrance."

"A big rock overhead came loose and almost hit us while we were working," Jonah said, looking at the three boys. "That's why we chased you off a while back. If you're not careful out there, you could get yourself killed by falling rocks."

The thought of being crushed to death by a loose rock was soon gone from the minds of the three teenagers, as they walked back to the car, talking about all that they'd just seen. Sam thanked the two men again, and then he and the boys drove away.

Back at the high school, Sam called the boys around him. Retrieving the small, shiny object from his pocket, he held it up so they could look it over. "I found this on the floor of the cave near the entrance. It's a tarnished brass button, with the letters CS centered inside a sunburst pattern stamped on the front, and some gray threads on the back."

"Does CS stand for Confederate States?" Doug inquired.

"That's right, boys. I think this little button is evidence that there was something on the floor of the cave when you all were out there the last time that's not there now. I don't know what happened to those crates, or caskets, or whatever you saw, but I think the sons know quite a bit more than they wanted to tell us today. I have no idea why they'd remove anything from the cave, and act so secretive about it. I guess we're not going to be able to solve this mystery until they're ready to talk.

"You're free to tell your folks about what we found today, but I believe we should try to keep the discovery of the cave quiet for now, until we find out more about what's going on. I don't want to have newspaper reporters from all over this end of the state descending on the farm until we get to the bottom of things. Now more than ever, I think that cave on their property is directly linked to the Battle of Eden Springs. Maybe the discovery of the cave will give me a start on the book about local history during the Civil War that I've been waiting to write."

Chapter 13

MARCH WEATHER was far more likely to resemble the proverbial lion than the lamb in West Virginia, and Doug had heard the wind whistling around the eaves of the house when he first woke up on Sunday morning, before getting out of his warm bed. JR was still curled up on his rug beside the headboard, watching him closely. Since providence had changed JR's situation from abandoned stray on the side of the road to full member of the Housman family, he kept an eye on Doug, sticking to him like glue

Doug could see cloudy gray skies, with trees swaying in the gusts, as he looked out the window. Dressing warmly, he went downstairs and out on the porch with JR at his heels to retrieve the morning paper. Glancing into the kitchen, he could see that his dad had started a pot of coffee and set a box of corn flakes out on the table.

"What's on the front page this morning?" Ed inquired, as Doug and JR came back into the house. "More news about Harry Truman's front porch addition to the White House, or Margaret's singing career?"

"I don't know. I'm keeping the comics and the sports section. I'll fill you in on Li'l Abner and what's happening in Dogpatch. You can have the rest of the paper, and tell me all about President Truman and what's going on in Washington. Not that I'm really dying to find out."

Sitting on a pew near the back of the church sanctuary later that morning, Doug's mind continued to wander from Rev. Seymour's sermon, delivered in his usual pastoral monotone. The warm temperature in the room created an overwhelming drowsiness, and Doug could not prevent his head from repeatedly drifting downward toward his chest. Each time it did, he could feel his father's elbow nudging him back to attention. By the time Rev. Seymour had reached the end of his long message, Doug could see that his dad's eyes were also starting to glaze. It felt good to return a jab, and see the sheepish look that came across his father's face.

On the sidewalk outside the church, Doug asked in a low voice, "Want to tell me what you got out of the sermon this morning?"

"I'm pretty sure that he told us we should all refrain from sinful conduct, but I may have missed one or two of the details." Ed pulled back in time to avoid his son's mock blow to the arm.

In the afternoon, the wind subsided, and the two were able to go out in the driveway, where Ed had mounted a hoop on the front of the garage, and play "horse." Doug was far better at shooting a basketball, and he enjoyed rubbing it in as he won game after game.

"You're missing a lot of easy shots, Dad. I guess you grew up a long time ago, shooting at a peach basket nailed on the side of the barn. You seem to be having a lot of trouble with this regulation backboard and hoop."

Ed refused to quit until he finally succeeded in putting a "horse" on his son, then quickly retired from the game as a winner.

Tossing the basketball in the garage, Doug picked up an old tennis ball, and took JR for a run in the vacant field nearby. Somewhere in the dog's mixed ancestry, there was a retriever's instinct, and each time he threw the ball, JR would take off like a shot and run it down, bringing it back for Doug to pry out of his mouth. The sun was getting low in the sky when they turned back toward home, JR trotting ahead, panting, still carrying the ball in his mouth.

Ed and Doug spent a quiet evening reading and listening to

the weekly *Jack Benny Show* on the radio. By the time the good radio programs were over, the Housman family, man, boy, and dog, was heading upstairs to bed.

It was an hour past midnight when the phone rang. Ed quickly glanced at the clock, then ran down the steps to the living room and picked up the receiver. When he answered, the caller identified himself as Tom Mackey, fire chief with the Eden Springs Fire Department.

"Mr. Housman, you need to get down to your office as quickly as possible," Tom said. "I'm afraid I've got some bad news for you. A fire has broken out in the Madison Sign Company part of the Compton Building, next to your office, and spread into your place. We didn't get called out until twenty minutes ago, and the fire had a big jump on us before we got a crew on site. We're doing everything we can to contain it at this time."

Ed put down the phone and went back upstairs, where he saw Doug coming out of his bedroom. "Anything wrong?" Doug inquired apprehensively, knowing phone calls at late hours rarely bring good news.

"I'm afraid so. I just don't know yet how bad it is," Ed replied, pulling on his shirt and pants. "That call was from the fire department. My office building's on fire, and I'm heading down there as fast as I can. If you can get dressed quickly, you can go with me. Just leave the dog in the garage."

In only a few minutes, Ed and Doug were out the house and in the car, speeding downtown. From the curb near Ed's office, flames could be seen licking from the windows and through a gaping hole in the flat roof of the old two story brick building. They created an eerie flickering red glow, punctuated by the flashing lights of the two fire trucks parked out front, a pumper, and a hook and ladder vehicle. The firemen had smashed windows to get access to the fire inside, and water gushed from two hoses into the interior of the building.

The lights and the loud voices of the firemen had started to attract a crowd of neighbors, who clustered in small groups a short distance away, watching the action and talking to each other. After half an hour of hard and dangerous work by the fire fighters, the flames had been contained, but heavy, acrid smoke continued to pour from the now-gutted building. By the time another hour had passed, the flames were out, and only wisps of smoke continued to drift through the cold night air.

Tom Mackey walked up to Ed, introducing himself as the fire chief who had called earlier, saying, "I think we pretty much have it out now, but there's a lot of damage to the building. The fire has weakened the structure so badly it's unsafe for anyone to go in, and the water and ashes have made a big mess inside. I'm going to keep a couple of my men down here the rest of the night to make sure it doesn't flare up again, and to prevent anyone from disturbing anything inside."

"I appreciate your securing whatever's left of my office," Ed said. "The file cabinets and office safe contain a lot of private documents. What do you think could have triggered a fire down here at this time of the morning?"

"Like I told you on the phone, it appears to have started next door on the Madison Sign Company premises," Tom replied. "The building seems to have the most damage right along the wall between their place and yours. We'll have an investigator down here tomorrow to see if we can figure out what caused it. It could have been the electrical wiring, or maybe some stored chemicals in their place caused spontaneous combustion.

"Apparently, no one was in or around the building at the time the fire broke out. The building would have burned to the ground if some lady hadn't gotten up and looked out her window. Fortunately, she saw the flames, and called us. Normally everyone around here is asleep at that hour. You live here, so you know that in this town we roll the sidewalks up at 9:00.

"I'm really sorry about the damage to your business. We'll try to help you get your office safe and files out on the sidewalk a little later, and we'll salvage anything else inside that we can. It'll be a lot safer for us to enter the building in daylight, after the smoke clears out, and we can see what we're up against."

Ed glanced at Doug, shoulders slumping in exhaustion. "I don't think we can do anything more here tonight. It looks like my office suite took an awful lot of damage. I'm certain that the entire building is a total loss, and that I'll have to find new office quarters pretty quickly. Tomorrow morning, I'll report the fire to the insurance company, and call Carolyn and tell her what's happened. Then I'll be back down here with the fire department to see what can be salvaged from inside."

Seeing the worried look that came over Doug's face, Ed quickly added, "This is a big disruption to my law practice, but at least no one was hurt or killed tonight. It could have been worse."

As they walked back to the car, Doug said, "I'd like to stay off from school tomorrow and help down here anyway that I can. We sure seem to be having a lot of bad luck lately. You almost got wrecked in your car last week, and now your office catches on fire."

"I have the same feeling about a bad run of luck for us, if that's what you call it," Ed replied. "There's an old saying that things happen in threes, and we sure don't need another calamity after all of this. Anyway, I'll take you up on your offer to help. I think your teachers will understand if you miss a day of school tomorrow. I'll write an excuse for you if you need one."

Ed called Carolyn just after sunrise, telling her what had happened during the night. "I'm sure you'll want to drive down to look. Later, when the files are moved outside the building, we'll have to look them over and go through the contents to determine what can be saved. I'm going to start work now to see if I can line up new office quarters."

A secretary called Laura to the phone to take his call a short time later, and he heard her usual cheery greeting. "Laura, I need your help. My office burned early this morning." He told her about the fire, adding, "If you can help me find some suitable office space, you'll be a life saver."

She exclaimed, "I heard the fire trucks go by early today, but I had no idea where they were heading. I'm terribly sorry to learn the fire was in the Compton Building."

"I was sound asleep and totally unaware of anything until I got that wake-up call from the fire chief," Ed replied. "It makes me cringe whenever the phone rings late at night or early in the morning like that. It's always someone delivering bad news."

"But try to look at it another way, Ed, it's good no one was inside when the fire broke out."

"That's exactly what I told Doug. Things would have been infinitely worse if someone had been seriously hurt or killed. But at this moment, I'm still having a little trouble looking on the bright side."

"Maybe I can help make you feel a little better. I think we may be in luck finding you a suitable office space," Laura continued. "There's a similar size suite that was vacated by a loan agency two weeks ago only a block south of your current location. There's also office furniture and equipment stored by the previous tenant that may be suitable for you, should you need it. I can pick up the key, and meet you there in an hour, if you want to take a look at the property right away."

By the time Ed and Doug arrived, they could see Laura waiting in her white station wagon, parked in front of a small one story brick office building. Laura stepped out of the Olds as Ed and Doug approached. Ed introduced Laura to him, and she reached out to him with her hand and a warm smile, "Doug, it's nice to finally get to meet you, although I wish it were under different circumstances."

"I'm pleased to meet you, Mrs. Jackson," he replied, taking her hand awkwardly while looking her in the eye, and then quickly glancing down.

"I'd prefer it if you'd just call me Laura. I hope we redheads don't need to be so formal with each other." Unlocking the door of the building, Laura led the way inside. The two vacant rooms appeared to be slightly larger than Ed's current office suite. "I think the rent for this property is probably in the ballpark of what you've been paying down the street."

"It looks like this would work as well as anything we could find on such short notice," Ed commented. "I'm sure we're not going to be able to reoccupy our old office anytime soon, and probably never. I'm ready to sign a lease agreement now."

Laura, and Ed and Doug, drove separately to the scene of the fire, where Ed saw that the firemen had done more for him than required. His badly damaged furniture, metal file cabinets, and even the small steel safe had been wheeled out on the walk in front of the building and covered with tarps. Recognizing the fire chief, Ed walked up and said, "Thanks for getting the fire out as quickly as you did, and for moving my belongings out of the building. I appreciate everything you've done for me."

Tom took Ed aside. "Please don't repeat this to anyone. My fire investigator has already taken a preliminary look around inside, and the cause of the fire appears very suspicious to him. There's strong evidence that an arsonist broke into the Madison Sign facility early this morning and deliberately set the fire, right where we thought, at the wall adjacent to your office suite.

"It'll take more time to determine exactly what took place, but it at this time we're almost ready to rule out any accidental cause for the fire. I've reported this to Chief Spencer at police headquarters."

"Why in the world would anyone want to burn the Madison Sign business?" Ed inquired.

"I have no idea. I'll be talking more with the owner later today to see what he can tell me. But to be sure we don't overlook anything, I also have to ask whether you know of anyone who might have a reason to deliberately burn you out."

"I can't think of anyone who would have a motive to do that to me."

"Are you sure about that? Sheriff Daniels told Chief Spencer about someone deliberately trying to wreck you not long ago. I don't mean to worry you, but you might want to give this some more thought, and try to see if you can think of anyone who might have a serious grudge against you." The two men said goodbye, and Ed walked away, his head spinning.

Carolyn and Ed spent long hours throughout the remainder of the week going through the smoke and water damaged files, getting things back in the best order possible. Late Friday afternoon, Ed was finally able to prop his tired feet up on his new desk. As he surveyed the results they'd accomplished, the phone rang.

"Ed, this is Earl Daniels. I wanted you to know something that was reported to me this morning by a resident on the outskirts of town. He said his dog started barking around midnight this past Sunday, and when he went out to shut him up, he saw a dark colored panel truck high-tailing it past his house, heading north out to the highway. He just learned that a fire broke out downtown about that same time, and he thought he should report what he had seen to the police department and me.

"Since Chief Spencer hasn't told the local newspaper reporters that he suspects arson, we're lucky the man bothered to call in. The truck sounds a lot like the same one you described to me that ran you off the highway. I just wanted to call to alert you that whoever drives that truck may still be somewhere in our area."

"Good Lord!" Ed exclaimed. "Tom Mackey asked if some-one might have it in for me, and now it sounds like he may be on the right track. But even if the arsonists are the same men who were in the truck that ran me off the road, I still don't have any idea what their motive could be. I got a pretty close look at one of them that day, and I'm positive that I never saw him before in my life."

Chapter 14

A FEW OF Doug's classmates were still standing around their lockers after the last class on Friday, talking over plans to meet later at the canteen. He picked up his jacket and geometry book as the hallway cleared, and made his way past Principal Stoner's office and out the door. The cool breeze felt good to him after a day inside the stuffy school building, as he made his way across town to his dad's new office. Ed and Carolyn were completing the finishing touches, including hanging several pictures on the walls when he walked in.

"Starting to look like you've always worked here," Doug commented. "This may turn out to be a better set-up than your old office. What's left that I can help with?" Ed winked at Carolyn, and asked him if he would mind cleaning the lavatory. "If I'd known what position you were saving for me, I would have definitely walked a lot more slowly coming over here," Doug joked, vigorously scrubbing the toilet with Old Dutch Cleanser. "I think I'm much better cut out for courtroom work."

There was still some unpacking to be done after he finished with the bathroom chores, and when that task was completed, the three decided to call it quits for the day. By the time Doug and Ed had left the office and dropped by Gil's for dinner, it was almost 8:30 when they pulled into the driveway at home. "I think I can still catch up with my buddies at the canteen. Can

I have the car?" Doug asked.

Ed tossed his car keys to Doug. "Drive carefully, and don't put any dents or scratches in the car. And be home by 11:30."

Doug circled the crowded canteen parking lot several times before he found a space. Inside, he saw that that the usual Friday night crowd had arrived earlier, and the party was in full swing. He could feel the energy generated by the boys and girls, with the pool and ping-pong tables all in play, the unmistakable Johnnie Ray hit *Cry* cranked up on the Wurlitzer in the corner, and the animated sound of teenagers laughing and talking. He located Mike, Ronnie, and Wayne, paired off with their girl friends, sitting at a table across the floor. Mike spotted Doug at almost the same time, motioning for him to come over and join them. As Doug slipped into a vacant chair, Mike leaned closer to say, "Things may get a little rowdy here tonight. A bunch of the seniors have made a beer run, and they're slipping out in the parking lot to knock it down. Your best bud, Lennie, is here, and he's already got a load on. You can see him hanging out over there on the other side with your secret crush."

Doug looked across the room, where he saw Len talking to Vickie. They were standing close together facing each other, and Len had one arm around her waist. She was looking up at him smiling, apparently hanging on every word he said. "She must really enjoy his beer breath up close," Doug commented. "I guess if you're the senior star on the football team, girls will go for you regardless. They seem to have a thing for bad boys."

A little later, someone played *Unforgettable*, and Ginny invited Doug to dance. During the time Mike and Doug had developed a best buddy friendship, Ginny had become a surrogate sister to Doug, trying to help him overcome his shyness. Knowing how to make Doug relax, she glanced at him as they walked out on the floor, asking, "Do you want to lead or should I?"

"I think it's my turn tonight, Ginny. You got to lead last week. You want to know something? If Mike hadn't already talked you into going steady, I'd be knocking your door down trying to get you to go out with me."

Ginny laughed, "Big talk, coming from a very bashful boy. But I'll let you in on a little secret: if Mike and I weren't going steady, I just might be interested."

Doug couldn't keep from watching Len and Vickie out of the corner of his eye throughout the evening. Several times, he saw Len leave the room to go out into the parking lot, then come back a short time later. As time passed, it appeared to Doug that Vickie was no longer smiling as much, or trying to stand so close to him. Although the two were still hanging out together, they were no longer looking at each other in the same way. Doug noticed that they walked out of the canteen together around 10:45, then thought no more about it.

Realizing that his curfew hour was creeping up on him, Doug bid his friends goodnight. Pulling the collar of his jacket closer, feeling the cold March breeze cutting across the dimly lit parking lot, he hurriedly walked to his dad's car. He started the engine and was about to back out, when he heard someone knock on the glass beside him. Rolling down the window, he saw Vickie standing beside the car. "I need a ride home," she said. "Can you take me?"

Doug leaned over and opened the passenger door. Vickie slid in, closed the door, and pushed down the lock. Glancing over at her, Doug could see that her make-up was smeared and her hair mussed. It appeared that she'd been crying, and was still on the verge of tears. "Are you OK?" he asked.

"Yes. All I want to do is just get home."

There was no conversation on the way. Doug kept his eyes straight ahead, but he could sense that something was badly wrong. Vickie seemed to be extremely hurt and angry, barely in control of her emotions. When they drove up in the long driveway beside her house, Vickie unlocked the door and stepped out of the car. Turning to face him, she said, "Thanks for driving me home. You're a nice boy, Doug." She wheeled around and ran up the walk and into the house without looking back. The front door opened again, and a man Doug assumed to be her father stood in the doorway for a few seconds, glaring toward him angrily before going back inside.

As Doug shifted into reverse and backed out toward the end of the driveway, a black Ford suddenly pulled in behind, blocking him. He peered intently into his rear view mirror, but the headlights of the other car blinded him, making it impossible for him to distinguish who was driving the coupe. When he turned his head around to look behind, he saw that it was Len Hacker getting out of the car, starting to walk toward him. Doug was totally unprepared when Len came up beside him, jerked open the car door, and spit out, "You wanted in on this, and now you are. Get out of the car!"

Before Doug knew what was happening, Len grabbed his jacket, yanked him out of the seat, and drove his right fist into his stomach just below the ribs, knocking the wind out of him and doubling him over. Pulling his right arm back, Len hit him again solidly with a round-house blow to the cheek just under the left eye, knocking him back against the car. Half stunned, Doug dropped into a low crouch, watching Len pull his right arm back to strike him again.

Reacting purely from instinct, Doug dropped his head and drove forward as hard as he could, delivering a spearing blow with the top of his head directly against Len's unprotected face. The impact was hard enough to make Doug step back, dazed. The result was immediate, dramatic, and decisive. A crimson spray covered Doug's jacket, and he could see blood pouring out of both sides of Len's nose, down his face, and dripping from his chin onto the ground. Len was no longer preparing to hit him again; his only concern now seemed to be slowing the profuse bleeding from his nose with the front of his shirt. "You little son of a bitch! You broke my nose," he growled.

At that moment, the man Doug had seen standing in the doorway earlier burst out of the house and came running toward them. "You punks get the hell out of here! I'm calling the police. If I ever see either of you around here again, or if you come anywhere near my daughter, I'll beat the crap out of both of you!"

Len's tires squealed and smoked as he spun the rear wheels of his coupe backing out of the driveway, and again as he ran through the gears, tearing off down the street. Doug was close behind him, adrenalin pumping through his veins, wasting no time in putting as much distance as possible between himself and Vickie's furious father.

Doug's left eye was closing quickly, his ribs hurt with each breath, and the goose egg on top of his head throbbed. Anger and resentment overwhelmed him, and he was barely able to control the impulse to break down and cry. Things are really screwed-up when you try to help a girl out by giving her a ride home, and you end up getting your butt whipped by her boy-friend, then get threatened and run off by her old man. "The hell with all of them," he said aloud.

Inside the house, Doug found JR asleep in the garage, and his dad already in bed. Climbing the stairs quietly, he dropped the car keys in a tray on the top of the dresser in his dad's bedroom with-out turning on the light, intending to say nothing about what had just taken place. But he realized while showering that he needed someone to talk to. After slipping into his pajamas, Doug went back into his father's room and woke him. "Dad, something bad happened tonight that I need to tell you about." Flipping on the light switch, he told Ed everything that had just occurred.

Seeing Doug's swollen eye and bruised face, Ed sat straight up in bed and listened closely. He wanted to call the police and report an assault, but Doug pleaded with him not to.

"It's like a fight in the locker room. I don't want anyone at school thinking that I can't take care of myself, and that I go running to my daddy to take up for me. If Len starts to come after me again, I promise I'll tell you. But I believe his broken nose is going to keep him from starting any trouble with me for a while, and maybe by the time it's mended, this will all have blown over."

Doug's heart pounded when he heard the phone ring a short time later. He was sure that Mr. Vicelli had reported the fight in his driveway to the police, and that someone was now calling to learn more about his involvement.

When Ed answered the phone, he heard an unfamiliar voice on the other end. "Is this Mr. Housman?" the man inquired. "This is Tony Vicelli. I'm sorry for calling you so late, but my oldest girl Vickie insisted. She tells me that I owe your son Doug an apology for the way I yelled at him and threatened him this evening."

Tony went on to report what he had been told by his daugh-ter after the fight in front of his house. "Vickie's been going with some boy in the senior class named Len Hacker for a while now, but that's all over. Tonight while they were at the canteen, he and some of his friends got hold of some beer, and he had too much to drink. Before he'd drive her home, he started trying to pull some things on her in his car out in the parking lot, and she got out and asked your son to give her a ride home.

"Apparently, that made the Hacker kid pretty mad, and he followed them over here to the house and tried to give your son a beating. I'm not sure who got the worst of it, because when I went out to run them off, the Hacker boy had the worst looking broken nose I've ever seen. I didn't know until later that your boy only got mixed up in the fight because he was helping Vickie. That's why I'm calling to apologize. If you'd like, I'll talk to him, too."

"That won't be necessary, Tony," Ed replied. "Doug's going to feel a lot better after hearing that you called to apologize. He felt like he'd done the right thing by driving your daughter home when she asked him, and he was pretty upset that all he had to show for it was a beating. Thanks for calling."

"Doug, come down here a minute," Ed called upstairs. "You're going to feel a little better when I tell what that call was all about."

For the rest of the weekend, Doug remained out of sight at home, trying to avoid questions about what had happened to him. By Monday, the swelling had gone down, and his left eye was open again. Only a large, dark bruise around his eye and on his cheek remained to show where he had been struck.

At school on Monday, he encountered several friends as he approached his locker. Freddie was the first to spot the black eye. "Dawg, what in the world happened to you?" he inquired. "How'd you get that shiner?"

"I got up in the night and ran into a door in the dark," Doug replied, trying to discourage further questions.

"Seems like everyone's been running into doors in the dark lately," Mike commented. "I heard Len Hacker showed up today with a white adhesive tape strip across his face holding his nose in place."

Doug's friends seemed to buy the story, and they headed off to first period class. Mike lingered behind, saying quietly, "I started to call you over the weekend, but decided you might want to be left alone. Vickie told Ginny what happened Friday night in the parking lot at the canteen and out in front of her house. She feels really bad about getting you involved in the fight and everything else that went on. She told Ginny she made her dad call your house to apologize. How'd you land one on Len's nose to keep him from beating you to a pulp?"

"I'm still trying to figure that out myself," Doug said. "Everything happened so fast. I was just reacting like you do when you're firing off the line to block someone in football, and somehow I speared him in the face with the top of my head. Does anyone else know about this? I don't want it to get back to Len I'm bragging about breaking his nose, and end up with a rematch."

"It's going to get out one way or the other," Mike commented. "But it's not out yet, and I promise, my lips are sealed. By the way, Ginny gave me a note I'm supposed to pass on to you." He reached in his pocket and dug out a sheet of paper torn from a composition book, folded several times. "We better head for class, or we'll be late."

As Mike walked ahead, Doug unfolded the paper and read the message, hand-written in pencil. "Doug, I'm sorry for all the trouble I got you into Friday night. Thanks for taking me home from the canteen. I'm glad you weren't hurt bad in the fight. Vickie."

Chapter 15

CAROLYN AND Ed started the week in their new quarters, open for business at the normal time. "We both lost a lot of nice things we'd been keeping at work for a quite a while," Carolyn commented. "But I found another good picture of Frank at home, for my new desk."

Ed received the first call at the new office later that morning. Picking up the phone, he recognized the voice. "Good morning, Mr. Housman. This is Robert Simpson speaking. Last week while you were moving to your new office, Clarence Henderson and I both received calls from Mr. Thorpe. He said he'd been unable to reach you, so he'd come directly to us, wanting to know if we're ready now to sign a sales contract for our farms. I told him both of us were still considering his offer, but hadn't talked any more with you.

"He went on to remind us that his offers were based on our homes being in good condition. The Hendersons and us know there's no fire department where we live out in the country, and you never can tell when lightning or something else will catch a house on fire and burn it to the ground. We hadn't thought much about it up until now, but seeing how your office building burned down in town even with the fire department right on the scene, it helped get Clarence and me thinking that we ought to go ahead and make a decision now. I think we've made up our minds, and we're both ready to sell."

Ed replied, "As I told you and your wife, and the Hendersons, the decision whether or not to sell your farms is strictly up to you. If you'd like to meet and discuss this further, I'd be glad to. But if you've thought this over carefully, and have already made up your minds, I'll talk to the Hendersons, and then start on the sale contracts for each of you."

Hanging up the phone, Ed spoke to Carolyn, "Well, it looks like Barker Mining has two more pieces of their jigsaw puzzle falling into place. The Simpsons and Hendersons are definitely going to sell. I've learned that three other large tracts of land in that same general area sold recently to other buyers who are probably Copperfield agents for Barker Mining. I suspect the only remaining piece of property needed now for their mining operation is the Buchanan farm."

Ed spent a number of hours working with Carolyn to produce the sales contracts for the Simpson and Henderson farms. It wasn't until Thursday that he was finally prepared to meet with the Buchanans to present the new will and power of attorney for Gideon's signature.

When Ed dialed their home, he heard Myrtle Spencer's voice on the other end of the line. "Good morning, Myrtle. Could I please speak with Mr. Buchanan?"

Myrtle replied, "I'm sorry to tell you that Mr. Buchanan hasn't been feeling well for several days. He's in bed, and he isn't able to come to the phone."

"Have you reported this to Dr. Jannsen?"

"No, I haven't, Mr. Housman. I was expecting he'd be back on his feet any day now. I didn't think he needed the doctor to look in on him."

"I believe we need to give Dr. Jannsen a call right now. If he's available to make a house call this afternoon, I'll be out with him to see Gideon." Incredibly poor judgment on Myrtle's part to let something like this go, he thought to himself.

Ed phoned Dr. Jannsen and reported what he had learned from the family housekeeper. "Myrtle should have called me when she first saw that Gideon was having trouble," Dr. Jannsen exclaimed. "This may be very serious. Let me get my nurse to cancel my appointments for this afternoon, and I'll be ready to go."

Dr. Jannsen pulled his car in behind Ed's a short time later. When they arrived at the Buchanan home, Myrtle met them at the door, and led them back to Gideon's bedroom. The old man was lying on an ornate walnut four poster bed, propped up by pillows, his mouth open and his eyes almost shut as though dozing. Although he attempted to respond when Dr. Jannsen spoke to him, he seemed very confused, and sounded incoherent when he tried to speak.

As Ed and Myrtle stood to the side, Dr. Jannsen examined Gideon, checking temperature, blood pressure, respiration, and other vital signs. Finishing his exam, he stood and shook his head, "This is a real puzzle. I can't find any sign of a disease. There seems to be nothing that has changed since I last examined him, except for his mental state. I'm beginning to wonder if he might have suffered a stroke."

Myrtle moved toward the door as if to leave, then stopped to rearrange some folded towels on a nearby table.

Moving closer to the doctor, Ed inquired in a low voice, "What can we do for him? I brought along some very important papers he asked me to draw up for him to sign, but he's obviously in no condition now to do anything like that."

"I could have an ambulance take him back to the hospital in town. But I'm not sure that would be in his best interest. He's never been away from this house and his family. It might be better to keep him here and have Myrtle and his sons keep a close eye on him, and see if his condition starts to improve. I can drive out in the afternoons and check on him after my regular office hours. But if he shows any signs of taking a turn for the worse, we'll have to get him to the hospital."

"I'd appreciate your keeping me informed about his physical and mental condition," Ed responded quietly. He started to say something more, but stopped when he sensed that Myrtle was taking in every word of his conversation with Dr. Jannsen.

As they left Myrtle behind and walked together up the dark hallway, Ed continued, "I know that Gideon wouldn't object to my confiding in you about his personal affairs. I brought the revised will and power of attorney with me today that he felt to be so urgent. Until I can get the documents signed, his estate is in jeopardy, due to the current will and executor. I need to know the minute Gideon becomes rational again, assuming that he will."

Outside the house, squinting as their eyes adjusted to the sharp sunlight, Ed and Dr. Jannsen were joined by Daniel and Jonah, whose faces reflected obvious concern for their father.

"Boys, I don't know what's happened to your pa," Dr. Jannsen said. "I can't find anything physically wrong with him. I want you to call me at work or at home if there's any change in his condition, either better or worse. Otherwise, I'll see you again tomorrow afternoon about this time." He jotted two phone numbers down on a note pad, tore off the sheet, and handed it to them. "Ed, I'll let you know if Gideon improves enough to meet with you. I understand the need to get his affairs in order."

Ed received a call late in the day from a man he had not expected to hear from again. "Ed, this is Tony Vicelli. I hope you'll excuse me for bothering you at work. What I'm calling about is an opening here at my store for a boy to work part time after school and on Saturday, and your son Doug came to mind. The job involves bagging groceries and making deliveries for me. Maybe some other general work that needs to be done, like stock work, sweeping floors and hauling out the trash. The pay would be a half dollar an hour. If he's interested, he can come by tomorrow after school and talk to me. I guess the reason I thought about your boy is that I still feel I owe him something for what he did for my daughter the other night."

"I appreciate your calling, Tony. I'll talk to Doug when I get home, and tell him about the job. I'm almost positive he'll be interested. Part-time work in this town for boys seems to be hard to come by. If he's not interested, I'll have him call you tonight. Otherwise, he'll be by your market to see you tomorrow after school."

At dinner that evening, Ed told Doug about the events of the day, including his visit to the Buchanans, and his surprise in finding Gideon so confused. Then he remembered the last phone call of the day. "There was one more thing I meant to tell you. Tony Vicelli called right before I left the office. He's looking for a boy to work part-time for him in the afternoons and on Saturdays, for a half buck an hour, doing general grocery store chores like bagging groceries, making deliveries, and cleaning up around the place. Your Good Samaritan deed Friday night got you a job interview with him after school tomorrow, if you're interested."

"I'll say I'm interested," Doug responded. "My buddies and I have all been keeping our eyes open for part-time jobs since basketball season ended, and there's nothing anywhere in town. I'll go straight from school tomorrow to talk to Mr. Vicelli. The part about making deliveries sounds like fun. I hope that means driving his truck, and not riding my bike around town. But I confess, I'm going to be a little nervous when I first go in to talk to him. The last encounter I had with him, he was mad as a hornet, and threatening to beat the heck out of me. You want to wish me good luck?"

Chapter 16

As the school day wound down on Friday, Doug nervously twisted his pencil in his hand, thinking about what was facing him. When the bell rang, he grabbed his jacket and headed out of the door toward the Fresh Harvest Market. He could not shake off his apprehension as he walked across the parking lot to the entrance. Inside the store, he saw an attractive blonde standing at the cash register, and over in the produce department, a stocky, dark-haired man taking oranges from a crate and arranging them on a display counter. Approaching the check-out counter, Doug inquired, "Can you tell me where I can find Mr. Vicelli?"

The woman glanced up and replied in a pleasant voice, "I'll bet you're Doug Housman. I'm Ingrid Vicelli. That's my husband over in the first aisle, stocking produce. You and our oldest daughter Vickie are classmates at Tyler, aren't you?"

"Yes, ma'am, I'm Doug. She's in most of my classes," Doug replied awkwardly. "Mr. Vicelli left word with my dad for me to come by after school today and see him if I was interested in a part time job. I'm definitely looking for work."

Ingrid called to her husband, "Tony, Doug Housman's here to see you."

Tony sized up Doug up as he approached. Then reaching out with his broad hand, he said, "Nice to meet you, son. Let's go back in my office and talk for a few minutes." Sitting in the tiny store office, face to face, he carefully explained the work, hours, and pay. "Are you sure you want to work here, and do you think you can handle the job?"

"Yes, sir."

"Well, then, you're hired," Tony said, giving him a friendly pat on the shoulder. "You can start tomorrow at 9:00, helping me get some goods set up out in front of the store. There's plenty to do around here to keep you busy."

Doug breathed a huge sigh of relief as he walked out of the office. The interview had not been nearly as stressful as he had imagined. Just as he started to leave the store, Ingrid motioned for him to come over. "I didn't want you to get away before we could talk. I want to tell you how much I appreciate what you did for Vickie the other night, bringing her home from the canteen. I'm glad to see you're going to be coming to work here with us."

Walking home in the cool afternoon air, Doug found himself humming the catchy tune *Heart and Soul*. After lagging behind his buddies in the tenth grade as the only boy without a steady girlfriend, he now had something lined up that the others were all still hunting, a good part-time job. I can't wait to tell Mike and the gang about this, Doug thought. It'll make them eat their hearts out.

"I got the job, Dad," Doug exclaimed, as he burst through the door.

"Congratulations, son! I was about your age when I got my first real job. Did Tony Vicelli turn out to be as intimidating as he seemed to you the other night?"

"No, he was very friendly to me today. But I still don't think I'd want to get on the wrong side of him." In the kitchen, Doug set the dinner plates on the table. "What are you going to do around here tomorrow while I'm at work?"

Ed suppressed a laugh. "It looks like a nice sunny weekend. I had thought about taking Laura for a drive along the New River, but I waited too late to ask her again. One of the ladies who works in her office told me she left at noon with friends for a weekend at the Greenbrier. She sort of let the cat out of the bag that Laura was going with Dan Wohlford and his brother and sister-in-law."

"You're going to have to improve the speed of your game, Dad," Doug joked. "I don't think you'll ever score any points with Laura if you're that slow bringing the ball up the floor. It looks to me like Dan Wohlford knows how to run the fast break. And I sure don't have the experience to coach you."

"I suppose I could use a good coach," Ed replied good naturedly. "Oh, one other thing you might be interested to know about your new boss. I recently learned that his wife, Ingrid, is Dr. Jannsen's daughter. In a small town like this, it seems that everyone's related."

At the store the next day, Doug was surprised to find a new member of the family at work behind the checkout counter. Vickie was standing next to the cash register, with her hair pulled back in a pony tail, wearing red pedal pushers, a white blouse, and store apron. She greeted him cheerfully, as though he were a regular employee, "Good morning, Doug. You can get an apron in the storage closet beside the office."

In the store setting, away from the peer pressure of high school, Doug found it easier to talk to her, but still difficult to make direct eye contact. "Thanks. Your dad told me he wanted me to help him move some things out front, first thing this morning. I'll grab an apron and see him to get started."

Tony Vicelli proved to be a boss who expected the same non-stop activity from his employees that he demonstrated. Doug unpacked, sorted, cleaned, boxed, and carried, all under close supervision, and almost without stopping. But he found himself enjoying the demanding pace of the new job, and took pride in showing that he could handle whatever work his boss threw at him, quickly and well. "What do you want me to do now?" he frequently asked, as he completed one task after another.

By late morning, Tony moved him to the checkout counter to bag groceries while Vickie rang them up. Doug soon learned that heavy canned goods needed to be packed into more than one grocery bag. When he overloaded his first one, it split from top to bottom. Vickie stopped to help him corral the cans rolling across the floor. "I did the same thing when I first started working here last year. Cans went everywhere! The lady buying the groceries and Dad weren't too happy with me."

Between customers, she asked, "How do you like Mr. Powell as a math teacher? I'm having trouble in his geometry class. I did a lot better in algebra class last year with Miss Anderson as my teacher, and ended up with a B+. She could explain things so they made sense to me. With Mr. Powell, a lot of it just seems to go over my head."

Doug straightened unconsciously, hands on hips, a math whiz coming into his own. "I don't think Mr. Powell can get the concepts across as well as Miss Anderson. I know that I learn a lot more from studying the book at home than I get out of his class. Anything in particular that's bothering you now?" he asked, for once looking into her blue eyes.

"Yeah, I don't understand polynomial equations, and how they define curves. Mom and Dad have forgotten any geometry they ever knew, and I don't feel comfortable asking Mr. Powell for help after school. At this point, I don't think he could get anything across to me in a way that would be very helpful. I'm really struggling."

"If you'd like, we could go out on the loading dock at the back of the store at lunchtime, and I'll try to explain some of the basics," Doug offered, feeling a degree of self-confidence he had never before experienced around her. "You'll need to have them down pat, before you can handle the more advanced part you're having trouble with now."

"That would be nice of you," she replied appreciatively. "I brought an extra sandwich with me today, and you can have it."

Later that morning, the remaining two members of the Vicelli family showed up, fourteen-year old Sandra and ten-year old Tony, Jr. Unlike Vickie, both had their father's black hair and dark eyes. It was obvious that Vickie had gotten her blonde hair and blue eyes from her mother's side of the family. When she saw Doug looking at her sister and brother, she laughed, "We're really blood kin. When people see me and hear my name is Vicelli, some of them think I'm adopted."

At lunchtime, Tony let Sandra take over the checkout counter, and Vickie followed Doug out onto the loading dock. Using wooden crates for seats and a work table, and a stubby yellow pencil to write on a brown paper bag, Doug spent the next forty-five minutes reviewing basic geometry with her. She grasped the concepts much more quickly than he had expected. "Mr. Powell must be a pretty poor math teacher if he can't get this stuff across to you. You seem to have a good handle on the fundamentals already."

'Thanks. Maybe you ought to think about a career as a math teacher after high school and college. I think I've learned more from you today, sitting out here scribbling on a brown paper bag, than from Mr. Powell during the last month, with him writing on all three of his blackboards."

In the afternoon, Doug helped Tony with orders that had been phoned in during the week, filling bags and boxes with groceries for customers. His boss explained, "We call back and let them know what the groceries come to, and they have cash or a check waiting when we deliver. We have one special customer that has his bank send us a check to pay the account at the end of the month, and that's Gideon Buchanan. We only deliver that far out because he and his wife can't get around."

Doug joined Tony for the weekly grocery delivery run at the end of the day. After making in-town deliveries, they drove out to the farm and up the long private road to the Buchanan house. Doug looked across the fields, in the direction of Chimney Rock, noticing two men working with a team of horses near the top of a low hill in the distance. Tony slowed the truck to get a better look. The men seemed to be using a horse-drawn grader equipped with a wide blade to move dirt, preparing a flat area near the crest. "I wonder what in the world they're doing up there," he commented. "It doesn't look like they're plowing. It's the wrong time of year for that, anyway. You plow fields in the fall, so the winter freezes will break up the clods."

Dust swirled behind them all the way to the house, where they parked close to the back door leading into the kitchen. Myrtle Spencer was waiting to receive the delivery. "Are Mr. and Mrs. Buchanan doing any better today?" Tony asked.

"No, sir. They're both still sleeping a lot." She nervously shifted her weight from foot to foot and tugged at her apron, her gaze somewhere above Tony's head.

Ready to head back to the store, Doug and Tony saw a late model Chrysler sedan drive up. Tony hesitated in starting the truck, watching to see who might be coming to visit. When the car doors opened, Doug caught sight of three men. The driver had brown hair and appeared to be the age and size of his dad. The other two men looked older, one with gray hair, and the second almost bald. The gray-haired man was carrying a briefcase and camera, and the bald man was holding a small black bag.

"I'd like to know what that visit's all about," Tony said, starting the engine. "I recognize the driver. He's a nephew by the name of Julian Grant. I've run into him out here once before. But I don't recognize either of the others. I may ask my father-in-law what he knows. It looked like one of the visitors was carrying a doctor's bag, and I'm almost certain that he doesn't practice medicine around here."

The "Closed" sign was hanging on the front door when they returned to the store. After picking up papers from the parking lot and hauling the trash can to the alley behind the building, Doug started toward home, kicking a tin can along the street as he went. JR spotted him as he came within sight of the house, and bounded out to meet him.

"How did your first day on the job go?" Ed inquired, as the two entered the house.

"Really great," Doug replied. "I didn't have any trouble with anything my boss threw at me, and I got to work with Vickie part of the day. Guess who we saw while we were finishing up our grocery deliveries to the Buchanans?"

When he went on to explain the chance encounter with Julian Grant and the two strangers, and Tony Vicelli's comments afterwards, his dad's curiosity was evident. "I'm glad that Tony was going to talk to Dr. Jannsen about seeing them out there," Ed said.

After dinner, Ed called Dr. Jannsen, inquiring, "Did your son-in-law just call to tell you who he saw at Gideon Buchanan's house this afternoon? I wanted to find out what you make of it."

"I just got off the phone with him," Dr. Jannsen replied. "I have no idea why Julian would bring in another doctor look at Gideon or Hester without contacting me first."

"I could offer one logical explanation," Ed said. "If I were the executor for that estate, laying the groundwork to prove that the Buchanans are no longer competent to handle their own affairs, I'd try to get an expert medical opinion on record documenting their condition, witnessed by a legal expert, with supporting photographs."

"Exactly the same thoughts passed through my mind," Dr. Jannsen responded. "I don't believe that those three were out there with benevolent intentions toward the family."

Chapter 17

THE SIMPSONS closed on the sale of their farm on Tuesday morning, and the Hendersons followed that after-noon. William Thorpe and the attorney for Copperfield Enterprises drove down from Beckley for the day to meet with each party in Ed's office. The Simpsons and Hendersons were reconciled to the sale of their homes, and were pleased to get such high prices for them. Of the participants at the closings, only Ed felt a strong sense of misgiving, knowing that two more tracts of pristine farmland outside of town were now in the hands of Barker Mining.

After the second meeting ended, and the Hendersons and Thorpe and his attorney had left, Ed drove to the court house. When he pulled into the parking lot, he spotted the familiar white Oldsmobile station wagon. Crossing the lobby, he caught sight of Laura walking toward him.

She approached him with a smile, saying, "Ed, how nice to run into you like this. I haven't seen you for a few days. Have you gotten everything organized and running like a Swiss watch in your new office?"

"The move's gone a lot more smoothly than I expected," Ed replied, trying to conceal the resentment he felt since learning of her weekend with Dan. Feeling no inclination to return her smile or engage in friendly small talk, he added, "By the way, since it's a matter of public record now, I can tell you that the sales of the Simpson and Henderson properties to Copperfield Enterprises are complete. Copperfield and Barker Mining have a major foothold north of town, and I'm sure we haven't seen the last of their land acquisitions out there. If you'll excuse me now, I've got to run down to the Clerk's office before they close for the day. Good to see you again."

For a moment, hurt and puzzlement flashed across Laura's face. But she quickly concealed her emotions behind a polite mask, and replied coolly, "Nice to see you again, too." Then stepping to one side, she continued past him, the sound of her heel taps on the terrazzo floor echoing through the room.

Watching her walk away, Ed felt a sudden loss of interest in his mundane task down the hall, but also no desire to return to his office. He recalled a similar feeling from years ago, when he had hurt a girl in his fifth grade school class by spitefully telling her he didn't want to come to her birthday party. Allowing time to be sure that Laura had left the parking lot, he retreated to his house.

After dinner that evening, Ed sat back in his chair to look at the new Time magazine, but instead gazed about the room, visibly distracted from the article he had set out to read. Something troubled him, and he could not seem to shake it off.

"What's wrong, Dad?" Doug inquired, looking up from his homework. "You look like you have a lot on your mind tonight."

"I don't know. I'm still bothered about my role in helping to sell those two farms to a company fronting for Barker Mining. Sometimes in the legal profession, you get involved in legitimate business transactions you personally find troubling, and this is one of those times.

"But probably what's bothering me even more is how I acted when I ran into Laura today. I think I let some petty jealousy cause me to be unfriendly, and she really didn't have it coming. I'm going to call her and get this off my chest."

He put down the magazine, and dialed Laura's home number. Hearing her answer, he said, "This is Ed. I wanted to call you and apologize if I came across as rude when I ran into you at the court house earlier today. I had some things on my mind, but that shouldn't have had any bearing on how I acted."

"I'm glad you called. I didn't think you seemed your normal, friendly self this afternoon. You seemed to be all business, as though I were just some sort of professional acquaintance. If I'm permitted to ask, what was on your mind?"

"I'm not sure I want to get into that now," Ed said. "How about just accepting my apology and putting all this behind us."

"I accept your apology, but I think it might be good for us to clear some things up, so we don't walk away with any misunderstandings. What was bothering you? Was it the fact that someone in my office told you I had gone for the weekend to the Greenbrier with Dan and his brother and sister-in-law? I reserved my own room there before we left. You could have asked me what plans I had for the weekend, and I would have told you. I have no reason to try to cover something up. You knew that I had gone out with Dan a few times, and he's aware that you've also taken me out a couple of times, too."

"I know that we're not like a couple of kids going steady, Laura," Ed countered. "But I really enjoy your company. Maybe I come across as being a little jealous and possessive, but the truth is that I'm not interested in winning some kind of sportsmanship award by sharing your free time with Dan Wohlford or anyone else. I believe we'd better drop this discussion now, before I put my foot in my mouth, and have to apologize for something else."

"I don't think a lawyer like you is going to get himself into trouble by talking too freely," she continued, but with a lighter tone in her voice. "I appreciate your opening up and letting me know what was bothering you today. I confess that I was hurt by the way you acted at the court house. I started to say something to you at the time, but bit my tongue instead. Maybe that was a mistake on my part. Thanks for calling me tonight, and letting me know what's been bothering you. If you were just displaying a little male jealousy, you're forgiven."

"I'm glad to hear you say that," Ed replied. "Let's pick up where we were before I almost spoiled things between us today. We're friends again, right?"

"Special friends," she replied. "Bye now."

The phone rang shortly after Ed and Laura hung up, Dr. Jannsen on the other end of the line. "I had a call this afternoon from Myrtle Spencer. She said it was extremely important that she talk to me privately as soon as possible. I couldn't get her to tell me what was on her mind, but I don't think it had anything to do with the health of Gideon or Hester. I told her I planned to come out to the house on Friday afternoon, and I could speak with her then.

"She asked me not to say anything to anyone about her calling, but I thought you needed to know, since you're now as deeply involved with the Buchanans as I am. One thing Myrtle mentioned is that Julian Grant has brought another woman out to the house to work with her part time. Myrtle doesn't know the other woman, and she thinks she may have just moved here from out of town. Anyway, I thought if your Friday afternoon was open, you might want to go with me and get your own reading on Gideon's mental condition."

"I'm going to clear my calendar for Friday afternoon, and we can ride out together," Ed replied. "If Myrtle has something urgent she wants to discuss with you, and it has nothing to do with the people she's caring for, I wonder what in the world could be troubling her?"

★

Harold Akers had earned a reputation throughout the community for being a proud landowner and hardworking farmer who was always ready to pitch in and lend a hand to a neighbor. Early in the morning, he rolled out of bed while it was still dark outside, slipped into warm work clothes, and headed downstairs to fix breakfast. Putting on a heavy jacket and red plaid hunting cap, he stepped outside to feed and water his Llewellyn setter in the dog run beside the house. As the sky turned spectacular shades of orange in the east, he glanced across the rolling fields and saw Myrtle Spencer's house a half mile away.

Walking toward the dairy barn, he spotted his prize four-year old Guernsey bull, Big Dan, standing in the securely fenced field out beside the road. Then a large, unnatural looking form on the ground caught his eye. Walking back toward the road to get a better look, Harold felt his stomach drop. When he got within fifty feet, his worst fears were realized. Lying on the ground, beside the bull, was a mauled and obviously dead body, dressed in a blood spattered long gray coat.

Running back toward the house, Harold called out to his two teenage sons, "Jimbo, Tommy, get out here on the double! Something bad's happened! I need you out here right now." The boys came running out of the door, still putting on their jackets, and the three rushed toward the gate leading into the bull pasture.

"I'm going to try to walk over and grab hold of the ring in his nose," Harold explained. "You boys will have to distract him if he starts to turn on me." Harold entered the field and approached the bull, but Big Dan was in no mood to let him get close, throwing up dirt with his hooves and bellowing ominously, warning him to back off. When the bull lowered its head and started toward him on the run, Harold sprinted away and vaulted the gate to safety.

"You want me to go in the barn and get a couple of pitchforks to drive him back, Dad?" Jimbo asked.

"He's mighty stirred up this morning. I'm not sure that pitchforks would do the job, unless we want to take a chance on sticking him hard enough to really hurt him. I'm going to go get the tractor."

Hurrying to the barn nearby, Harold climbed onto the seat of his John Deere and fired up the engine. Gripping the wheel with shaking hands, he purposefully back-tracked to the nightmare come to life in the pasture.

"Tommy, I want you to open and shut the gate for us. Stay on your toes, because he'll be right on our heels when we come back out of the pasture. Jimbo, you've got the dangerous part. I want you to stay right behind the tractor. I'm going to drive him far enough back for you to pick up the body. Then I'll try to keep the tractor between you and the bull as we back out through the gate."

Following instructions, the younger son opened the gate, while the older boy followed closely behind the tractor toward the gray clad remains. The bull lowered its massive head and shoulders, charging into the front of the tractor again and again, trying to overturn it. "Watch out, Dad! He lifted the front wheels off the ground that time!" Jimbo cried out.

Finally, Harold was able to drive the bull back just far enough for the older son to pick up the corpse. With Harold maneuvering the tractor as a shield, they backed out of the pasture together. "Quick, open the gate," Jimbo shouted. As the tractor came through, Tommy slammed the gate shut, leaving the angry bull behind.

"Good job, boys. You can put the body down on the ground, now, son," Harold said, his voice trembling. "Let's see if we can tell who it is."

When they placed the body on the ground and turned it over, Harold exclaimed, "Oh my God, it's Myrtle Spencer!" Tommy backed away, spun around, and vomited. Jimbo, who had been wiping the coagulated blood from his hands, crouched low to the ground, and also emptied his stomach on the grass.

★

Ed had experienced premonitions before, and from the time he entered the office on Friday, he recognized a familiar sense of apprehension. His subconscious anxiety proved to be well founded when the call came from Dr. Jannsen later that morning.

"Ed, something's happened that has changed all of my plans for today. I got an urgent call early this morning from Harold Akers, a neighbor of Myrtle Spencer, telling me she'd been killed in some kind of farm accident, and that I was needed out there right away.

"When I drove up, I saw Myrtle's body on the ground, with Sheriff Daniels and two of his deputies beside it, and Harold and his boys standing nearby. Harold said that it looked like Myrtle had taken a shortcut across his place walking home from work at the Buchanan's place yesterday evening, and she made the mistake of going through the pastures where he keeps his Guernsey bull. From the condition of the remains, it appears that she was knocked down and trampled to death around dark, and her body remained out in the field with the bull until Harold spotted it this morning. He had to use his tractor to drive the bull away, so he and his sons could get the body out to where they could identify who it was. I believe Myrtle had been dead for over twelve hours by the time I looked at her."

"Good Lord!" Ed exclaimed. "How could a sensible woman like Myrtle walk into a field with a bull? She must have known he owned that animal, and how dangerous it was. Surely there was a fence and closed gate to keep people out."

"There was, Ed. She had to open the gate to let herself in. And the strangest thing about all of this is that she had a shorter, more direct path to her home without even cutting across that field. Neither the Akers or any of the other neighbors within earshot heard her cry out for help. Sheriff Daniels is still scratching his head, trying to figure out what might have happened. I've been asked to provide a medical examination of her body, to see if I can help shed any light on this accident. We haven't had a farm fatality around here for a long time."

"Even the timing of the accident seems strange," Ed observed. "You get a call from Myrtle earlier this week saying she urgently needs to talk to you privately, and the evening before you're to meet with her, she's killed by a neighbor's bull. I'm sure you and Sheriff Daniels are going to give Myrtle's death a very hard look before you rule that it was an accident."

"We certainly will. It's good that Julian Grant has someone lined up who can help the family now that Myrtle's gone. I think that I still need to visit them today, and get to know the new housekeeper. Hopefully, she had time to learn the ropes while she was working with Myrtle. Gideon and Hester need a lot of special care, particularly while we're trying so hard to get Gideon back to a rational state of mind."

"I can still go with you if you like. Why don't I meet you at your office in the mid-afternoon, and you can ride out with me."

At the Buchanan house, Ed and Dr. Jannsen were met at the door by Agnes Harper, who identified herself as the new housekeeper. She appeared to be younger and smaller than Myrtle, a haggard woman who had not led an easy life. Following her into Hester's bedroom, both men saw that the old woman's fragile health condition was unchanged, as she continued to lie sleeping fitfully. Moving down the hall to the adjacent bedroom, they found Gideon to be as lethargic and confused as during the previous visit, obviously still incompetent to sign any legal documents.

"They're both about the same as they were when I was here

before, working with Myrtle," Agnes volunteered.

After Daniel and Jonah came up from the barn, Dr. Jannsen took them aside with Agnes, and gently informed the three that Myrtle Spencer had been killed the previous evening in a farm accident. Both sons seemed shaken to hear the news, and were obviously distraught as they left the room. Agnes listened without showing emotion, though the color drained from her face. "I suppose you'll need for me to start to work full-time now?" she inquired nervously. Dr. Jannsen nodded.

Daniel caught up with them as they were leaving, carrying an old leather satchel with a broken strap. Handing it to Dr. Jannsen, he said, "This belonged to Myrtle." Drawing a deep breath, Daniel walked away before Ed or Dr. Jannsen could speak a word of comfort, a tear slipping down his weather-beaten cheek.

On the way back to town, Dr Jannsen pushed the satchel across the car seat toward Ed. "Would you please take a look inside for me and see what she kept in the bag?"

Opening it, Ed found an assortment of items, including clothing, a hair brush, a mirror, a small framed photograph of two people he assumed to be Myrtle's parents, a stubby yellow pencil, and a Blue Horse spiral-bound composition book with many handwritten notes, showing evidence of several ripped-out sheets.

"Nothing of any value here," he commented. "Myrtle obviously didn't leave many worldly goods behind at the Buchanan home. I feel sure that most of her belongings are back at that empty house where she lived. She must have led a terribly lonely life living all by herself way out in the country."

Chapter 18

D R. JANNSEN arrived at his office early Friday morning, dreading the task ahead of him. Performing autopsies and pathology reports as a contract coroner for Madison County was never pleasant work, and it was infinitely worse when he knew the victim personally.

Rolling a stainless steel table bearing the body of Myrtle Spencer under a low hanging light, he began. Visual examination disclosed only minor sign of external bleeding, either on the clothing or the body. He attributed this to the fact that the bull had been dehorned, and therefore Myrtle had not been gored. Experience with similar accidents involving large livestock had taught him that fatal injuries were usually inflicted after the victim was knocked to the ground, then trampled or crushed under the weight of the animal.

It soon became apparent that Myrtle had been mauled in such a manner, causing many broken bones, and massive internal injuries. There was a large contusion where the bull had driven its head against her chest, and hoof marks showed on various parts of her body and clothing. But continuing his examination, Dr. Jannsen saw a group of deep bruises on her back and legs that did not appear consistent in shape with either the head or hooves of a large bull. The black pattern appeared almost like a circular shape between two somewhat irregular horizontal bars, with the lower of the two far more pronounced. At this point he realized where he had witnessed similar bruises before. It had been two years earlier, when a pedestrian walking along the highway had been struck from behind, killed by a hit and run driver.

Striding into his office while composing his thoughts, Dr. Jannsen phoned Sheriff Daniels office. "Earl," he said, "I've completed a preliminary examination of Myrtle Spencer's body, and I'd like for you to come right over so I can show you what I've found. There's physical evidence that Myrtle was run down from behind by a motor vehicle before she was thrown into the field with the bull. I don't think that we're looking at a farm accident now. I think we may be looking at a homicide."

There was a brief hesitation, and then Sheriff Daniels replied, "Dr. Jannsen, I'm not completely surprised by your findings. I never could understand in the first place why Myrtle would have gone through that gate and cut across the field with the bull. The walking distance would have been about the same if she'd just stayed on the road. I'll get my deputy, and we'll be over in a few minutes to get some photographs."

Waiting for Sheriff Daniels to arrive, Dr. Jannsen dialed a second number. "Ed, I think your curiosity about the strange timing of Myrtle Spencer's death was well founded. Earl Daniels is on the way over here now. It appears to me someone may have run Myrtle Spencer down on the way home from the Buchanan's place, then dumped her body across the fence into the field with Harold Akers' bull to cover up the crime. I don't think any of us understands how the pieces of this puzzle fit together, and until we do, maybe those of us who have recently been involved with the Buchanans should stay on the alert."

"I appreciate your call," Ed replied. "There's never been any progress by area law enforcement people in finding out who ran me off the highway last month, or who may have burned down my office building. That's all happened since I took on the Buchanans as clients."

Sheriff Daniels arrived shortly afterward, accompanied by a deputy carrying a camera. Following Dr. Jannsen to the examining table, they lifted the sheet and examined the contusions on Myrtle's legs, buttocks and back. For the next hour they collected forensic evidence, including photographs, sketches, and measurements of the pattern of bruises.

"You can see what I was telling you," Dr Jannsen said to them. "There's no way a bull made those bruises on her back. She was run down by a motor vehicle."

"I'm sure you're right," Sheriff Daniels stated. "I believe Myrtle was hit from behind while she was walking. The pattern of bruises looks like it was stamped on her legs and back by the bumper and grille of a car or truck. The injuries to her face may have resulted from being knocked to the ground."

Focusing on the coarse circular black shape centered between two irregular dark horizontal bars, he continued, "I think it's clear that the heavy lower bruise was made by a bumper. It appears likely the circular one in the middle was made by the grille. The upper one probably was caused by the front end of the vehicle above the grille.

"I have something in my driveway at home that probably would produce a similar pattern: my '51 Ford pickup. Last year, Ford came out with a large one-piece grille for their trucks, and the body style is about the same this year. There are a lot of them on the road. I wouldn't rule out the possibility that the vehicle that ran Myrtle down was a late model Ford truck."

Sheriff Daniels and his deputy returned to their headquarters. Using their own photographic lab dark room, they printed glossy photos showing Myrtle's injuries. Before the end of the day, they had completed their report, ruling the death to be vehicular manslaughter or homicide. As they were wrapping up, Earl glanced over toward his youngest deputy and inquired, "What's wrong, Billy? Looks like something's been bothering you all afternoon."

"I keep thinking about the Spencer woman. She reminds me of the aunt who raised me, skinny, and stooped over with arthritis. My aunt used to tell me she felt like a horse that'd been rode hard and put up wet. This poor old woman looks like she's had the same kind of tough life. I hope I can help catch whoever it was that ran over her."

Daniels issued a bulletin to area law enforcement agencies to be on the lookout for cars or trucks showing heavy damage to the front bumper and grille from a possible hit and run. "Whoever ran her down is going to have a hard time covering it up. Repairing that vehicle's going to take a lot more work than knocking a few dents out of a sheet metal fender with a rubber hammer."

Chapter 19

FEELING THE euphoria that only the sight of clock hands approaching 3:00 can bring, Mike caught up with Doug at his locker, and grabbed him by the shoulder. "Dawg, I've got the deal of a lifetime for you. I've got a date with Ginny tonight, and we're going to see *High Noon* at the Lyric. Ginny has a friend, and wants to know if you'd like to double date with us. What about it?"

"Who's the other girl? Someone who looks like Debbie Reynolds?"

Mike rolled his eyes. "Since when did you get to be so picky, Romeo? I'm not aware that there are a whole lot of girls in our class beating your door down wanting to go out with you."

"I'd still like to know who it is," Doug persisted. "Didn't Ginny tell you?"

"No, dummy, it's a blind date. I think the girl is some friend of hers in the junior class, but I'm not sure. You're not intimidated by older women, are you?"

"No, but first I'll have to check with my receptionist to see if I'm open for tonight," Doug replied. Sticking his head into his locker and then pulling it back, he replied, "The older woman is in luck. I had a cancellation, so I'll be able to work her in. When will you coming by the house to get me? The first feature starts a little after 7:00."

"Don't start worrying about the details," Mike assured him.

"We'll come by for you plenty early to make sure you don't miss the Daffy Duck cartoon."

Doug turned Mike's proposal over in his mind as he hurried home from school. Why had Mike and Ginny waited to the last minute before inviting him to double date with them on a Friday night? But on the other hand, if he turned the blind date down, would he chance missing the opportunity to meet someone who could turn out to be really special? After mulling it over, he concluded that he had made the right decision.

That evening at supper, Ed stared at him inquisitively, asking "Why are you bolting your meal down like that? Have you got something planned for later?"

"I sure have, Dad," Doug shot back, downing the last of his milk. "You and JR are on your own tonight. Mike has me lined up with a blind date, and I've decided you just never know when you're going to meet Miss Right."

"Have a good time. I'll hold the fort down here with the dog until you get home to tell us all about your evening."

After stepping out of the hot shower and toweling off, Doug splashed on some Old Spice lotion, strictly for the manly fragrance, since he had never shaved a day in his life. Pulling his favorite clothes from the closet, he donned khaki pants, his new brown and white plaid sport shirt, and brown loafers. Running a comb through his short red hair, he glanced in the mirror, speaking to the dog. "How do I look, JR? Think the mystery girl will mistake me for Tab Hunter?" Then looking back into the mirror again, he answered his own question, "Not too likely."

Mike's loud blast of the car horn in front of the house brought Doug running down the steps and out the door. Settling into the back seat, he immediately inquired, "OK, Ginny, tell me who's your mystery friend I'm going out with tonight?" Ignoring his question, she turned the radio up louder, pretending not to hear him as they drove off.

When they reached a neighborhood of large brick homes and spacious lawns, Mike slowed to turn into a long driveway leading to a house with a wide front porch. "Hey! This is where the Vicellis live," Doug exclaimed. "I was only here once before, but if I live to be a million, I'll never forget this driveway."

"You're on your own now, Dawg," Mike commented. "Go on

up to the door and see if she's ready."

Doug walked to the front door and rang the bell. Ingrid greeted him at the door with a smile, saying, "Come in, Doug. Vicky will be down in just a few minutes."

In the living room, Tony was sitting in a comfortable chair, his feet up on an ottoman, watching the news. He glanced up at Doug, and said in a joking way that Doug had never heard from him before, "Sit down, son, and make yourself comfortable while you wait. You're going to learn that women are never ready on time."

Having worked around Vickie's parents, Doug felt a little more at ease. Still, he was not totally relaxed trying to carry on small talk with the two of them in their home, particularly when Tony was his boss and all business at the store.

Fortunately for him, Vickie soon came down the steps into the living room, a white sweater setting off her blonde hair and bright smile. "Hi, Doug, I'm finally ready. I guess Ginny and Mike are waiting out in the car, so we'd better go." The thought flashed through Doug's mind that years later he would still remember how pretty she looked, lighting up the room where he sat nervously visiting with her folks, waiting for her to appear.

In the front seat of the car, Ginny was in the middle, close to Mike, "helping him drive," as their friends would say. In the back seat, Doug and Vickie sat much further apart. As Mike pulled out into traffic, the four were laughing and talking, a comfortable familiarity enveloping them.

That all changed when a car pulled up beside them at the traffic light a block away from the theater. Looking over, Doug recognized four boys in the senior class who hung out with Len Hacker. Just as the light turned green and the other car accelerated away, one of the boys rolled down his window and loudly yelled something unmistakably rude and vulgar: "Hey, Vickie, I hear you put out."

Her smile disappeared as if she had been struck. "Those are some of Len's friends," she said in a shaken voice. "Since I broke up with him, he's tried to get back at me by spreading lies around the school. He and his friends have made some really ugly comments."

"Just ignore them," Ginnie interjected. "They're just a bunch of crude jerks. No one believes anything they say. Let's go on to the movies, and not let them spoil the evening."

Doug did not know how to react. Everything had happened so quickly and unexpectedly, and there seemed to be no way to make things right, the way they had been just a few minutes earlier. Instinctively, he reached across the back seat for Vickie's hand. She glanced over at him, hurt and embarrassment stamped on her pretty face, and he felt her clasp his hand firmly.

The full house at the Lyric was exceptionally quiet throughout the movie. Gary Cooper was perfect as Sheriff Will Kane, forsaken by everyone including his Quaker wife, waiting for the return of the Miller Gang. As the clock moved inexorably toward the showdown at high noon, Vickie reached across and put her hand on top of his. When the lights came on after the exciting climax, Doug walked beside her out of the theater, the theme song of the movie still running through his head.

The parking lot at Gil's was crowded when they stopped off for chocolate shakes. Doug glanced around, glad to see that the car with Len's friends was nowhere in sight. Later, when Mike drove them back out to the Vicelli's home, Doug opened the door for Vickie and walked beside her up to the front door under the porch light. "I had a good time tonight," she said.

"I did, too," he replied. "I'm sorry we ran into those jerks on the way to the theater. I hope it didn't ruin the evening for you." Then, summoning up his nerve, he put everything on the line and asked the big question, "Would you go out with me again?"

Returning to the car, Doug slipped into the back seat, Mike and Ginny snuggled together in front. "Were you surprised when you found out your blind date was going to be Vickie?" Ginny asked, laughing. "I was afraid that if Mike let you in on the secret, you'd chicken out and wouldn't go."

"You could have knocked me over with a feather," Doug replied. "This was an evening I'll never forget."

The rest of the way home, Vickie's brief reply on her front porch ran through his mind again and again, crowding out all other thoughts. "Those boys didn't spoil anything for me, Doug. Sure, I'll go out with you again."

Chapter 20

Clerk of Court Shirley Baker caught up with Ed on Monday. She motioned for him to follow her to a corner where they could talk without being overheard. "Ed, I may be overstepping my authority, but I know that you've done some work for Gideon and Hester Buchanan, and I think there's something you should know. Julian Grant just filed papers today to have the Buchanans and their two sons declared incompetent to handle their affairs, and to appoint him as executor of their estate.

"Rumors fly inside this building, and the word going around is that Julian has the opportunity and every intention to sell their property quickly. A hearing's been scheduled for the third week of April in front of Judge Kirk. I don't know of anyone except yourself and their doctor who might be able to look out for their interests."

"Shirley, I'm not as surprised to hear this as you might think," Ed replied. "I anticipated something like this might be in the works, but didn't expect it to happen quite so quickly. Thanks for making me aware of it. I wish the hearing was to be held before Judge Wine instead of Judge Kirk, but that's out of our hands. If there are any new developments you feel comfortable discussing with me, I'd appreciate hearing from you."

Walking down the hall to the pay phone, with no one within earshot, Ed dialed Dr. Jannsen's office. "Arnold, I think that the other shoe has dropped. I'm over here at the courthouse, and I've just learned that Julian Grant has started legal proceedings to take over the Buchanan estate." He then related everything that he had just learned. "Unless Gideon makes a dramatic recovery in the next few weeks, I think Julian will have little trouble proving that Gideon, Hester, and their two sons are incapable of managing their own affairs, and that as the appointed executor, he should be authorized to make all their decisions."

"Ed, I still don't know what's causing Gideon to remain so confused," Dr. Jannsen replied. "I haven't seen any improvement in his condition in recent days. But I promise you that I haven't given up, and I'm still looking for other things I might be able to try in order to snap him out of this.

"I still have Myrtle's satchel at home. I wanted to look over the contents before I turned it over to Sheriff Daniels, and last night I found the time. The notebook has a lot of reminders Myrtle made to herself about the medicines I've prescribed for Hester and Gideon over the past couple of years, including one as recently as this January. But the page after the most recent entry has been ripped out of the book. Looking at the next blank sheet, I could see where her pencil left impressions in the paper, and I tried to make out what she had written. It looks to me like '1- morning, 1- afternoon.' I've gone over all the medications I've prescribed for Gideon and Hester, and that note makes no sense at all. I'm still perplexed as to why she jotted something like that down."

"It sounds like the timing for some ongoing prescription medicine, doesn't it?" Ed observed. "Let me know if you solve the puzzle."

When Ed returned to his office that afternoon he found several phone messages left by Carolyn. Laura's was the first call he returned. "Thanks for calling me back, Ed. I wondered if you'd like to stop off at the café downtown after work today. I know I'm asking at the last minute, but I haven't talked to you for a few days, and I thought it would fun if we could have dinner together."

"That sounds good to me, too. I think the special today is fried chicken, and when I was growing up, I only got that on

Sundays or when company came to visit. Would you like to meet around 6:00?"

Later, at their favorite table, they settled back comfortably, and Laura asked, "Have you heard anything new about the investigation of Myrtle Spencer's death? The newspaper reported it as a possible homicide, and I can't even remember the last time we had one of those in these parts."

Leaning close, Ed replied, "I don't know any more about Myrtle's death than you've already read in the paper. But there are some things going on that you might be interested to know.

"Dr. Jannsen's stymied by Gideon's condition and doesn't know what to do next. Until Gideon's mind clears, there's no way in the world for me to help him execute a new will and power of attorney. And there's a real urgency to that now, with the upcoming hearing before Judge Kirk. An incompetency ruling would result in his nephew becoming executor for the estate, with the authority to sell the farm.

"Looking back, from the time you told me about a coal discovery north of town, and an unknown party trying to buy up land, bad things have happened to those of us who've tried to help the Buchanans in one way or another. I'm beginning to wonder if we're looking at a lot of small parts to one large jigsaw puzzle, although I can't be sure. But if you step back and try to see how everything might fit together, something jumps out at you. There's one person who has a lot to gain, depending on how things play out in the days ahead, and his name is Barker."

After the meals arrived, Ed abruptly changed the conversation. "All we've been talking about this evening is unpleasant situations. Before we go any further and ruin a good dinner, tell me how things are going with you. You haven't been back to the Greenbrier lately, have you?"

Laura's forehead wrinkled, and she looked down at the table for a few seconds. Glancing up at him, she inquired, "Is that your subtle way of asking whether I've gone out again with Dan Wohlford?"

Ed shifted uncomfortably. "Yes, I suppose it might be."

Still looking him in the eye, but now with a mischievous grin, she continued, "Do you really think that's any of your business?"

"Probably not. You may not realize it, but this is starting to become a pretty uncomfortable experience for me. I usually get to ask the questions during a witness interrogation."

"Well, if we're going to handle this like a courtroom case, Counselor, I would like to object to your question as completely out of order. However, to cut through all of your legal mumbo jumbo, I'll give you a simple answer: no

"I hadn't planned to get into my personal life tonight, but since you've brought up the subject, I'll go ahead and tell you something. Dan has gotten much too serious, far too quickly for me. The last time I went out with him, he brought out an engagement ring with an enormous diamond. I turned him down.

"I'm learning that Dan is someone who can't take no for an answer. Since that evening, he's called me several times a day, at work and at home. I've made up excuses to avoid contact with him, and I've even tried taking my phone off the hook at home. It's gotten so bad I really wish we'd never been introduced. That's 'how things are going with me.' And no, I haven't been back to the Greenbrier."

Glancing down, Ed replied, "I was half joking when I asked you the question. I'm really surprised to hear how Dan's acting, because he has the reputation around town of being a very likeable guy. Obsessive personalities can sometimes be hard to spot. I'm sorry he's started harassing you."

Looking back up at Laura, he continued, "But to be honest, I'm glad that you aren't seeing him now. I feel like I'm way too old to be competing with another man for a lady I think so much of."

"I appreciate your listening to my troubles, and your kind words. And if it will make you feel any better, you don't have any competition to worry about."

Ed glanced away, not wanting to show just how much that remark meant to him. Trying to conceal his feelings, he quipped, "As I've gotten a few years older, I've begun to think that competition is highly overrated."

He followed Laura out of the café onto the street, just as the sun was settling low in the sky, and headlights were piercing the dusk. They were still talking as they walked to her car, unaware of people passing by on the street. Gently turning Laura by the arm to face him, he pulled her close for a long kiss. As he closed the car door for her and walked away, Ed noticed an older couple who had stopped on the sidewalk and were staring at him. Taking a second glance, he noticed that the woman was smiling.

When he got home, Ed found that Doug had finished his homework and was already in pajamas, listening to a radio program. "Did you find anything for supper in the fridge?" he asked.

"Not the kind of food or the dining experience you had," Doug replied, laughing. "But the leftovers from Sunday dinner weren't so bad." Turning down the radio, Doug got to the point, "How's Mrs. Jackson getting along? Did you kids have a good time?"

"Yeah, we talked some about what's been going on out north of town. She had read all about the Myrtle Spencer homicide in the paper. I filled her in on where I stand with the Buchanan will. That sort of thing."

"That's all you talked about while you were with her tonight?" Doug asked. "Sounds like a pretty boring dinner discussion between two people who haven't spent much time together lately."

"Oh, I don't know. We may have gotten into a little personal conversation," Ed answered. "I'm going upstairs to read for a while. Good night."

"See you in the morning," Doug replied. "Oh, by the way, you may want to wipe the lipstick off your face before you turn in, so it doesn't come off on the pillow case."

Chapter 21

SAM BARRY asked Doug, Mike, and Ronnie to stay after history class on Thursday afternoon. He called the three boys around his desk as soon as the other students cleared the room, saying, "As you've heard, all classes have been cancelled tomorrow afternoon because of a faculty meeting with the school superintendent. I've arranged to be excused, and I'm planning to go back to the Buchanan farm to scout the place out again. The sons have agreed to show me around like they did before. I'm hoping that as they get to know us better, they'll start to open up and talk about what they're trying to do. I'm wondering if any of you would like to join me again and see what else we may be able to discover."

Doug glanced at Mike and Ronnie, and both nodded. "I think all three of us are in. Do you want us to meet you here in the parking lot like we did the time before?"

"That would be fine. Better wear old clothes, and bring your flashlights." Opening his desk drawer, he withdrew an envelope and pulled out the tarnished brass button with the CS insignia he had found in the cave on the previous trip. "I've been anxious to go back out there for one reason, and that's to try to find any remains, including the body of the Confederate soldier this button belonged to. Everything that was taken out of that cave by those two men must still be on their property somewhere. And there aren't many places where they could have concealed objects as big as caskets. One of the barns or sheds on the place is a possibility. We'll all need to keep our eyes open."

The three boys joined Sam at noon on Friday, and rode with him out to the farm. As they drove up toward the house, Doug pointed to the hill rising above the fields in the direction of Chimney Rock, saying, "When I was out here a couple of weeks ago helping Mr. Vicelli deliver groceries, we saw Daniel and Jonah working with a team of horses at the top. It looks like they've leveled an area up there as big as one end of our football field."

Sam slowed the car to get a better look. "I wonder what all they turned up when they graded the crest of that hill. Some of the old timers believe that high ground is the spot where the Union troops were dug-in during the battle. One man showed me a collection of fired minie balls he found up there when he was young."

Both men were waiting in the yard when Sam pulled up in front of the house. "Good to see you again," Sam said. "Your folks doing any better?"

"Ma and Pa sleep most of the time," Jonah replied. "Agnes gives them their medicine every day, but it hasn't seemed to help."

"You want to go back out at the cave again?" Daniel asked. "No one's ever seen it but y'all."

"Yes," Sam replied. "And this time we'd like to have you show us around your barns on the way out there."

Sam, Doug, Mike, and Ronnie followed the long strides of Daniel and Jonah along the path leading from the house in the direction of Chimney Rock. As they got closer to the cluster of old farm buildings, they could see the warped gray board walls and sunlight glinting from the rusty corrugated sheet metal roofs. Upon reaching the barnyard, they looked around the outside and inside of the barns, a corn crib, and several livestock sheds.

"Are these all of the buildings here on your farm?" Sam asked.

"This is all of 'em," Jonah responded. "Some of 'em don't get much use nowadays. They're getting old and rundown."

"How about that one across the fence next to the old apple orchard?" Sam inquired. "That one that's leaning over to the side. Could we look around it?"

A worried look came across Daniel's furrowed face. "Not

safe to go in that one. The boards in the roof are rotten, and something might fall on your head and hurt you."

"I understand. I just want to get a little closer look, but I promise not to go inside."

Moving toward the open door of the building, Sam peered into the dark interior, but was unable to see more than a few feet past the entrance. Reaching into his pocket, he pulled out a flashlight and directed the beam inside. He spotted a collection of old farm equipment, scattered wooden boxes, several large barrels turned on their sides, and warped planks tossed into a pile. Aiming the flashlight further back, he detected something that stood out from the disorderly accumulation of junk closer to the door. At first glance it looked like stacks of rough-hewn boards. But a closer look gave him an entirely different perception of what he was seeing. He could hear Doug's voice running through his mind again: 'It looked like rows of wood crates as big as caskets.'"

"I guess we've seen about everything here that we were curious about," Sam said to Daniel in a matter of fact voice, putting the flashlight back in his pocket. "Let's walk on out to the cave now and look around again."

At the foot of Chimney Rock, Sam and the boys searched the ground outside the entrance to the cave, but found nothing of particular interest. Moving to the dark opening under the overhanging slab, they used their flashlights to sweep the cave floor with narrow beams of light, hoping to spot signs of human activity from earlier years. But there was nothing to be seen in the cave except their own tracks previously left in the dirt.

Sam did not press the two men to go inside again. The front chamber had been searched during the previous trip, and exploring the cave further to the back would be unsafe for any of them. "I'm ready to go now," he remarked.

Following the two men on the twisting path toward the house, Sam broke the silence. "We noticed that you've been working up on the hill across the field. Have you turned up anything remaining from the Civil War battle?"

Jonah nodded his head. "You want to see?"

"I certainly do. I teach history at the high school, and studying that battle is a hobby of mine."

Back at the house, Daniel and Jonah held the front door open for the four visitors to enter the cold, dark front room. Moving stacks of cardboard boxes aside, they led the way up the dusty curved staircase to the second floor. Water damage from the leaky tile roof of the house was obvious. In several places, piles of fallen plaster lay on the floor directly below exposed wood lath in the ceiling.

Walking down the hallway across warped boards, they turned to the left and entered a room with two large windows. Despite an accumulation of dirt on the glass panes blocking much of the light, the room was bright enough to allow them to see the sparse furnishings inside, including a long oak table and eight ladder back chairs, two with broken legs. The most curious objects in the room were sitting next to the table, two brass bound trunks with rounded tops and broken leather straps.

"These were Grandpa's," Daniel said, pointing to the trunks. "He kept things here he found on the ground after the fight. When Pa, Jonah, and me find bullets and things out there in the dirt, we bring them here and put them in Grandpa's trunks."

Jonah opened both trunks and lifted the trays out onto the table. Sam noted that the trays contained a variety of ordnance in several calibers, including fired lead minie balls as well as unfired cartridges. He also saw a straight razor, a harmonica, several belt buckles, a pocket watch, and many sizes and types of metal buttons from uniforms.

The trunks were filled with larger items, including canteens, a coffee pot, belt knives, a pistol, and a knapsack, together with a number of belts, caps and other parts of blue and gray uniforms.

The object that caught Sam's eye was a cracked leather pouch with CS stamped in large letters on the flap. Lifting it out carefully, Sam raised the flap, and observed that the initials JTE had been burned into the rough unfinished leather on the back side. Inside the pouch, Sam could see several documents, written on brittle, yellowed paper in faded black ink. Sam could barely contain his excitement as he carefully riffled through the fragile papers. "Would you loan this to me if I promise to return it next week unharmed?"

Daniel and Jonah stepped to one side to confer in whispers. Then Jonah returned and replied, somewhat apprehensively,

"Don't let nothing happen to it. That belongs to Pa."

"I promise I'll take good care of it," Sam repeated. Cradling the pouch in his arms as though it were a delicate piece of china, he followed the others out of the room, continuing out to the car.

Sensing the perfect opportunity to get additional information from the two men, Sam approached Daniel, and without beating around the bush, said, "We're all very curious to know what you two are planning to put on top of the hill back there. Would you be willing to tell us?"

Daniel and Jonah glanced at each other, and Daniel delivered a brief, straightforward answer, "A graveyard. That's what Pa wants us to do."

"Who will be buried in the graveyard?" Sam asked, concealing his surprise at their candor.

"We'll tell you before long," Daniel said, ending the discussion.

Realizing that he had gathered all of the information that the Buchanan sons were willing to share at that time, Sam thanked them, saying "We appreciate your showing us around again, and letting me borrow these papers to look over."

As he and the three boys got into the car, Sam handed the car keys to Doug. "How about driving us back to the school. I want to get a look at what's inside this pouch right away."

While the boys talked, Sam became lost in his own world, carefully inspecting the fragile documents. Although the ink was faded, the handwriting from an earlier era proved to be both neat and legible. By the time they got back to the parking lot, Sam had completed a quick scan of the contents of the pouch, and couldn't wait to share the discovery with his three students. "I need look these letters over a lot more carefully before I go jumping to conclusions, but there seem to be some extremely important papers here.

"It appears these letters may be the final communications to Captain Jason Taylor Early from his uncle, General Jubal Anderson Early. From what I was just able to read, I gather that Captain Early was leading a company of Confederate soldiers under orders from his uncle to make a fast, covert move up the south branch of the Potomac River to strike and destroy Union rail lines at the north end of the Shenandoah Valley. There's no indication that the Confederate command was aware of a larger Union force which had moved south through Abner Gap, and was positioned directly in Captain Early's path. This would finally explain the setting for the Battle of Eden Springs. And Captain Early's death in the encounter would provide an explanation as to why the Confederate forces retreated in disarray."

As they got out of the car, he added, "There's something else we found out today. I'm almost certain Daniel and Jonah moved the caskets out of the cave to that abandoned apple storage building next to the old orchard. And I'm speculating that's why they're excavating for a cemetery up on top of the hill. I believe they're preparing a fitting burial place for the battlefield victims in accordance with their father's wishes."

Walking across town gave Doug time to mull over Sam's explanation for recent events occurring on the Buchanan property, both at the cave and on the hilltop nearby. At home, Doug caught up with his dad in the kitchen. "You won't believe what went on today. We found out that Daniel and Jonah are building a graveyard up on the hill where that Civil War battle took place. And they loaned Mr. Barry a leather case with some papers that help explain the Battle of Eden Springs."

Doug provided a colorful run-down on everything that he had seen and heard during the day, including what Sam Barry had said. "Do his opinions make sense to you?"

"He gives the most logical theory behind the Battle of Eden Springs I've heard from anyone to date," Ed replied. "And also the most believable reasons for those men doing all of that work to reopen the lost cave on their property, and to plan a cemetery on top of that hill."

Lifting a pan off the stove, Ed added, "I remember when Sam challenged you and your buddies to be detectives and help find out what was going on at the Buchanan place. It sounds like you've been very successful."

Then he added, "I wish the law enforcement people around here were as good at detective work as you boys and Sam Barry."

Chapter 22

LATE MONDAY, Carolyn's phone rang with a call from Earl Daniels. "It's for you" she called out to Ed, "Sheriff Daniels is holding on the line."

"I had a call from State Police Headquarters early today," the sheriff began. "Saturday morning a group of boys was hanging around an abandoned rock quarry between Princeton and Pearisburg, plinking at tin cans with their .22's. The water in the pit is clear as glass, and one of them spotted a truck looking like it was parked on the bottom under about sixty feet of water. They walked over to an Esso station and told the owner, who called the state police. One of their rescue teams spent most of the day Sunday getting a cable attached to the truck and winching it up where they could take a look at it. Fortunately, there were no bodies inside. But one thing that really got their attention was when they saw it was a new dark blue 1952 Ford panel truck without license plates."

"You think it could be the same truck that two men were driving when they ran me off the road out north of town?" Ed asked.

"That's a possibility that crossed my mind. There's more to the report. There was a blown out tire and broken shocks and springs where the truck landed on its wheels at the bottom of the quarry. But there was also a mashed in front bumper and grille."

"But the truck I encountered didn't make any contact with

me when it forced me off the road. And if it had, the damage would have been on the right front side."

"I realize that. But that's not all I learned. Caught up in the grille almost out of sight, they found a torn piece of gray wool cloth, a heavy kind of fabric. The scrap had several very small dark brown stains that hadn't come out despite soaking for a long time under water at the bottom of the pit. The state police believe it could be spattered human blood. Their lab is running a test today."

"Do you think that truck could be the hit and run vehicle involved in Myrtle's death?"

"The state police seem to be thinking along those lines. There was some speculation based on the pattern of bruises on Myrtle's body that something like a Ford truck might have been involved. The vehicle serial number on the truck had been filed off, but the state police lab technician was still able to etch it out. It turns out the truck was stolen off a dealer's lot in Wheeling back in January. Someone cleaned up the truck and wiped off all the fingerprints before pushing it over the side into the quarry, so there's no way to identify the people involved yet."

"Will your department be working with the state police on the investigation?"

"Yes, and that's why I called you. There's a question of who has jurisdiction, because it's uncertain where the hit and run occurred, or whether Myrtle was still alive when she was thrown in the field with the bull. The state police have requested that you and I look at the truck where it's impounded in Princeton, to see if we can bring anything to light that might help in the investigation. I have some other business that takes me up that way tomorrow, and I wondered if you would be willing to drive up and meet me there. I can give you the address now."

"I'll plan to join you at after lunch tomorrow at their headquarters in Princeton. OK if I bring someone along for the ride with me on the drive over?"

When the call ended, Ed told Carolyn about the truck in the rock quarry. "I'll be driving over to Princeton in the morning, and I won't get back until mid-afternoon. The only other thing coming up that will take me out of the office this week is the

Buchanan hearing in front of Judge Kirk on Friday. And I don't even know how big a role I'll be permitted to play in that hearing, since Gideon was unable to give me power of attorney before he became disabled."

Ed dialed Jackson Realty before lunch, catching Laura on the way out the door. "Any chance you could take the morning off tomorrow and drive over to Princeton with me? There's a used truck I want to show you."

"And just why would I want to waste my time and go all the way to Princeton to look at a used truck?" she inquired curiously.

Ed gave her a brief update on the new development in the Myrtle Spencer homicide.

"I'm so glad to hear there's finally some progress in solving her murder that I'm more than willing to risk a commission. Sure, I'll ride along with you. What time do we need to get on the road?"

"I'll plan to come by for you at 7:30. We can have lunch after we get there. I promise you, nothing but the best."

When he got home that evening, Ed encountered a typical scene of Housman domesticity. The radio was tuned in to a popular music station, and Doug was talking on the phone, with JR pawing at his leg, trying to get his attention. Ed quickly pulled together a supper of scrambled eggs, bacon, and toast. He had the meal on the table when Doug hung up the phone and came in to join him.

"Looks like I overslept," Doug joked. "Thanks for fixing such a great breakfast."

"Just be thankful you're getting fed. Think of all the starving children in China. Who were you on the phone with?"

"Vickie called me. Who'd have ever thought that anything good could come from a math class. She's having trouble with the geometry assignment due tomorrow, and I was trying to help her out."

"I told you studying hard would pay off for you someday, but I confess, success with the ladies was not exactly what I had in mind. By the way, I'll be going out of town tomorrow morning. I've been asked to look at a truck being held in Princeton that could be connected to my recent encounter out on the highway, and even more likely, the one involved in the Myrtle Spencer hit-and-run."

"I wish I were going with you tomorrow. But I don't seem to have as much interest in skipping school these days, particularly math class. I just hope Mr. Powell keeps creating a world of confusion the way he does now, and makes geometry as clear as mud for a certain classmate."

When Ed drove up in front of Laura's apartment the next morning, she was watching for him through the window, and quickly ran down to the car. "Good morning, Ed. You're running a few minutes early, as usual. I just had time to finish breakfast."

Ed caught a breath of Laura's light cologne, a clean floral fragrance, as she slipped into the seat beside him. The summery scent lingered as he steered the car toward Princeton.

"How's the Eden Springs real estate tycoon doing this morning?" Ed asked. "Judging by looks, I would assume incredibly well."

"I'm doing just fine, thank you. Truthfully, it's good to get away from the office this morning. Dan asked me earlier if I would go to lunch with him today, and he still hasn't learned the meaning of the word 'no.' Unfortunately, we real estate tycoons can't have unlisted phone numbers, so it's difficult to hide from him."

"I'm sorry he's still being a problem. Well, that's not totally true, and I promised you no more fibs. Actually, I'm glad you classify him as a problem. You already know how I feel about competition."

At noon, they stopped at a small diner on the outskirts of Princeton, comfortably settling on adjacent stools at the counter. "You want the Moon Pie and RC Cola I promised?" Ed joked.

The no-frills diner seemed like a throwback to a prewar era, with the lunch specials printed in chalk on a small blackboard behind the counter. "Eating in one of these places really takes you back a few years, doesn't it?" Ed remarked.

"Speak for yourself, Housman," Laura laughed. "I'm way too young to remember the good old days you're always talking about."

When they arrived at the regional headquarters, Sheriff Daniels and an older man wearing a West Virginia State Police uniform were waiting for them inside. The uniformed officer introduced himself as Captain William Stanley, and he invited the three visitors to follow him to the back of the building.

In a brightly lit garage bay, under rows of bright overhead lights, Ed saw a dozen cars and trucks, some with major collision damage. Captain Stanley led them over to one side by a row of windows, where a dark blue Ford panel truck was parked. "That's the vehicle," he commented. "Does it look familiar to you, Mr. Housman? Think it could be the same one you encountered?"

Ed walked out ahead of the truck, and then over to the right side, trying to recreate the same view of a dark panel truck he had seen earlier. "I believe it's the same make and model vehicle," Ed replied, "but there's nothing that jumps out at me to tell me this is the same one."

The three men were surprised when Laura, who had been walking slowly around the truck, inspecting it from all sides, observed, "The '51 and '52 Ford trucks look a lot alike, Ed, especially from the front." Walking back to study the vehicle head on, she continued, "The damage to the center of the bumper, the pushed-in grille, and the broken hood latch, look to me like this truck hit something dead center, the size of a deer, or maybe a person. Finding that scrap of cloth makes it easy to rule out an animal."

Curiosity visible, Captain Stanley inquired, "If you don't mind my asking, Mrs. Jackson, where did you pick up your knowledge of motor vehicles and collision damage?"

"I worked in my uncle's garage in Parkersburg during summers while I was going to school," Laura replied. "I've spent a little time under the hoods of these things."

"You never cease to amaze me," Ed commented. Turning to the captain, he continued, "This could be the truck that ran me off the road, but it's impossible for me to make a positive ID. I'm sorry."

"I have something I'll tell you in confidence," Captain Stanley advised the pair. "We have the lab test results back from that scrap of cloth found caught-up in the grille. The spots turned out to be type O human blood, the same as Myrtle Spencer's. And the scrap of wool fabric exactly matches the hole found in her coat. We're absolutely certain this truck was used in the hit and run homicide. But we still have nothing like a set of fingerprints to indicate who was driving it."

"I'm surprised that whoever stole and operated the truck was able to wipe off all their fingerprints," Ed replied. "It would be hard not to miss one or two. Anyway, I'm sorry I couldn't be more of a help today."

Heading toward home, Ed glanced at Laura and said, "I wasn't surprised to learn that the impounded truck is the same one that was used in the murder, because of the scrap of cloth Earl Daniels told us about earlier. But I'm still trying to get used to the idea that you're a former auto mechanic. Somehow, you don't look like you belong in a garage."

"You might be surprised to find quite a few wives and daughters with their own auto mechanic's toolboxes," Laura replied. "All the women in garages today aren't necessarily hanging on the wall, posing on the fronts of cheesecake calendars."

When they pulled up in front of her apartment, Ed turned off the engine, and with a deadpan expression said, "My Ford's way overdue for a lube job and an oil change. Can I leave it here with the keys in the switch for you to service today? I can come by and pick it up some time tomorrow."

"Sorry, Ed, but I've retired from the auto service and repair business, and I won't be able to help you with that. You'll probably have to take your Ford down to the Texaco to get it lubed. I'm afraid I'd have trouble now getting down on a creeper and rolling up under your car, and I'd never be able to get the dirt out from under these long nails if I did." Then reaching over to him, Laura slipped her arm around his neck, and snuggled closer to him, adding in a soft voice, "But maybe I can make it up to you in some other way."

"Darn! I really had my heart set on a free grease job and oil change," Ed responded, trying to keep from laughing, holding Laura's arm to keep her from strangling him.

Chapter 23

Waiting outside the courtroom for Dr. Jannsen on Friday afternoon, Ed watched the comings and goings of attorneys and clerks, defendants and plaintiffs. Judge Kirk came into sight, along with a tall stranger in a well-cut charcoal suit.

"Jesus, Bill, I thought you'd snagged a catfish when you hooked that big brookie. I thought for a minute it was going to break your rod. What'd it weigh- three pounds?"

"Closer to four," Kirk grinned. "You'll have to drop by my office and look at it. It's right there on the wall beside the rack I took off that twelve point buck, when we were up at the hunt club together last fall."

"I'll do that. And you and Kathryn should drive over for a drink sometime. Anne wants to show off the new television set. RCA, thirteen inch screen. You'll feel like you're at the movies."

"Great, I'll tell the Missus to call her. See you inside." With that, the judge entered a side door leading into his chamber.

The stranger glanced at Ed, checking for his reaction, sliding a hand along the part of his closely cropped gray hair. When he passed Ed to enter the courtroom, their eyes met, and he nodded briefly. Ed knew that he'd met Grant's hired gun, the one with friends in high places.

After Dr. Jannsen arrived to join him, the two men went inside and took a seat. They saw Julian Grant, together with the tall stranger Ed had observed in the hallway, and an older man, seated at the front of the room, directly in front of the bench. Over to one side, the bailiff was flipping through an old copy of Field and Stream, waiting for the judge. When he saw the judge enter, he called in a loud voice, "All rise!"

The first hearing on the court docket involved Julian Grant's petition. Judge Kirk listened with a detached demeanor as the petition was read, almost as though viewing a movie he had seen earlier, one where he already knew the ending.

The two men with Julian turned out to be retained experts from Bluefield. The gray-haired man was an attorney and a senior partner in a law firm known to have strong ties to the coal mining industry within the state. The balding man was a psychiatrist, specializing in geriatric medicine.

The case presented was well organized, thoroughly documented, and persuasive: Gideon Buchanan was a ninety-one year-old man who had been comatose and mentally unresponsive for over a month. His wife was only a year younger, and extremely fragile, physically and mentally. The two sons were also in advanced years, and portrayed as uneducated and socially backward, incapable of handling affairs in their own home, or of managing and operating a 2500 acre farm. The family home, Roseanna, was depicted as having deteriorated almost beyond the point of repair, as shown by enlarged photographs. All assertions were backed up by expert professional opinions.

When the gray-haired attorney had finished presenting his case, Judge Kirk asked, "Is there anything else to come before the court before I make my ruling?"

Ed stood and replied, "Your Honor, Dr. Jannsen and I have been professionally assisting the Buchanan family, both before and after Gideon Buchanan experienced his current mental problem. Dr. Jannsen can find no physical cause for his condition, and we feel optimistic that his mind will clear again in the weeks ahead. If so, it would permit him to have a voice in any required changes to the family's situation. Therefore, we are appealing to you for a continuance of sixty days before you rule on Gideon Buchanan's competency."

Judge Kirk looked at Ed dispassionately, replying, "Mr. Housman, I think your optimism regarding the prognosis for Mr. Buchanan's mental recovery is poorly founded. I am hereby ruling that Mr. Buchanan, and his wife, and both sons, are incompetent to conduct their own affairs, and that Mr. Grant is empowered to act for the family in all legal matters as delegated by power of attorney. This case is closed." He punctuated his decision with a sharp rap of his gavel on the sound block.

Outside the courtroom, and out of earshot of bystanders, Ed spoke to Dr, Jannsen, "That quick ruling in Julian's favor was what we both anticipated. Judge Kirk has a reputation for leaning toward the side of the wealthy and politically connected. It's pretty obvious that Julian doesn't have the kind of money to bring in top legal and medical gunslingers from out of the area like he had with him today. I'd bet my life that he's being bankrolled by Barker Mining, and that Judge Kirk knows it. As the old saying goes, 'cash talks,' even if it's passed under the table. Have you got any medical tricks left up your sleeve that might help bring Gideon back to rationality, assuming that there's still time to save the Buchanan estate?"

"I've been giving it a lot of thought, Ed, and I've decided to try something different," Dr. Jannsen responded. "There's a nurse in town named Gertrude Estep, who works part time. She was a WAC during World War II, and she's capable and honest as the day is long, in addition to being tough as nails. I'm going to see if she'll stay at their home for a week and take over all the medical care for Gideon and Hester. At this point, I'm willing to pay her out of my own pocket. Agnes Harper can shift duties and concentrate on the domestic work. Gertrude may see something that I'm missing by not being out there full time. I think I need to act now, before Julian takes charge, and we no longer have any say in how things are done in that household. I expect that he'll find out right away from Agnes what I'm doing."

"It sounds like a good plan to me," Ed said. "I've got some homework to do, now. If Gideon recovers, another hearing's going to be required to rule he's of sound mind and capable of handling his own affairs again. That will certainly be necessary in order to validate the new power of attorney and will that I have ready for him to sign. Somehow I'll have to make sure that Judge Wine presides, not Judge Kirk. And that part might be very difficult."

Leaving the courthouse charade behind him, Ed was relieved to get back to his office. Carolyn was anxiously waiting for him to return, and almost before the door had closed, spoke out, "How'd things go?"

"Exactly the way you and I expected," Ed replied, in a resigned voice. "Judge Kirk looked like he had his mind made up to rule Gideon incompetent before the hearing even started. The only thing that can save the family now is for him to make a quick turn for the better. Dr. Jannsen's going to put a nurse with him around the clock for a week, to be sure he's getting the correct medication. If that doesn't work, I believe Julian Grant will soon be calling all the plays, and Dr. Jannsen and I'll be relegated to riding the bench on the sidelines."

"Sorry it went like that, even though that's what you told me would happen. By the way, Laura phoned while you were out, and asked if you'd call her back."

Ed dialed the number for Jackson Realty from memory, and when he heard Laura pick up, quipped, "Your nickel."

"Ed, I was driving back toward town today just this side of Abner Gap, and I saw something big going on at the former Henderson farm. Where that tract of land backs up to the Norfolk and Western rail siding near the foot of Pine Ridge, there's a lot of road building activity. I could see a crew of men working with bulldozers and a number of dump trucks. It looks like they're starting to build a haul road across the Henderson land over toward the adjacent Simpson farm, directly in line with the Buchanan property. A pickup truck turning in toward the construction site had the black diamond logo on the side, so I assume the road crew works for Barker Mining."

"Things are moving even faster than I expected," Ed replied. "It looks like Barker may get the opportunity to add the Buchanan farm to all of that other land he's bought in recent months. I don't think he'd be spending money putting in a road now unless he's totally confident he's got the keystone lined up for his strip mine operation.

"Judge Kirk ruled Gideon incompetent today, just as we all expected. He's put Julian Grant squarely in the driver's seat to handle the Buchanan estate in any manner he pleases. The only positive development I can report is that Dr. Jannsen has hired a very capable nurse named Gertrude Estep to move in with the Buchanans and take care of them around the clock.

"But as far as heading off a coal mining operation in the valley, things are looking pretty bleak right now. I feel like we're in a football game going into the fourth quarter, down by three touchdowns, with no new plays left to call."

"Don't start to lose your confidence and give up now, Ed," Laura chided him. "It's not over yet. As I recall, football games go on for a full sixty minutes, and we're still in this one until the final whistle blows.

"When you mentioned the name Gertrude Estep just now, I started trying to recall where I've met her, and now I remember. Several years ago, she bought an older home in town through my agency. The seller failed to disclose a problem with water flooding the basement during heavy rains. Gertrude went to see him, and the two almost came to blows. It wasn't long afterward that he paid to have drain tile installed all the way around the house. Whether you know it or not, you just got a tough new player on your team."

★

Just at sunrise on Saturday morning, Gertrude Estep drove her rusty Plymouth coupe into the driveway and took her battered cardboard suitcase from the trunk. She strode across the front porch in her no-nonsense white oxfords, and the house soon reverberated from the force of her strong hands on the heavy brass knocker. Daniel and Jonah both came out to see who was there, dressed as though they had already been up for some time.

"I'm Gertrude Estep," she said, firmly shaking hands with the two men. "You boys must be Daniel and Jonah. I'm taking over the nursing duty for your pa and ma, starting now. Can you take me back to their rooms?"

"Dr. Jamison called to tell us you'd be coming this morning," Daniel said. "But he didn't tell us you'd get here so early. Agnes don't usually get here 'til later."

"I figured that," Gertrude responded. "And when she gets

here, I'll tell her she can fix your breakfast, take care of the house, go pick up hickory nuts, or whatever else she wants to do. I'm going to be doing everything for your folks this week. You boys just need to show me where I can sleep and clean up."

The men led Gertrude through the dark interior of the house to Gideon's quarters. As they entered his room, he stirred restlessly in bed with his eyes partly open, seemingly unaware that both sons and a stranger had just entered. Gertrude observed that although his white hair and beard appeared scraggly and unkempt, he was reasonably clean, much the same as other older patients she cared for. His gown and bed sheets appeared to have been recently laundered. A portable toilet seat with white enamel pot standing beside the bed was empty and sanitary. On top of the adjacent nightstand, Gertrude identified an array of health care products ranging from cough syrup and aspirin to mouthwash and diuretic pills.

"Is there any other medicine that Dr. Jannsen has your pa on?" Gertrude inquired. Jonah shook his head.

An hour later, Agnes arrived and quietly let herself into the house. In Gideon's bedroom, she was startled to almost bump into Gertrude, and she stepped back in surprise. Agnes had not expected to encounter a strange woman attending to Gideon, one in a white nursing uniform, who stood a head taller and forty pounds heavier than she.

"Good morning," Gertrude said, taking charge of the situation. "You must be Agnes Harper. I'm Gertrude Estep, and I work for Dr. Jannsen. I'll be taking care of Mr. and Mrs. Buchanan this week. You'll be able to take it a little easier for a while, and just handle the cooking and cleaning for the boys."

Agnes appeared flustered by Gertrude's comments. She clasped her shaking hands together, and a pink flush crept over her sallow complexion, as she stammered, "But I'm the one who's supposed to give Mr. and Mrs. Buchanan their medicine. That's what I was hired to do."

Gertrude stared at Agnes, replying in a commanding voice that came from her earlier years as a WAC sergeant. "Well, there's been a change in orders for this week. What medicine are you giving them that you're so worried about ?"

Agnes was at a loss for words, nervously shifting her weight from foot to foot, finally managing to get out, "Just the medicine on their nightstands." Wheeling around, Agnes rushed from the room up the dark hallway toward the telephone on the wall, and quickly dialed a number.

Gertrude walked to the doorway just out of sight, and listened closely. Although Agnes spoke in a low tone, the empty corridor transmitted her telephone conversation toward Gertrude like a voice tube.

"Mr. Grant, there's a woman here now who says she's a nurse working for Dr. Jannsen. She won't let me give the Buchanans their morning pills. I don't know what to do. I think we're in trouble." There was a silence while Agnes listened to a voice on the other end. Then she replied, "That's good. I'll see you in a little while."

As soon as Agnes had hung up and headed to the kitchen, Gertrude went to the same phone and dialed a familiar number. When she heard a voice on the other end, she spoke quietly, "Dr. Jannsen, I think you need to come out here just as quick as you can. There's something strange going on. Agnes just called someone named Grant and told them to get right over here. I think it's about some medicine that she's been giving the Buchanans, and I'm suspicious it could be something that you didn't prescribe." After listening for a few minutes, Gertrude replied, "Yes, sir, I'll be looking for you and Mr. Housman shortly."

When Gertrude returned to Gideon's room, she was surprised to see that he was staring up at her with both eyes open, but still not seeming to comprehend what was going on around him. Standing close to his bed, smiling, she spoke in a gentle voice, "Good morning, Mr. Buchanan."

Gertrude was astounded when Gideon replied in a weak, husky voice, "Where am I? Who are you?"

★

Chapter 24

D R. JANNSEN was pouring a second cup of coffee on Saturday morning when he got the call. Taking a single swallow, he emptied the mug into the kitchen sink, then phoned the Housman home number penciled on the front of his phone book. When Ed answered, stifling a yawn, Dr. Jannsen said, "Can I come by and pick you up now to drive out to the Buchanans'? Gertrude Estep just called, and asked for us to get out there right away. Gertrude isn't an excitable person, and when she tells me something's urgent, I treat it like a real emergency."

Ed was waiting outside, watching for him when Dr. Jannsen arrived. As they drove off, Dr. Jannsen told him what Gertrude had said during their brief conversation. He added, "Julian Grant may not be far behind us when we get there. I wish there was some way to delay him, so we could have some time alone with Gertrude and Agnes to find out what's going on. Do you have any ideas?"

Ed sat quietly, mulling over the question, and then an idea struck him. "Let's ask Daniel and Jonah to create some kind of a diversion. Maybe they can rig up a barricade at the entrance to the drive leading up to the house and make it look like they're working on their road. The fence will prevent Julian from cutting across the field in his car, and he'd have to walk in. I think he'd be reluctant to leave his car down near the highway and come up on foot."

The two men saw Daniel and Jonah watching them from the porch as they pulled in and parked. Ed called out to them, "We need your help right now, and there's no time to waste. There'll be another car showing up out here before long. We want you to keep the driver from turning off the highway onto your private road and coming up to the house. Block your drive with some sort of barricade, and make it look like you're doing maintenance work. Do you trust us enough to do what I'm asking? We're here trying to help your pa and ma." Daniel nodded.

Jonah's comment surprised Ed. "Mr. Grant's on his way out here now to cause a problem, ain't he? Neither of us like him a lick." The two men started to walk away, and then Jonah dug in the pocket of his coveralls, pulled out two objects, and handed them to Ed. "We found these stuck in behind the dresser when we was cleaning out Myrtle's room yesterday. It's like she was keeping them hidden away."

Ed looked at what Jonah had just given him as he followed Dr. Jannsen into the house. One object was a small Bayer aspirin bottle half full of white tablets, and the other a folded scrap of paper that appeared to have been torn from a spiral-bound composition book. A note scribbled in pencil on the paper read: "1-morning, 1-afternoon."

Outside Gideon's room, Ed glanced down toward the end of the hall and saw Agnes standing in the kitchen doorway, watching them anxiously, her hands clenched together in front of her.

Gertrude was waiting for them when they stepped into the bedroom. "He's been coming and going ever since I talked to you. For a while he made some sense when he spoke, and he even asked me about his wife and his sons. It looks like he's become as weak as a kitten from lying in bed so long with no proper nourishment and no exercise. Those may be the biggest things wrong with him right now."

At just that moment, Gideon opened his eyes to squint at them, and in a voice no louder than a whisper, said, "Dr. Jannsen, good to see you, sir." The words were no more than out of his mouth when his eyes closed again, as though he had nodded off.

"I'd say he was more lucid just then than I've seen him in the past month," Dr. Jannsen observed. "It would be good if we could get him to take a little nourishment, maybe something like chicken broth."

"I'll go in the kitchen in just a few minutes and see if I can find something easy for him to swallow like that. But unless I'm the one opening the can, I'm not going to feed him anything in this house."

Ed touched Dr. Jannsen's arm and said, "You need to look at what one of the sons gave me outside when we first got here. He said that he and his brother found both of these yesterday, hidden behind the dresser in the room where Myrtle Spencer stayed." He handed Dr. Jannsen the aspirin bottle and scrap of paper.

Dr. Jannsen's reaction was electric. He quickly walked to the window for better light, studying the penciled note. "That piece of paper clearly was torn out of the composition book in Myrtle's satchel," he said. "I could make out her identical '1-morning, 1-afternoon' writing inprinted on the sheet of paper underneath." Unscrewing the cap on the aspirin bottle, he poured several of the pills into his hand, and observed in a controlled voice, "These certainly aren't Bayer aspirin tablets. I'll get the pharmacist to double check me on this, but I'm almost positive what we have here is barbiturates, what most people call sleeping pills."

"Barbiturates! Well, I'll be damned," Ed exclaimed.

Standing on her toes to look over Dr. Jannsen's shoulder, Gertrude commented, "They look like sleeping pills to me, too, and I've administered quite a few of them to patients. That explains why Agnes was such a nervous wreck when she found me out here this morning. She figured out she couldn't give the Buchanans their usual knock-out pills any more."

"Now that you've gotten Gideon off the sedatives, I wonder if he'll snap out of this any time soon," Ed mused, as Dr. Jannsen begin to carefully examine the feeble old man. "I still have the power of attorney and will ready for him to sign."

Dr. Jannsen continued to check Gideon's responsiveness to light, sound, and touch. After a thorough examination, he stood and observed, "I'm not sure how much of a recovery he'll make, or how soon. At his age there's always a risk of senile dementia. And after being kept in a sedated state for such a long a period of time, he may have suffered some irreversible brain damage. I think we're going to have to wait and see how he comes along now that we've taken him off the drugs and are starting him back on solid food. We'll just have to hope for the best."

While the three stood by his bedside, discussing his condition and the prognosis for his recovery, Gideon slept soundly. Maybe he dreamed of days ninety years before when he was a child growing up following the worst war in American history. Maybe he remembered his courtship of Hester when she was a local dark-eyed beauty, or the miraculous birth of their twin sons almost too late in their married life. But whatever passed through his mind, his gaunt face wore a peaceful smile.

★

Daniel and Jonah pulled open the sagging door of the old tool shed, picked up a coil of rusty barbed wire, a pair of old fence pliers, a long handled shovel, and their worn leather work gloves, then walked quickly toward the highway. At the end of the unpaved road, the two men dropped everything they were carrying, and leaned over with hands on hips to catch their breath. For the next twenty minutes, they built a simple but effective barrier to prevent any automobile from driving by. Cutting off a long length of barbed wire from the coil, they attached the ends to fence posts standing on opposite sides of the drive. Handling the wire carefully with gloved hands, they stretched it back and forth across the road a number of times, and shoveled just enough gravel over it to both hold it in place and partially conceal it.

They had not been finished long when a dark, late model Chrysler sedan approached from the direction of town, traveling toward them at a high rate of speed. As the driver turned off the highway onto the gravel road, Daniel held up his hand, signaling for the car to stop. The automobile skidded in the loose gravel almost up in front of the men, and the driver rolled down his window. Daniel and Jonah had recognized the car from the time it came into sight, and they were not surprised when a very angry Julian Grant stuck his head out and yelled to them, "What the hell are you two doing? I need to get by right now."

Jonah glanced over toward his brother, then looked at Julian, and replied in a slow drawl, "We're working on the fence. You can't get by 'til we finish."

"How long will it take you to you get that damn piece of

barbed wire out of the road?" Julian said, with quickly mounting impatience.

"It shouldn't take us no more than an hour," Daniel replied.

"You dumb country hicks. I'm not waiting here any longer while you two screw around. Get out of the way. I'm driving on in." Starting the engine, he drove forward between the two fence posts, but immediately the hiss of escaping air signaled that his right front tire had been punctured.

Julian backed the car up, and climbed out to look. When he saw the flat tire, he was livid with anger. "Damn you! Now I've got to change the flat."

It was obvious that he had never changed a tire before, as he fumbled around in frustration with the jack and lug wrench, while the two men silently stood by and watched. Finally getting the spare tire mounted, he was just throwing the tools and flat tire back in the trunk when he saw Agnes running down the road toward him, panting as though she were about to collapse.

Rushing past Daniel and Jonah without even looking their way, she ran to Julian, and between gasps for breath, exclaimed, "We've got to get out of here right now. Everything's gone wrong up at the house. They found Myrtle's bottle of pills that we've been hunting for, and now they've figured out what's been going on. The worst part is Gideon is starting to wake up and talk."

"Shut up," Julian snapped. "They can hear everything you're saying. Just get in the car, now!"

Julian slid back under the wheel, slammed the door, and backed out of the gravel road onto the pavement without bothering to look in either direction. With the gas pedal mashed to the floor, and the rear wheels spinning, he accelerated the Chrysler up the highway away from town, north toward Abner Gap.

Watching the car speed out of sight, Daniel turned to Jonah, and a faint smile crossed his face, as they worked together to quickly remove the barbed wire from the gravel road. "Did you hear Julian call us dumb country hicks?"

"I heard him. And we both heard everything Agnes had to say, too."

★

"I'm going back to see what I can find out about all of this from

Agnes," Ed called out as he headed from the bedroom. "I really don't expect her to come clean, but anything she tells me will be admissible as evidence in court if she's arrested. I suspect Agnes has only played a small role in keeping the Buchanans drugged, but undoubtedly she knows a lot about who's pulling the strings and what they're up to."

Ed was surprised to find the kitchen cold and drafty, and he didn't understand why until he noticed that the back door was standing wide open. Agnes was nowhere in sight. Her coat and purse were gone from the hook beside the door, and her apron was lying on the floor nearby.

Striding back up the hallway to the front porch, he could see an automobile near the entrance to the gravel drive. He watched the dust fly as the car backed out onto the pavement, and drove away at high speed. As the cloud of dust cleared, he saw the two men coil something that looked like a length of wire taken from the gravel roadway, then pick up their tools and start up the road toward him.

When they reached the house, out of breath, Jonah exclaimed, "We blocked the road just like you asked us to. Before Julian got here, we took some barbed wire and laid it across the road in the gravel, like we'd been working on the fence."

Daniel interrupted, "He got mad as a hornet. Told us to get out of his way, and called us dumb country hicks. When he tried to run past us, he got a flat tire, and had to put on his spare. By that time, Agnes come running down the road, real excited. She told Julian you'd found Myrtle's pills and figured out what was going on. She jumped in the car, and they took off like a scalded dog going out the highway."

"You did everything exactly right. Now you may want to go in and see your pa. He's starting to come around a little, and you may even be able to talk with him."

Ed followed Daniel and Jonah into the house, where he called the sheriff's office. "Earl, can you come out here to Roseanna right away? There's been a crime committed against the senior Buchanans, and it could be related to the Myrtle Spencer homicide. We'll be on the look out for you shortly."

As they waited, Ed, Dr. Jannsen, and Gertrude stood back and watched the two men talking to their father. Gideon seemed to respond to the boys better than the three of them. Sometimes he would answer Daniel and Jonah in a rational manner, and at other times with comments that made no sense. But it was obvious that the sons were elated at his improvement, and that both were trying to hold back tears.

The sheriff and two of his deputies arrived at the house shortly afterward, and Ed and Dr. Jannsen explained what had just taken place. Handing the pill bottle and note to Earl, Ed said, "The two sons found these hidden in Myrtle's room, and Dr. Jannsen and Gertrude are both confident the Bayer aspirin bottle actually contains sleeping pills. Dr. Jannsen and I believe that Julian Grant was paying Myrtle Spencer to keep Gideon and Hester drugged with barbiturates. We think that after her death he brought in Agnes Harper to continue sedating them up right up until the time Gertrude arrived. Daniel and Jonah overheard a conversation between Agnes and Julian this morning that seems to corroborate all of this."

Ed continued, "Agnes fled the house an hour ago, heading north with Julian. I'll ask Daniel and Jonah to come over here, and repeat the conversation they overheard between the two of them before they drove off." The sons then took turns telling their story to the sheriff.

After the two men had finished, Earl directed his attention toward Ed and Dr. Jannsen, replying, "I know that all this may seem black and white to you at this moment. But, Ed, you in particular as an attorney, must see that this is not an open and shut case. Myrtle Spencer was hired to take care of the Buchanans by Dr. Jannsen, not Julian Grant. The sleeping pills, assuming lab tests show that's what they are, appear to have been in her possession. And Myrtle is dead, so we may never know what she was up to. There's no conclusive evidence that Agnes Harper was in possession of barbiturates, or was involved in giving any illegal drugs to the Buchanans. And the only evidence that Julian Grant is behind any of this seems to be his suspicious conduct today, and the conversations that the boys overheard between him and Agnes. I'm sure he'll deny everything."

Standing at the nightstand beside Gideon's bed, Earl reached between the larger bottles of cough syrup and mouthwash, and lifted the small bottle marked "Bayer Aspirin." He unscrewed the cap and emptied the pills into his hand, holding one tablet close to his eye. It was clearly marked, "Bayer," top to bottom and side to side.

Looking intently at Ed and Dr. Jannsen, he said, "Unless we can locate Agnes, and get her to confess that she's been giving illegal drugs to the Buchanans, we really don't have much to go on. We'll try to track her down and question her. And we'll go over to Julian's home today, and if he's there, we'll question him. I doubt he'll open up and tell us very much. But I can assure you, we'll be looking very closely for any possible tie-in between what we've just found out, and Myrtle Spencer's death."

Dr. Jannsen took Gertrude aside and asked, "Are you afraid to stay out here alone tonight with the family, after all of this?"

"I wouldn't have said this with the sheriff listening just now," Gertrude replied. "But I keep a government model Colt .45 in my suitcase under my pajamas. I'll be just fine."

When Ed got to the office on Wednesday, he could no longer contain his curiosity about how things were going at Roseanna, and he called Dr. Jannsen.

"Good morning, Ed. I just got off the line with Gertrude a few minutes ago. She told me that Gideon's wide awake, but not as alert as we'd hoped he'd be by now. He seems to be eating a little better and is regaining some strength. She's encouraging the sons to spend as much time as possible with him, and she thinks he's making a little progress in recognizing people, and understanding what's going on around him. Have you talked again with the sheriff?"

"Earl came by here late yesterday and told me that he and his deputies couldn't locate Julian until Tuesday around noon, when he finally showed up at his home. Julian claimed that he'd been away on business, and was just getting back to town. When Earl questioned him about Agnes Harper, he said that she'd quit her job, and asked him to drive her to the Trailways bus station in Beckley. He claimed that she'd almost had a nervous breakdown from the long hours she'd put in taking care of the Buchanans, and she was acting irrational when he dropped her off.

"He went on to say that he handed Agnes fifty dollars for back wages, and that she walked off alone into the bus terminal. Julian alleges he hasn't heard from her since, and he has no idea where she may be now. Earl remarked that afterwards, he contacted Trailways in Beckley, and the agent had no recollection of anyone fitting Agnes's description buying a ticket or getting on the bus there."

"Tell me, did the sheriff have any more information about the pills that were in the Bayer aspirin bottle?" Dr. Jannsen asked.

"Yes, he did. You and Gertrude were dead right. The tablets are barbiturates. But Julian denied any knowledge of the bottle and the note that Daniel and Jonah found behind the dresser. Earl still holds the opinion that the conversation the men overheard between Agnes and Julian is hearsay. I tend to agree that in a court of law, it wouldn't be enough to conclusively link Julian with sleeping pills used to drug the Buchanans."

"It looks like we're mired down in the mud until Agnes is found, doesn't it, Ed? In the meantime, I plan to ask Gertrude to stay on with the Buchanans for a few more weeks."

"Having Agnes arrested and brought in for questioning is the key," Ed agreed. "Her testimony could break this whole thing wide open. But I don't think either of us likes having to sit back and wait."

Chapter 25

WHEN DOUG arrived at the store, a steady stream of customers was going and coming. Late afternoon business was usually good, as people dropped by for last minute purchases for dinner. Doug put on an apron and began to bag groceries for Ingrid at the checkout counter. "Glad to have some help, Doug," she said. "We're starting to get pretty busy."

A few minutes later, Doug was happy to see Vickie enter the store, and ask her mother, "Want me to take over and spell you for a while?"

Ingrid handed Vickie her store apron. "Since you're here to give me a break, I'm going to see if I can help your dad with some of the bookkeeping back in the office." As Vickie stood beside her mother, Doug was reminded of one of his dad's favorite expressions, apples don't fall far from the tree. Vickie's mom could almost pass for her older sister, a very attractive, blond-haired sister.

"Hi, Doug," she greeted him. "We never ran into each other in class today." As she began to ring up grocery orders, he moved closer, breathing in a floral fragrance, completely lost in the moment. He was snapped back to reality when she inquired, "How'd you do on the geometry test that Mr. Powell handed back today? He gave me a B, which was better than I had expected."

"I think I got about the same thing. Some of the problems

were pretty hard, weren't they?"

Vickie glanced at him with a mischievous grin. "I was just waiting to see what you'd say. Mike told Ginny that you were the only boy in class that turned in a perfect paper and got an A. What's the matter with you? Are you afraid all the other kids will start to call you a brain?"

Doug grinned sheepishly. "If I had a choice, I'd much rather be the star on the JV basketball team like Mike. Not sure why, but math just seems to come easy to me. I don't spread that around."

"You've really helped me with my geometry homework during Saturday lunch breaks out back on the shipping dock," Vickie continued. "I can't imagine why you're so secretive about having a gift for math. A lot of us in Mr. Powell's class would like to have your problem."

Late in the afternoon, Tony and Ingrid came up to the front of the store, and she took over again at the checkout counter. Tony took Doug aside, saying, "I need for you to make one delivery before we close. Gertrude Estep just phoned in an order and asked if we could deliver it to the Buchanans today. You've been out there with me, so you know the drill."

Doug picked up the heavy cardboard box of groceries, noting a wide assortment of canned goods on the bottom, topped off with fresh fruit and vegetables, and several loaves of bread. He was starting out the door when he heard Vickie ask her dad, "Is it all right if I ride along? I've never seen Roseanna up close." Her parents glanced at each other, and then her father nodded.

Doug placed the box of groceries in the back of the delivery truck, and he and Vickie slid into the worn front seat, careful not to snag their clothes on the protruding springs. As he pulled out into traffic driving north, she turned on the radio, and dialed in a favorite station, just in time to catch the disc jockey playing *Why Don't You Believe Me*. "Do you like that song?" she inquired.

"I sure do," Doug replied. He didn't bother to tell her that he would have given her exactly the same answer if she had tuned in to another station with Kate Smith singing *When the Moon Comes Over the Mountain*. "It was nice of your folks to let you ride along on this delivery run. I'm starting to feel more relaxed around your dad now that I've been working at the store for a while, but I'm still not as comfortable around him as I am your mother."

"I know how you feel. My dad can be a little intimidating at times. He keeps a pretty close eye on me and my sister. Len Hacker came by to pick me up on a date one night, and he blew his horn in front of the house, wanting me to come out. Dad went out on the porch and told Len if he ever pulled that again, it would be the last time he'd ever come back on his property. I had a big crush on Len then. He was a senior, and the star athlete in school. It took me a while to see what a jerk he was. Dad and Mom never liked him, and maybe I was just being a little rebellious by going out with him."

"Well, that's one thing your dad and I have in common. I dislike Len more than anyone I've ever run into at school, either in Charleston, where I used to live, or here in Eden Springs. I really try to steer clear of him, especially since that night out in front of your house."

Vickie dropped her head, momentarily reliving what had gone on that night. "I'm sorry I got you into that fight. And looking back, I'm sorry for the way I acted around you before that."

As they turned into the long gravel road approaching the old home, she commented, "I've always thought that big old mansion looks like something out of *Gone With the Wind.*"

"Yeah, it's easy to picture Rhett Butler and Miss Scarlet standing on the porch between those big columns."

Doug parked in front of the house, picked up the box of groceries, and they walked together up onto the front porch.

The front door opened before they could knock, and a large-framed lady dressed in a white nursing uniform walked toward them, smiling. "I'm Gertrude Estep," she said. "I had a call from the market telling me you were on your way out here to deliver my order. I understand you're the Housman boy and the Vicelli girl. I know both of your folks."

"Yes ma'am, we are," Doug replied. "Do you want me to carry your groceries into the kitchen? The box is full of canned goods, and it's pretty heavy." Gertrude led the way through the front room and down the dark hallway to the kitchen, where Doug set the box down on the floor. "I guess we'd better be going back now," he said.

Vickie turned her head from side to side as they returned to the front door, staring with great curiosity at the ornate wood trim, elegant mantels, and spectacular curved staircase. On the porch, she glanced toward Gertrude and asked, "Doesn't it bother you staying out here alone after dark?"

Gertrude folded her arms across her chest and laughed. "This probably looks like a haunted house to you. I admit, it gets a little quiet around here after the sun goes down. Late at night you notice the wind blowing around the corners of the house and hear a lot of boards creaking, like someone's walking around upstairs. But there are two burly men to keep me company, and a couple of old folks in poor health to keep me busy. I guess I handle the solitude about as well as anybody could."

Walking to the truck, Vickie commented, "I think Gertrude's a brave woman to stay out there alone at night. Maybe I've seen too many vampire movies, but when I went to bed, I'd be thinking about Count Dracula fluttering into the room, hovering over me. I'd be afraid to close my eyes."

"Freddie Palmer's about as bad as you. I can scare the pants off him on camping trips by telling him I hear something late at night, watching us, moving around in the brush just out of sight."

Looking back across the fields toward Chimney Rock, Doug noticed something different near the top of the hill in the distance. When he and Tony Vicelli had come out to make a delivery in March, he had seen the two sons working there with a team of horses. Weeks later when he came back with Sam Barry and his friends, they had observed that a flat area had been graded on top of the hill. Now he could see what appeared to be a rail fence surrounding much of that space, with a pattern of white objects inside. Turning to her, he asked, "If I let you in on something, will you keep it a secret?"

Doug went on to tell her about the discovery of the lost cave, the wooden crates believed to be caskets for victims of the Battle of Eden Springs, and Sam Barry's discovery that the Buchanan sons were creating a cemetery on top of the hill. "It'll make us a half hour late getting back to the store, but if you're game, I'd like to walk up to the top of that hill and get a look at what Daniel and Jonah have done."

Without bothering to answer, she opened the door of the truck and jumped out. Jogging side by side across the field through the grass, they soon reached the foot of the hill. "I think you're in better shape than I am," Doug said, stopping for a minute to catch his wind. Breathing heavily, the two continued up the slope to the top, stopping peer around them.

The crest of the hilltop had been graded flat and was now turning green with newly planted grass. A chestnut split rail fence with a plank gate circled the leveled area. In the center, arranged in two long rows, lay twenty-two low mounds of fresh dirt, each marked with a rustic white cross. "The sons told Mr. Barry the truth, didn't they Doug?" she said softly. "They've built a cemetery up here on the top."

"Obviously, that's what it is," Doug replied. "I can see that each of the crosses has a number marked on it. It looks like the Buchanan family has tried to preserve the identity of the person buried in each grave."

The two lost track of time as they wandered among the graves, wondering aloud who was lying beneath each mound of dirt, and what story each could tell about his life in an era ninety years ago. Vickie observed, "Some of the numbers painted on the crosses are blue, and some are gray. It seems strange to think that these Union and Confederate soldiers who fought each other in the Battle of Eden Springs ended up buried together, here in a place that looks like a family cemetery."

"I never thought about it like that," Doug admitted. "But Mr.Barry says that's why we study history, to understand things and learn from mistakes. Maybe other people who come up here will stop and think the same thing."

Doug suddenly became aware of the time, realizing just how late they would be getting back. "If you've seen everything, let's head down to the truck and drive back to the store, before you're dad comes out here looking for us."

When they got back, it was past closing time, and Tony was waiting for them in the parking lot. He was smiling, but Doug sensed that beneath the smile, he was all business. "When you go off somewhere with my daughter, son, just be sure you get her back safely and on time."

"I'm sorry, Mr. Vicelli," Doug apologized. "We were looking around out in the country, and the time slipped up on me."

As Doug walked away, his complexion matching his hair, Vickie followed him to the street. "I wish Dad hadn't talked to you like that. He didn't mean anything by it. I think he really likes you."

She started to turn back toward the store, and then stopped to face him, adding, "I wish that I could be there tomorrow when you talk to Mr. Barry and tell him what we found up on the hill." Impulsively, she put her arms around Doug's neck to give him a hug, then spun around and returned to the store.

Chapter 26

"**W**ILL YOU and your faithful dog JR be able to survive if I'm away from home this weekend?" Ed inquired, as he and Doug moved into the living room after dinner on Friday evening. "There's a meeting of the southern West Virginia realtors at Bluestone Lake this Saturday, and Laura invited me to go with her. I'll only be gone from Saturday morning until Sunday afternoon. She's already reserved two rooms for us at the lodge."

"I think that the fearless dog and I can make it on our own while you're away," Doug replied. "We'll try to hold out until you get back. Do you really look forward to hanging out this weekend with a lot of people in the real estate business you don't even know?"

"I'd prefer to be going there with just Laura, and not have to stand around talking with a lot of strangers," Ed admitted. "She told me that Dan knows she'll be there, and she's worried that he may show up and create a problem, so I sort of felt obligated to accept her invitation. But Bluestone Lake is a beautiful place, and we should be able to get away from the crowd at least part of the time to enjoy ourselves."

Doug had left for work at the market by the time Laura drove up on Saturday morning. Ed slid into the front seat beside her and quipped, "Did you have time to give your Olds a tune-up before you picked me up?"

"Yep, I adjusted the timing and tweaked the engine idle speed up a little bit, so I think it'll get us there safely," Laura replied. "We auto mechanics never take a chance on breaking down beside the road. If that's all the information you need about the car, I have something else to tell you.

"Yesterday I received word about two local real estate transactions, and I suspect both are related. A reliable source tells me that that a contract is pending to sell the Buchanan farm, lock, stock, and barrel, to a company in Beckley. And in what seems to me a curious coincidence, a buyer from out of town just closed on the purchase of a run-down two story stucco bungalow on the south side of town that I've been unable to move, although I've been showing it to low income families for the past two years."

"Well, what do you know!" Ed exclaimed. "It sounds like Julian didn't waste any time getting the ball rolling, and he's moving at full speed to unload the Buchanan property before poor old Gideon can recover. If he moved the Buchanans into a house in town, it would certainly clear one of the last obstacles for him in transacting a quick sale of the farm to Copperfield Enterprises, and indirectly to Barker Mining. You don't have any idea what price has been put on the farm, do you?"

"I don't have any numbers, but I hear that the price per acre works out to be much less than the Simpsons and Hendersons got for nearby farm land that's not nearly as valuable from a commercial standpoint, especially in light of all of the timber on the Buchanan property. When you hear about property being underpriced like this, you suspect that money may be getting passed under the table from the buyer to the seller's agent. Julian could be getting a very large cut for his part in this sale."

"This is incredibly frustrating. I've been standing by with a new power of attorney and will for Gideon that would save his farm, but his recovery is progressing so slowly that everything may be over before he becomes legally competent to sign the documents. What we definitely seem to be heading for now is a Barker Coal strip mine development, destroying an historic civil war battlefield site, and putting a permanent blight on this entire region."

After a minute of deliberation, Laura glanced over at Ed. "What you just said started me thinking. Are we missing an opportunity to keep a strip mine operation from being developed? In other parts of the country, like Gettysburg, Civil War battlefields are being preserved. I know that the Battle at Eden Springs wasn't a pivotal event in the course of the war, but we've recently learned something about why it was fought, and what took place there is a part of our history during that era. Do you think we could possibly get some sort of historical site designation to prevent industrial development, like mining?"

"I haven't gone through anything like that before, so I'm just talking off the top of my head. In my opinion, obtaining historic site protection would be a very time consuming political process. You could probably drum up a lot of public opposition to a strip mine through organizations like the United Daughters of the Confederacy. But there are no existing zoning regulations to stop it, and Robert Barker has shown before that he's in business to make money, not friends. Furthermore, he seems to have some very powerful state politicians in his hip pocket."

"I guess that wasn't a practical idea," Laura said in a resigned voice.

"Getting historic site protection may seem impractical, but let's not toss the idea out just yet. I know that Doug's teacher is studying the history of this area during the Civil War era. Apparently, he has a circle of friends in the academic community with similar interests in learning about and preserving historic landmarks. I'll talk to him when we get back to town and see if he has any suggestions."

By the time they arrived at the lodge overlooking Bluestone Lake, realtors from around the region had began to check in. Ed was surprised at how many of them already knew Laura. When he and Laura received their room keys, he discovered that her room was conveniently located on the first floor, while his room was on the second floor near the back of the building.

Later that morning, a short realtors association business meeting was held in the lodge auditorium. At the conclusion, Ed and Laura split up and went back to their rooms to change into casual clothes.

When Laura reappeared, she was wearing blue pedal pushers and sandals. The sun deepened small freckles on her arms, now bared by her short sleeve blouse, as they walked hand-in-hand down the path to the nearby boat house and dock. Taking two worn wooden paddles from the boat house attendant, they carefully settled into the low seats of a dented aluminum canoe and paddled out onto the lake, Laura sitting in the bow and Ed in the stern.

"I haven't been in a canoe in the last five years, not since Bill died," Laura commented. "But I think that paddling a canoe is like riding a bicycle: once you learn, you never forget how."

"I worked as a counselor at a nearby Boy Scout camp when I was a teenager," Ed replied. "I got in quite a few hours paddling around in one of these things during those two summers. I think you're absolutely right. Once you learn how to handle a canoe, you're good for life."

They paddled across the lake with easy strokes until they reached the other side, where they moved in close to the bank, sitting and talking in the shade of an overhanging tree. "I guess this is just about as good as it gets," Ed commented. "I imagine that boys have been bringing their girlfriends here for years, getting off to themselves, enjoying the solitude just like us."

"You're starting to sound romantic," Laura laughed, shifting her weight to one side and turning around in her seat to face him. "You're not thinking about putting down your paddle, and coming up here to be close to me?"

"I just might do that," Ed said playfully, dropping his paddle into the bottom of the canoe. Pretending to get up from his seat, he shifted his position slightly to the same side. It wasn't much of a shift in weight, but it was enough. The canoe started to slowly tip to the side, gaining momentum as it went, until it completely flipped over upside down, dumping them over their heads in the cold lake water.

They both came to the surface, sputtering and laughing, as they swam over to the swamped canoe and grabbed hold of the side. "Once you learn how to handle a canoe, you're good for life, aren't you, Ed? " Laura said, unable to suppress a giggle. "What kind of stunt was that you just pulled?"

"Now don't start blaming me. It was your fault that we rolled the canoe. You were the one who started everything by inviting me to come up and sit beside you." Putting his hand on her shoulder, he pulled her away from the canoe, wrapped his arms around her, and pulled her under the water to kiss her.

When they surfaced again, Laura was sputtering to catch her breath and laughing uncontrollably. "That's a first for me, and I'm forty years old. Tell me, have you been watching a lot of Tarzan movies lately? Are you starting to think I'm Jane?"

Holding on to the gunwale of the canoe side by side and kicking, it took only a short time for them reach the bank. Together they pulled the canoe up on the shore and rolled it over on its side to dump the water out. Ed stared at Laura's long red hair streaming down against her face, and observed with a slight smile, "I declare, you remind me of a pet chicken I had when I was a kid. It was a Rhode Island Red hen. I named her Lucille. When her feathers got wet out in the rain, they were about the same dark red color your hair is right now."

"You can forget everything I said earlier about you having an Irishman's charm, Housman," Laura retorted, starting to laugh again. "Having you compare me to your pet chicken is not exactly the greatest compliment I've ever received. And hearing you say that, only a few minutes after trying to drown me, I would have to say your timing isn't the best, either."

You're taking it all wrong, Laura," Ed said, fighting a grin. "I thought the sun rose and set on Lucille."

They carefully launched the canoe, and with steady strokes, propelled it back across the lake to the boat house. The attendant came out to take their paddles and helped them pull the canoe out of the water. Seeing their wet clothes, he couldn't resist having a little fun at their expense. "If you two come back tomorrow, I'll give you free beginner's lessons in how to handle a canoe."

"I'll pass on the offer," Laura replied. ""But I'd like to sign up my friend here for the whole series." She slipped her arm through Ed's, and they walked together up to the lodge, still dripping, drawing amused looks from other guests.

When they reached her room, leaving wet tracks behind them, Laura opened the door. Glancing back over her shoulder, she said, "Come on in. I have a couple of bath towels, and we can both dry off. We're ruining the carpet, standing here with half of Bluestone Lake running off us."

"You really want me to come in like this, soaked to the skin?" Ed inquired, watching her as she entered the room. "I'll get water all over the floor if I do. Maybe I should just go upstairs and change into some dry clothes."

"I've invited you in," Laura answered softly. "It's up to you."

He followed her into the room, and without turning around, quietly pushed the door closed with his foot. Watching Laura kick off her wet sandals to stand barefoot on the carpet, Ed could not resist quipping, "Lucille used to walk around barefoot like that a lot."

"That's enough talk about Lucille," Laura chided him. Walking into the bathroom, she returned carrying two large white towels, and handed one to him.

Taking his towel by both ends, Ed looped it behind her back, and gently pulled her close to him. As she stood against him, he toweled the water from her neck and shoulders. Looking into his eyes, without uttering a word, Laura slowly unbuttoned her wet blouse, letting it drop to the floor.

There was a beautiful sunrise breaking in the east on Sunday morning when they checked out. Ed carried their luggage to the white Olds parked outside and stood watching as Laura said goodbye to her friends before walking out to join him.

When they reached the main highway, Laura glanced at Ed, saying, "I've had such a wonderful time the past two days. Don't you wish life could always be this good? Why do we have to go back and deal with greed, corruption, and even murder, when we live in a place called Eden Springs?"

"You better read the book of Genesis again. People went wrong, and good times didn't last in the original Eden either. I think that going through life is like canoeing down an uncharted river. You relax and enjoy the smooth stretches where the water runs still, while anticipating that there'll be white water up ahead. But smooth water or rough, the trip is better if you have a mate on board with you. Assuming, of course, you have one skillful enough not to flip you over. That's the synopsis for my five hour course in Navigation and Philosophy," he added. Laura reached over and switched on the car radio, turning up the volume to drown out further conversation.

When they pulled into the Houseman driveway, Laura turned off the switch. Ed slid across the seat, putting his arms around her, and holding her close, neither of them saying a word. The moment was broken when JR came bounding around the house, barking and jumping against the side of the car. "I love you," Ed said to her, while opening the door and reaching for the dog's collar. Looking back, he could see Laura's lips frame the same words, just before she started the engine and backed slowly out to the street.

Doug was waiting inside when he entered the house. "How did you make out while I was away? Any big news?" Ed inquired.

"No, it's been pretty quiet," Doug answered. "But there were a couple of interesting things I heard while you were away. Ronnie Myers's dad told him that the new owners of the Simpson farm had a work crew doing a lot of blasting last week near the base of Pine Ridge, not too far from the lower end of Stony Creek. And yesterday afternoon while I was at work, Mr.Vicelli came back from delivering groceries to the Eden Springs Resort with some news. He said that the mineral springs there always runs crystal clear, but for the past few days the spring water has been coming up out of the ground muddy. No one can remember anything like that ever happening before."

As Ed carried his suitcase up the steps, Doug remembered something else, and called up to him. "Oh yeah, one other thing, there's a teacher's meeting coming up, so I'll have the day off from school this Wednesday."

"You just reminded me of something. I want to call Sam Barry and talk with him about the old battleground site north of town that you've told me he's so interested in. I need his help."

Chapter 27

Ed called Sam later that day. "Mr. Barry, I'm Ed Housman, Doug's dad, and I'd like to talk with you, if you have the time. Doug's told me about your interest in the history of this area."

A pleasant voice replied, "I have all the time in the world, Ed, and please call me Sam. Your son's one of my favorite students. He certainly gave you good information about my passion for the study of local history. What would you like to talk about?"

"Doug told me about your trip out to the Buchanan farm a couple of weeks ago, and some of the things you discovered while you were looking around that rediscovered cave and the old battleground," Ed began. "Recently, there've been some very important developments which impact that property, and I'd like to make you aware of them." Ed sensed from the complete silence on the other end that he had Sam Barry's full attention.

"For some time, there's been a credible rumor about the discovery of a very large and commercially valuable seam of coal lying under the entire valley bounded by Pine Ridge and Chestnut Ridge, up to Abner Gap, although strangely enough, nothing has been reported about this to date in the newspapers. As you know, the valley encompasses a number of tracts of land, the largest by far being the Buchanan farm. I've had a report from a reliable source that the sale of that property to a mining company is now pending.

"It follows that this will bring a strip mining operation into the region, destroying that green valley, and along with it, the Civil War battlefield. I'm one of several people who's become aware of this, and I'm looking for ways to head it off. I'd like to get your opinion and ask for your help. Do you think that preservation of the valley including the battlefield as a tourist attraction could possibly trump development of a strip mine, in the eyes of state officials?"

After a brief hesitation, Sam replied, "Ed, I doubt that it would. As far as the West Virginia economy is concerned, coal is indeed king. Wealthy mining company owners are big donors to politicians, and they help to keep them in office year after year, giving them a lot of clout when controversial decisions are made. But as far as enlisting me in this cause, I'm in it with you right now. There are a lot of fine people in these parts who take a long range view of what's the right or wrong type of development for this region.

"I've invited two of them who are old friends from the academic world down this coming Wednesday. Jack Barnes from WVU and Henry Claffey from VPI are both PhDs who head up the history departments at their schools. They're coming here to see what we've recently found at the battlefield site. Both men are pretty influential in this region, Barnes in particular. Would you like to join us on a field trip to the Buchanan farm, and fill them in on what we're facing out there? We're having breakfast at the Eden Springs Resort at 8:00, and driving out afterward."

"I'll take you up on that invitation," Ed replied. "I hope that your friends are as enthusiastic about preserving that battlefield site as we are."

Arriving at the busy dining room on Wednesday morning, Ed joined three men dressed in casual clothes seated at a side table. He recognized the short one with the crew cut as Sam Barry, having seen him at high school ball games earlier. Ed shook hands and exchanged introductions first with Sam, and then the other two.

After the waitress had taken their orders, Sam said to Ed, "The three of us had dinner together last night, and I took the liberty of filling them in on what you told me on the phone. They'd already heard the rumor of a big coal discovery in this area, but neither thought it was so close to Eden Springs.

Neither of them would like to see anything like a strip mine in the valley north of town, close to the old battlefield. They want to go out there this morning and see the site first hand, before we all put our heads together."

Ed smiled across the table at the two visitors. "You have no idea how good it is to have you coming in on our side."

"Jack and Henry shared some big news with me last night," Sam remarked. "There's recently been an exciting breakthrough discovery about the Battle of Eden Springs. I'll let them tell you about it."

Henry leaned forward, peering through the thick lenses of his horn-rimmed glasses. "I'll try to relate the story without getting into too much detail. This spring, a prominent Virginia family donated its collection of old Civil War documents to the VPI library. When the collection was archived, a letter was found, written in January, 1862, by a soldier in the Confederate Army, Sergeant Daniel O'Connor, addressed to his wife in Richmond. It was, to say the least, not your typical letter from a lonely, loving husband to an adored wife back home.

"In it, he accused his wife of committing adultery with his commanding officer, Captain Jason Taylor Early, alleging that he had been sent on risky military assignments several times earlier in order to get him away from home, so that Captain Early and she could be together. This begins to sound a little like the story of David and Bathsheba, doesn't it?"

"I'm intrigued," Ed replied. "Please go on."

Henry continued, his lanky frame angled forward, "Sergeant O'Connor told his wife that he was embarking on a dangerous military mission behind enemy lines with his company, under the command of Capt. Early. He went on to say that he believed that the Union Army had been tipped off about their plans, and that combat was almost certain.

"The sergeant told his wife that he did not expect that either he or Captain Early would return alive, adding that in the confusion of battle, soldiers are not only at risk of being killed by the enemy, but often die at the hand of their own comrades. After that strange remark, he closed without ever expressing affection for his wife, only instructing her to take good care of their three-year old daughter. Apparently, Sergeant O'Connor then gave the letter to a young private to deliver in the event of his death."

"What do you all make of this?" Ed inquired.

Jack now spoke up, nervously scratching his bald head, "We suspect that Sgt. O'Connor may have found some way to inform the Union forces that his company of Confederate troops would be moving north toward Abner Gap in January. It seems likely that's the reason the Yanks were well positioned and had dug in on the high ground when the battle broke out. And we think it's a distinct possibility that Sergeant O'Connor was the one who shot and killed Captain Early during the engagement. The loss of the commanding officer definitely aborted the Confederate mission, which was to destroy the Union rail lines on the north end of the Shenandoah Valley."

Henry interjected, "At that time, the Civil War was starting to become highly unpopular in the North. If the Confederate troops had succeeded in cutting those Union rail lines, leading to a few more military victories for the South at that time, the war might have swung the other way. From what we're now learning, we believe that the Battle of Eden Springs was a pivotal event that may have influenced the outcome of the Civil War, and that it was not just the minor historical footnote we've all assumed up 'til now."

Sam joined in, "Which brings us back to the battlefield site on the Buchanan farm, making it far more essential than ever to see that it's preserved as a historic landmark."

Sam glanced at Ed, adding, "There's one other thing I'd like to make you aware of. The owner of the Eden Springs Resort talked to us last night at dinner. He'd heard about the blasting on the Simpson farm near Stony Creek last week, and he's convinced that's what caused the mineral springs here to turn muddy for a few days. He told us several visitors checked out and left after it happened. If the springs run muddy for very long, it will put him out of business."

Jack rode with Sam, and Henry joined Ed, heading out the highway toward Abner Gap. Turning up the private road to Roseanna, they parked the cars and started on foot, walking in the direction of Chimney Rock toward the hill ahead. They covered only a short distance when Ed noticed the fresh deep-tread tire tracks in the dirt leading across the field in the same direction they were walking. As they got closer to the hill, the tracks could be seen continuing up the slope to the top. Ed commented to Sam, "Someone must have driven a Jeep up there. I don't think you could get up that grade through the grass and soft ground unless you had four-wheel drive."

As the four men climbed up toward the crest, Ed could see the Daniel and Jonah, working side by side up ahead. He called ahead to them, "Good morning. You two look busy. What's going on?"

"Someone came up here last night and tore everything up," Daniel replied in an exasperated drawl. "We had everything fixed up like Pa told us to, and now we're having to start over and do it all again."

Reaching the top, the four men could see what the sons were dealing with. Fresh, deep tire marks showed where twenty-two new graves, arranged in two straight rows, had been desecrated by someone driving back and forth across them. White wooden crosses were lying broken on the ground, the rail fence bordering the graveyard had been pulled down, and a wooden gate was smashed. Ed turned to Jack and Henry and said in a low voice, "These are the Buchanan twin sons, Daniel and Jonah. They've created some sort of a memorial cemetery up here on top of the hill for both the Confederate and Union victims of the battle."

Ed spoke quietly to the two sons, "These men are here to help us preserve your farm. I'd appreciate it if you would stop for a few minutes and tell the four of us about this cemetery, who's buried in these graves, where the bodies came from, and why you brought them here."

Daniel looked at Jonah, and replied, "Let's move over in the shade under the oak tree, and we'll tell you about it. Pa told us the story that was handed down to him." As soon as the six men had gathered out of the sun, the sons began to talk, each taking a turn.

Daniel started. "Grandpa was a man of peace, and he wanted no truck with war. He didn't like it when the two armies came onto his property and fought that battle. Grandpa told Pa they'd desecrated his land. When the fighting was over and everyone had left, Grandpa and the uncles moved all the bodies over into the cave below Chimney Rock, and blasted it shut.

"When army men came back later looking for the bodies, Grandpa didn't let on that he'd hauled them off and laid them away. But being a God fearing man, he started worrying that it was a sin for him to leave those bodies uncovered on the floor of a cave. A few years later, he and the uncles made caskets at the sawmill. They moved the rocks away so they could get back inside the cave, and put each soldier's remains in one of them wooden boxes. Then they closed up the cave like it was before."

Jonah picked up the story, adding, "But before he died, Grandpa told Pa he wished that he'd buried the men up here on the hill where most of 'em died, so people could come and see the terrible price that common men pay for wars. Grandpa told Pa that 'generals lead, and soldiers bleed.'

"Last year Pa sent us out to find the cave, so we could move those soldiers' bodies up here like Grandpa wanted. Pa said this graveyard should be preserved to honor all the men that was killed in the battle. We'd just finished marking the graves, and was going to get a preacher out here for a proper Christian service."

Daniel interjected, "Last night, we thought we heard someone drive up here, but they didn't have any lights on, and it was too dark to see them. We can tell by the tracks that it was an old army Jeep, and we think from the footprints that two men did all this mischief. It's good they didn't have time to tear up the graves. But it's gonna take us a while to get everything back the way it was before."

Jack spoke angrily, "It would take real scum to do something like this."

Ed responded, "Maybe the same scum who would commit a string of crimes to get their hands on a big tract of land with a coal deposit worth a king's ransom. Having a cemetery up here full of Civil War victims would be one more obstacle for someone trying to turn this farm into a strip mine. Anyway, while we're here, let's pitch in and see if we can help these men get some sections of this fence back up."

Helping the twins rebuild the fence was taxing work for the three academics and a lawyer. Stopping to catch his breath, Jack said, "I'm ready to pitch in and help drum up support to conserve the battlefield site, including this cemetery."

"I think all of us are," Henry replied. "I'll start making some phone calls when I get back to Blacksburg." Returning to work, he added, "Jack, how 'bout catching the other end of this fence rail, and helping me set it back up where it was."

Later, the four men wiped the sweat from their faces with handkerchiefs, and started back toward the house, leaving Daniel and Jonah working steadily to restore the graveyard.

"I don't know whether it's even worth reporting this to the sheriff," Ed commented to Sam. "The law enforcement people haven't solved a single crime since things started to happen out here. But for whatever it's worth, I guess I'll call Earl Daniels when I get home, and tell him about what we've seen."

When Ed arrived home, he found Doug outside giving JR a bath, using the garden hose and a bar of red Lifebuoy soap. "I thought baths were just for Saturday night."

"Not for family members who go out in a field and roll around on a rotten carcass," Doug laughed, rinsing the lather off the shivering dog with a cold stream of water. "Got to keep ol' JR smelling good. You haven't forgotten that the Eden Springs Chautauqua is coming up this summer. JR's a lock for best looking dog in the competition."

As soon as Doug turned off the spigot, JR shook the water from his coat, covering him with spray, then ran over in the yard and began to roll around in the dirt. "I don't plan to enter him in the contest for the most intelligent or best trained dog in show," he added.

"There's so much going on around here I had forgotten all about the Chautauqua being held this year," Ed observed. "Speaking of social events, the high school spring dance is coming up pretty soon, isn't it? Have you and your buddies started lining up dates yet?"

"My buddies have steady girl friends, so they're all fixed up," Doug answered. "But I need to get up my nerve and ask Vickie pretty soon. One of the boys in the junior class is starting to hang out around her locker after school, and I'm sure he plans to ask her to go with him."

"Leave JR out here in the yard so he doesn't track up the

house, and let's go inside and talk," Ed said, starting toward the door. "I learned some interesting new things today about the historical significance of that Civil War battle, and I think you'll be surprised when I fill you in."

"There's something you probably need to do first," Doug replied. "Laura wanted you to call her when you got home. She acted like it was important.

When Ed went inside, he dialed Laura's number. "I just got home, and Doug told me you called. Anything going on?"

"Yes, I believe there is," Laura answered. "I was at the court house today, and Shirley Baker took me aside. She's probably going way out on a limb for us, telling us things that she shouldn't be disclosing as a court clerk. But she wanted me to let you know that there's now a contract, signed by Julian Grant as executor, selling the Buchanan property to Copperfield Enterprises. The curious thing is that Julian seems to be hanging onto the contract, rather than having it recorded and the title to the property transferred. What do you make of that?"

"It's just a hunch, but maybe Julian's trying to put the squeeze on Copperfield Enterprises and Barker Mining for more money under the table. Otherwise, I'd expect that he'd want to complete the deal as quickly as possible, before Gideon recovers. If I'm right, and he's holding out for more bucks, he may be playing a very risky game, betting that Gideon doesn't get better, and that Robert Barker doesn't take the gloves off. Barker has the reputation of being a ruthless businessman that nobody with common sense wants to cross."

"I had somewhat the same thoughts," Laura replied. "Julian would be a fool to go against a powerful man like Barker. Now that I've told you why I called, give me a rundown on how things went with you."

"I learned a lot today. I found out that the Battle of Eden Springs may have been decided by a jealous husband who killed his commanding officer for seducing his wife, but that's a Shakespearian tragedy I'll get into when we have more time.

"And I found out that that the Buchanan sons have built a cemetery for the victims of that battle up on the hill near Roseanna. Someone vandalized it last night, and I suspect that it could be more dirty work connected to Barker's move for their farm. I'm planning to report what I saw today to the sheriff."

"Isn't it amazing how little that human behavior has changed over time?" Laura replied. "You're telling me that the outcome of that Civil War battle may have been determined by lust, infidelity, jealousy, and revenge. Shakespeare would have had a field day writing a play around all of that."

Before hanging up, she reminded him, "Don't forget to make that phone call to Earl in the morning." Then she added softly, "I love you."

"I love you more."

Chapter 28

O N THE way to school Friday morning, Doug cut down the side street to Mike's house, catching up with him under a maple tree in the front yard. "You're right on time, Dawg," Mike greeted him. "Only one more day of school, and we get a weekend off to just lay around the house."

"You mean unemployed bums like you get a day off to lay around," Doug joked. "Working men like me with regular jobs have things we have to do on Saturday."

Stopping to tie a shoe, Mike observed, "You realize we have less than three more weeks of school before summer vacation? I've got to get on the ball and find a job, or my old man will find one for me. He knows a mason working on a building downtown who wants someone to carry brick and mix mortar for him this summer, and that's hard work. By the way, Ginny reminded me the spring dance is coming up soon. Are you going to ask Vickie to go with you?"

"I've kind of been putting it off. The only time I've been around her was on that blind date with you and Ginny, except for school and working at the store."

"Y'all can double date with Ginny and me if you want. That way you'd get to sit in the back seat with her again."

"Thanks for the offer, Michael, but you and Ginny would probably have a lot more fun in the back seat than we would. Anyway, I'll try to catch up with her before class, and ask her if she'll go with me. If she says yes, I'm pretty sure I can borrow Dad's car. You drove the last time."

In the main hallway at school, a noisy, boisterous crowd of teenagers was waiting for the first period to begin. Approaching a group of friends, Doug spotted Vickie talking to Danny Baker, the boy in the junior class who got so much attention from the girls. At that moment the bell rang loudly, and everyone started moving quickly toward their classrooms. The instant Danny split off from her, Doug walked up and inquired nervously, "Hey, Vickie. Can I talk to you for a couple of minutes after first period?"

"Good morning, Doug," she replied, looking at him curiously. "What about?" There was no time for Doug to answer as they entered Mrs. Wilson's Latin class, and he headed for the sanctuary near the back of the room, while she took a seat nearer the front.

Doug spent the class period mentally rehearsing his invitation, giving only superficial attention to the teacher's animated pronouncement in Latin that "all Gaul is divided into three parts." He caught up with Vickie after class, just outside the doorway. Summoning up his nerve, he spoke quickly, "I was wondering if you'd go to the spring dance with me?"

Giving him a long look, she asked, "You waited pretty late to ask me, didn't you, Mr. Housman? You know, last week, another boy invited me to go with him."

It was exactly the answer that Doug had feared. He dropped his head and started to turn away, certain that that the other boy could be none other than Danny Baker.

At that moment, she added, "You must not want a date with me very badly." Doug turned, and saw her mischievous smile. "I told you another boy invited me to go with him. I didn't say that I accepted his invitation."

"I'm not sure what you mean by that. Will you go to the dance with me or not?"

He was completely taken aback when she answered, "Yes, I'll go with you. I've just been waiting for you to ask me. What took you so long?"

Doug tried to control his feeling of incredible good fortune. He had experienced a similar emotion before in a sixth grade baseball game, when he had taken a wild swing at a high fast pitch, not expecting to connect, and had knocked the ball over the outfield fence to win the game. "Great! That means we can double date with Mike and Ginny."

Trying to act nonchalant, he wheeled around and walked down the hall toward his second period class, almost running head-on into another student.

Later, Doug worked his way through the school cafeteria lunch line, joining his buddies who were already negotiating their usual complicated series of lunch bag trades. Wayne had swapped his Spam sandwich for Mike's peanut butter and jelly, but seemed to be considering whether he had made a bad trade. As Doug slipped into a vacant chair, Freddie swallowed a large bite from an apple, and said, "Dawg, I saw you talking to Vickie after Latin class. What in the world were you up to?"

"I was just checking to see what color dress she's wearing to the dance, so I'll know what kind of corsage to buy her," Doug answered in a matter of fact voice, holding his glass of milk like he'd seen Cary Grant handle a scotch and soda in *An Affair to Remember*.

"Only in your wildest dreams. Shirley told me last week that Vickie had already been asked by Danny Baker. You or any other boy in our class wouldn't even get a look after that."

"Well, Frederick, if you'd like to put a five dollar bet on it, you're on, and Mike can hold the money, but you're going to lose this one. Stranger things have happened than Vickie picking me over Danny Baker to take her to the dance. You know, once in a while, the underdog comes out on top. The New York Yankees usually win the World Series, but not every time."

"He's not shooting the bull, Fred," Mike added. "Ginny and Vickie are working up plans for the four of us to double date again. Our friend Dawg has greatly surprised us all."

"Honestly, I'm glad to hear that," Freddie said, putting his apple down. "I thought you might miss out on everything again this year. Maybe we can get a couple of tables side by side near the dance floor, so all of us can hang out together."

"I hear Mr. Barry will be the head faculty sponsor for the dance again this year," Wayne said. "He hits it off with everyone in the school, including the seniors on the dance committee. Usually, he lines up several teachers and their husbands or wives to hang out at the dance, and try to keep kids from sneaking out to their cars in the parking lot to drink beer and neck. Last year, Mr. Barry couldn't get enough teachers to volunteer, and he ended up asking some of the parents to pitch in and help out. I sure wouldn't want to have my folks at the dance acting as chaperones, trying to keep jerks like Len Hacker and his buddies in line."

Mike gave Doug a good-natured pat on the shoulder going up the worn wood steps from the cafeteria, saying, "I think I may have lucked into a summer job that'll keep me out of the brick masonry business. My old man talked to Mr. Hauser, the manager of the body shop at the Ford dealership, and he's got an opening for summer help to do prep work in their paint shop. After we get out for the day, I'm going by to talk to him."

"I'll walk with you after school as far as Dad's office downtown," Doug volunteered. "I've got a little time to kill, and I can ride home with the old man after he finishes work."

When the bell sounded to end the school day, Doug and Mike joined the stampede of students heading home. At Fourth Street, Doug veered off, calling out to Mike, "Good luck getting the job." Inside his dad's office, he heard the rapid staccato sound of a typewriter, and saw Carolyn seated at her desk in front of her Underwood. "Hey, Mrs. Carson. I just stopped by to see you and check up on Dad."

"Nice to have you drop in, Doug," Carolyn smiled. "Your father's on the phone, as usual. How did school go today?"

"Pretty good, thanks. Friday is every kid's favorite day, 'cause we know the weekend's coming up, and we'll get a break from classes. When I walk out the door on Friday, I always think about that old grade school rhyme, 'no more pencils, no more books, no more teacher's dirty looks.' I bet you felt the same way when you were in school."

"Some things never change, do they?" Carolyn laughed.

At that moment, Ed rushed out of his office, unable to contain his excitement. "I just got off the phone with Earl Daniels, and he gave me some great news. He got a call this morning from the State Police Headquarters in Princeton. It seems they went back over that Ford panel truck again, looking for any fingerprints that they may have missed earlier, and this time they hit the jackpot. They found one set of prints on the back of the rear view mirror, and another set just inside the rear door. With some help from the FBI, they've succeeded in matching them up to two men with long criminal records, including a number of major felony convictions. The prints belong to William Hurd and Jake Tolliver out of New Jersey. A bulletin's just been issued for their arrest in connection with the Myrtle Spencer homicide case.

"Earl asked me if I'd come by and look at the mug shots of Hurd and Tolliver just as soon as he gets them in, to see if I can identify either of them."

"Ed, what great news!" Carolyn exclaimed, rushing over to give him a hug. "This sounds like the break in the Myrtle Spencer murder case we've all been waiting on. I'm so relieved to learn that the police finally know who to look for."

"Feel free to give me another hug after you hear what else he told me. There's been a sighting of someone matching Agnes Harper's description in Charleston, and the police there have been asked to stay on the lookout. I may end up having to eat my words about the law enforcement people not getting the job done."

"I prefer the way they hunted down killers like Hurd and Tolliver in western movies," Doug chimed in. "The police ought to put a bounty on their heads, and tack up posters on telephone poles all around here with their mug shots, 'Wanted Dead or Alive'."

"I hope you're joking," Ed replied, grinning. "I'd like to think our law enforcement system has come a little way since those days."

"All of this good news calls for some kind of a celebration." Carolyn interjected. "Doug and I were talking a few minutes ago about Fridays being the best day of the week, and this is turning out to be one of the best Fridays ever. Since we don't keep champagne here in the office, what should we do?"

"We definitely need to celebrate," Ed agreed. "Let close up shop now and get the weekend started a little early." Reaching into his billfold, Ed dug out a twenty dollar bill, and slipped it into her hand. "This is a 'best Friday' celebration award. I'd like for you to take your sister to dinner and to share a bottle of wine at the Stafford Steakhouse tonight. I'll see you back here on Monday morning." At the door he called back, "Have a great weekend."

Ed draped his arm affectionately across his son's shoulder as they walked to the car. "Gil's hamburgers OK with you again tonight?" he inquired.

Doug nodded. "I guess anything's fine with us, just as long as it keeps both of us out of the kitchen."

★

Julian Grant drove to Bluefield in a light rain on Saturday. Arriving at mid-morning, he parked in front of an old two story brick building with boarded-up windows, and a rusty red and white sign lettered Walton's Machine Shop. A black Cadillac sedan and a light green Chevrolet pickup truck could be seen parked against the curb just down the street.

He tried turning the knob to open the sturdy wooden door at the entrance, but it was locked. Knocking several times but getting no response, he stood in the rain and waited. A few minutes later, he heard the sound of a deadbolt being retracted, then the door swung open. A stocky man with a boxer's flattened nose, wearing a ball cap, motioned for him to come in, then led him through a shop filled with large machine tools back into an office at the rear of the building.

Inside the office, two men dressed in dark suits were seated in folding chairs beside a table, one middle-aged and the other somewhat older. He recognized the younger of the two as William Thorpe. It was the unsmiling, heavy-set man beside Thorpe coldly staring through thick horn-rimmed glasses who filled him with a sense of apprehension.

"Mr. Grant, it's good to see you again," William Thorpe said with a faint smile, walking toward him with a well manicured hand extended. "I'd like to introduce you to the owner and president of our company, Mr. Robert Copperfield Barker."

Robert Barker remained seated and expressionless, but lifted his arm and reached across the table, displaying a massive gold ring with an onyx stone on one of his thick fingers. When Julian walked over to shake his hand, he was surprised at the strength of the older man's grip. Barker's demeanor took Julian back twenty years to his army drill sergeant, who had kept draftees in line by total intimidation.

Thorpe continued speaking, although there was no doubt in Julian's mind as to who was in charge of the meeting. "Mr. Grant, or if you'll permit me the liberty of calling you by your first name, Julian, I believe that you have the required signatures on the contract, and everything is in order as required to record the sale and transfer the deed for the Buchanan property to Copperfield Enterprises. Isn't that correct?"

"Yes, sir," Julian replied. "But I think in light of the extremely high value of the Buchanan property you're purchasing, and the low price I've arranged for you to pay, the 'sales commission' you're paying me should be considerably more than the amount you offered me earlier. My work in facilitating this sale has put me in serious jeopardy with the law."

"We negotiated the amount of your 'sales commission' months ago, Julian, and you were satisfied with it at that time," William continued. "We're not here today to renegotiate the fee we'll pay you. We're here to find out why you haven't already concluded the sale as we agreed. We certainly don't want to think that you've acted in bad faith, and are trying to squeeze more money from us before you'll complete your end of the bargain. You're not trying to do that, are you, Julian?"

"No, Mr. Thorpe, I'm not. But as I said, I've put myself at extreme risk with the law in working to have Gideon Buchanan declared incompetent, so that I could sell his land to you. I'm just asking you to pay me more because I've stuck my neck out so far."

Barker, who had been shifting in his seat with increasing impatience, suddenly spoke in a low voice with quiet deliberation. "Mr. Grant, I don't take well to people who renege on business agreements. Mr. Thorpe and I are going to go away today and give you a little more time to think about your position. You can get back to him with your answer." His back ramrod straight, Barker walked away without a backward glance, Thorpe scurrying at his heels.

"Mr. Thorpe, wait," Julian called out, starting to follow them. He had only managed to take a few steps when he found his way blocked by the stocky ex-pug in the ball cap. With a sick feeling building in the pit of his stomach, he watched a second man enter the office through a side door, large and muscular, a stubble beard on his face and tattoos on both arms, carrying a short length of metal pipe. "What's going on?" Julian asked in a high, quivering voice.

Before Julian could move, the stocky man with the ball cap pinned his arms against his side in a bear hug, and forced him across the office to the wood table. "Shut up. I don't wanta hear a whimper out of you," he muttered.

The larger man pulled Julian's left arm free, pinning it against the table. Then with one short swing, he struck Julian in the forearm with the pipe, breaking the bone with a sharp crack. Julian screamed out, moaning loudly, as he gripped his broken left arm with his right hand. The ex-pug released his hold, grabbing Julian by the back of his collar, half-carrying him through the building, and throwing him out through the front door onto the sidewalk. As Julian fell to his knees, light-headed with pain, he heard that sandpaper whisper, "Mr. Barker and Mr. Thorpe will be waiting to hear from you."

Fighting excruciating pain, Julian managed to unlock his car and drive to the home of a Bluefield doctor. A shot of morphine soon numbed his arm, but did nothing to relieve the fearful uncertainty that now engulfed him.

★

Chapter 29

"MY SISTER's still talking about that dinner you treated us to last week," Carolyn commented, as her fingers flew across the keyboard of her typewriter. "Sarah doesn't get to eat at the Stafford Steakhouse but once in a blue moon." She swiveled around in her chair to grab the phone ringing beside her. "It's Laura on the line for you."

Picking up the phone, Ed listened carefully to what she was saying, in a near whisper. "I'm in my office. I don't want anyone to overhear this conversation."

Ed pushed his door closed and returned to the phone. "OK, no one can overhear us now. What's up?"

"Yesterday, I did something at the court house that was definitely unethical, and probably illegal, trying to stall the sale of the Buchanan farm. When I went by the courthouse after lunch and ran into Shirley Baker in the clerk's office, she told me that Julian Grant had been in earlier, and that he'd brought the signed contract between him, acting as executor for Gideon Buchanan, and Copperfield Enterprises. She said that Julian seemed very tense, and he told her that all the clerical work to complete the sale and to transfer the title needed to be handled immediately. She mentioned his left arm was in a cast, and he was wearing a sling, like he'd broken a bone.

"Shirley told me the contract was still lying on top of one of her file cabinets. It almost seemed she had intentionally left it out and was calling it to my attention. We didn't talk about it any more, but I had no difficulty spotting where Shirley had placed it, and as I walked by the file cabinet on my way out, I brushed it off the top of the cabinet with my arm, and it dropped down behind, out of sight. The contract probably won't be found until the janitor cleans the office on Friday."

"Boy, oh, boy!" Ed exclaimed softly. "We must have a bad connection. I've missed everything you've said, except for something about the janitor cleaning on Friday. I'm sure it isn't important, so don't bother to repeat it."

"You don't have to worry about that," Laura added nervously. "What should I do now?"

"I think that you better go downtown and pick out your wedding dress," Ed replied. "I'm on my way over to the courthouse to get our license."

"I know that you're just trying to keep me from getting too worked up about all of this, but I'm definitely not in the mood now for one of your attempts at humor."

"I figure if we get married, I can't be forced to testify against my wife. That sounds like a much better plan than my going home to bake you a cake with a file in it.

"Look, I know you don't need me to be joking about this. I'm confident the contract will be found within a few days, and everybody will assume that it just got knocked off accidentally. I'm sure that everything's going to turn out fine."

"That's what I wanted to hear in the first place. I was looking for some much needed reassurance from a legal professional. I'll let you go now. Anything else you want to tell me before I hang up?"

"Yeah, I can think of three things. First, don't say anything about this to anyone other than me. Second, I think you showed a lot of spunk in taking the action you did, trying to stall the fleecing of a helpless family. Third, and most importantly, I love you more than you can ever imagine."

"Do I have to get sent to Moundsville in order for you to tell me that? I'd prefer to hear it while I'm still on the outside. And it's easier when I'm not peering out from behind iron bars to tell you that I feel the same."

"I promise, you're going to hear it more. Now, would you

please repeat that last thing you just said?"

A euphoric feeling of having regained something once lost in his life came over Ed as he put down the phone. Laura had declared her feelings for him before, but each time she said it was an affirmation that the future was bright. It helped him sort out the priorities in his life, making problems seem less daunting, and giving him confidence that there would soon be a turn for the better. Catching sight of Carolyn's knowing smile, Ed shrugged helplessly and laughed.

The expected call from Earl Daniels came that afternoon. "The mug shots of Hurd and Tolliver sent by the state police have just come in. Could you come over as soon as possible and take a look at them like we discussed? No one in my office has seen anyone around this area who resembles either of them."

"I'll be over within the next couple of hours," Ed answered. "It'll only take one quick look for me to tell whether either of them is the man I saw in the truck that ran me off the road."

Ed wrapped up his work for the day, then drove across town to the sheriff's department. Inside, a young dispatcher directed him to an office across the hall where he found the sheriff sitting at his desk.

"Thanks for coming over," Earl said. He produced a brown envelope and took out two photographs. "Here they are," he continued, laying both pictures on top of his desk. "These are two fine looking fellows, I'll have to say. The one on your left is William Hurd, and the other is Jake Tolliver. They have a string of convictions as long as your arm going back twenty years, ranging from assault and armed robbery to malicious wounding and second degree murder. Each of them has served time in prison on the east coast, and both are alumni of the Moundsville State Pen. Does either of them look at all familiar to you?"

"Oh, yes," Ed replied, his voice shaking with anger. "The one on the left, I believe you said his name is Hurd, he's definitely the man that stared me right in the eye all the time his partner was forcing me off the road. He was wearing a ball cap at the time, but his face was only a few feet from mine, and I'll never forget that tough, hard-eyed look he gave me."

"You're absolutely sure that's him?"

"Sure enough to swear it on the Bible in a court of law. If you can bring him in, I'm ready to be your star witness."

"Wait'll you hear the rest of what I have to tell you," the sheriff said with a smile. "I think these two men must really have it in for you. Last week, Chief Spencer had his detectives conduct another search of the former Madison Sign facility, and he found a clue the police missed right after the fire."

"What was it?"

"He dusted the outside door face again and found a partial finger print on the door latch near the lock that was jimmied. It matches the right thumb print the FBI has on file for Jake Tolliver."

"Then you're right about who they're out for. That pair has come after me twice." He hesitated for a moment, then continued, "Both of these attacks occurred very soon after I took on Gideon Buchanan as a client. That time frame also happens to coincide with Agnes Spencer's murder."

"It's pretty clear now that these two have been involved in all three crimes," Earl stated, leaning forward in his chair. "When we bring them in, we'll find out who put them up to all of this."

"You sound pretty confident about arresting them. Don't you think that savvy career criminals like Hurd and Tolliver will stay out of sight when they learn that they're wanted?"

"They've already shown themselves to be pretty brazen, Ed, and that just might trip them up. We're working in cooperation with the state police and the FBI on this manhunt, and that puts a lot of law men on their trail."

On the way home, Ed could not help looking more closely at the people he passed, trying to identify them, reassuring himself that they were only the usual residents of his community. In the back of his mind was a nagging apprehension that he couldn't seem to shake off. Somewhere on the loose, possibly nearby, were two ex-cons intent on harming him, undoubtedly with the goal of eliminating him as an ally to the Buchanan family. When he discussed the meeting with Doug and Laura later that evening, he managed to mask his concern, but it did not go away, staying on his mind until he turned in for the night.

Laura called him late Friday morning. "The janitor found

the missing Buchanan farm sale contract behind the file cabinet when he cleaned this morning, just as we expected. Julian's been all over Shirley this week, mad as a hornet about the delay in completing the closing. I feel bad about the abuse I caused her to take, but it bought us a few more days, and I'll make it up to her somehow. The sale is being finalized this morning, and Barker will get the title to the property. He probably won't be required to give the family more than thirty days to vacate Roseanna. What in the world are we going to do now?"

"I'm not quite sure. I'm going to need to check for legal precedents, but if we can prove that Julian used his power of attorney to sell the farm as part of a criminal conspiracy against the Buchanan family, we should be able to void the contract."

"Ed, do you read anything into the strange way Julian has acted in handling the contract? Remember how we talked about him dawdling around, seemingly in no hurry to complete the sale. Then when he did bring in the papers, he acted like it was a life or death emergency to wrap everything up and get the title transferred immediately."

"I remember. We'd speculated that he might be trying to shake Copperfield and Barker down for more money, and we agreed that going up against the owner would be risky business. I doubt that it's just a coincidence Julian's wearing a cast on his arm and working full speed to wrap everything up."

"The thought of someone deliberately maiming a person, even a slimy creep like Julian, makes my skin crawl. But I don't have any trouble believing that someone as wealthy as Barker could find ruthless people willing to do that kind of dirty work for him. You've already had an encounter with two people who wouldn't bat an eye at trying to injure or kill someone."

"You're right about that. But if we're to do what we can to protect decent people like the Buchanans, I'd better get back to work now. I'll talk to you later, hon."

★

"Pull in at that diner," Hurd barked, glaring at his partner behind the wheel. "I'm ready for a few beers. We'll be in Charleston by mid-afternoon, so you don't need to be in such a damn big hurry."

"You're always ready for a few beers," Tolliver growled back. "You've been drinking 'em all the way up here, and you almost got us pulled over by a trooper when you threw that bag of empties out the window. That was stupid as hell."

The two men had been in the truck together for hours, and were all over each other's nerves. Earlier, Hurd had demanded that Tolliver stop so he could "drain his radiator" for the third time, and Tolliver had moved the truck up the road a short distance, making him walk to catch up. Hurd wanted to fight him on the spot, and as big and tough as he was, Tolliver knew better than to take on an ex-pug. "Go on inside and get your beer," Tolliver snapped. "I'm not eating at this greasy spoon."

When Hurd returned with a brown bag full of Blue Ribbons, they continued to drive up the highway without speaking a word until they reached the Charleston city limits. "Do you know where the hell you're going?" Hurd asked.

"Damn right, I do," Jake replied in a no-nonsense voice. "Julian found out she's staying at the Earl Hotel over on Railroad Avenue and Watts Street. It's a flea bag hotel for winos and working girls. The only problem is I don't know where I pick up Railroad Avenue. I guess we'll have to keep our eyes open for the railroad tracks."

After driving back and forth across the city for half an hour, Jake finally stopped to get directions. A short time later, they pulled up in front of the Earl, which looked even more run-down than Jake had described. The six story brick fire trap appeared to have been last painted some time after World War I. The windows were dirty, many covered by torn shades pulled down despite the hour of the afternoon. A neon sign in the window of the lobby read, "Vacancy-Low Rates."

At the front desk Hurd and Tolliver saw a short bald man with a stubble beard, sitting on a tall stool. He said flatly, not bothering to look their way, "Cash only- All day or half day?"

"Neither," Hurd replied. "We're looking for a woman named Agnes Harper that we know's staying here. She's about five feet tall and weighs a hundred pounds, with black, stringy hair. What room's she in?"

"Our hotel policy's not to give out any information about who's staying here. But I might make an exception, if you've got some kind of emergency," the man replied, now giving them his full attention, watching to see if a green bill would come across the counter.

"You might want to either rethink your hotel policy, or decide what you consider an emergency," Tolliver growled, leaning across the counter. "I believe having that stool you're sitting on come down across your head might be one."

The clerk moved back from the counter, all the color drained from his face. "Room 522."

Hurd and Tolliver passed up the elevator, taking the worn wooden stairs two at a time. Walking down the dark hallway, they were approached by a chunky, middle-aged woman wearing heavy makeup, a dowdy cocktail dress, and an inviting smile. "Out of the way, Grandma," Tolliver commanded, watching her smile transform into an angry scowl as they passed.

When they reached room number 522 at the end of the corridor, they could see a pay phone on the wall just outside the door, with the receiver dangling on the cord. Looking back up the hall, they spotted the woman, who had stopped to glare at them. "You're too late. She's gone," the woman called out. They were unable to hear what she muttered under her breath in a spiteful voice, "Grandma helped her go down the fire escape."

★

Ed stepped outside the door to stretch his legs, enjoying the pleasant early May weather, feeling the contrast between the warm sunlight and cool breeze. He would have stayed longer to soak up the sunshine, if Carolyn hadn't called to him. "Can you please come in here a minute, I can't understand what this woman wants."

He had to listen very closely to hear out what the woman on the line was saying in a low, distraught voice. "Mr. Housman, I need help," she began. "I can hire you as a lawyer, can't I?"

"Let's start a little more slowly, and we'll see if I can help you," Ed replied. "What's your name, and where are you calling from?"

There was a long hesitation, and the woman started to cry, answering him between sobs. "Mr. Housman, this is Agnes Harper. I can't tell you where I am now, but I'm calling you from a pay phone. The police here are looking for me, and somebody else is hunting me, too. If they find me, I'm afraid they'll kill me, just like they did Myrtle Spencer. I'm running out of money, and I don't have nobody to turn to and nowhere to go. I need help, and I knew you were a lawyer."

Ed quickly recovered from his astonishment, responding, "Agnes, why don't you go to the nearest police station, wherever you are, and turn yourself in? That way you'll have the police to protect you if someone is trying to harm you. If you're ready to come forward and tell the truth, I'll be willing to travel to the town you're calling from, and take you on as a client, pro bono. That means at no cost to you."

"Mr. Housman, it's not that easy. I'm running from some bad people, and if the local police give me over to them for any reason, I'll end up dead, just like Myrtle. I want to turn myself in to you." There was a moment of complete silence before Agnes spoke again, this time in a frightened whisper, "I can't talk no more now. I'll call you back as soon as I can."

"Hold on a minute," Ed said quickly. "Let me give you my home phone number." Just as he finished calling out the number, he heard a click, and the line went dead, leaving him to wonder if she had caught what he had said. Ed tapped his fingers on his desk, in a quandary. He realized that he should report the conversation with Agnes to Earl Daniels, but knew that he couldn't without the risk of frightening her off and never hearing from her again.

"Carolyn, would you please come in here for a minute? You need to know that the person you couldn't understand just now was Agnes Harper. She's still on the run from the law, and she thinks she's being stalked by someone who wants to silence her. She's terribly frightened, and she's begging me to act as her attorney, and more importantly, as her protector. I intend to tell the sheriff, but not until I can speak with her again, and help her make plans to turn herself in under safe conditions."

"I respect your judgment, Ed, and I'll certainly do as you ask. But from my years of experience in a law office, I can't help but question why you're withholding this information from the sheriff. It concerns me that you may be creating a serious problem for yourself later when this all comes to light."

"I value your opinion, Carolyn. But the stakes are so high in trying to get Agnes to come in without doing anything to spook her off, I'm willing to risk a reprimand later. I don't plan to keep this information from the law indefinitely. I only want to hold off long enough to give her a chance to call back and plan to surrender at a time and place where she'll be safe, and I can advise her.'

"You're the boss. I'll keep everything you've told me about Agnes in strict confidence, and just hope she gets back to you soon."

At home Ed got much the same reaction from Doug. "I understand what you're doing, Dad, and why it's so important to be sure Agnes stays safe, but when I look at how involved you've become with the Buchanan family, it reminds me of the Uncle Remus story about Br'er Rabbit and the Tar Baby. You keep touching it, and each time it sticks to you a little tighter, 'til finally you can't let go."

"You show remarkable insight for a sixteen-year old," Ed replied, laughing for the first time of the day. "Let's try to get our minds on something else for a while. Time magazine and The Saturday Evening Post both came today. We can flip a coin to see who gets to read which."

But even Time and the Post failed to keep their thoughts from the phone, which stubbornly refused to ring, and finally they went off to bed, still wondering where a terrified Agnes might be hiding out in a strange town under the cover of darkness.

Chapter 30

A T WORK on Saturday morning, Doug watched as Ingrid switched on the overhead lights, then began putting money into the cash register, readying the check-out line for business. "Good morning, Doug," she said, glancing up at him. "Mr.Vicelli is back at the loading dock, receiving a truckload of fresh produce. You may want to go back there and get started by giving him a hand."

"Yes, m'am, I'll go back there right now and see how he wants me to help." Fidgeting for a few seconds, Doug got up his nerve, and inquired, "Mrs. Vicelli, can I ask you a question? I'm taking Vickie to the spring dance next Saturday, and I wanted to surprise her with a corsage. Dad said I need to know what kind of flowers she likes and what color dress she'll be wearing before I can place an order with the florist."

"That's sweet of you, Doug," Ingrid replied, closing the cash register and giving him her full attention. "Vickie has always liked the fragrance of gardenias, so they would make a nice choice for her. As for the corsage color, I went shopping with her last week and helped her pick out a pretty powder blue satin dress for the dance, so white gardenias would be perfect. Is that what you needed to know?"

"Yes, m'am, it sure is. I've never taken a girl to a school dance before, and all of this is new to me." Turning toward the back of the store, Doug noticed that Sandra had come in and was absorbing every detail, ready to give a full report to her big sister. "Hi, Sandra," he said as he walked past her.

"Hi, Doug," she replied, following his progress down the center aisle with wide eyes.

When it was time for Ingrid to take a break, Sandra took over the cash register. She began checking out customer purchases quickly in an experienced manner that surprised and impressed Doug, who was now bagging with the speed born of recent practice.

"How'd you manage to learn all the different prices and to ring up groceries so fast?" he asked with genuine curiosity. "I'm pretty fair at math, but I couldn't remember what everything costs, and I sure couldn't check out people nearly as fast as you do."

Sandra glanced at him, blushing, appreciating both the attention and the compliment. "I've been helping out here since last year. After you do this for a while, you memorize what a lot of our stocked items sell for. When it comes to ringing them up and making change, I'm not as fast as Mom yet, but I'm almost as good as Vickie."

Ingrid returned to take over the cash register a short time later. When there was a break in the steady line of customers, she confided, "I probably shouldn't tell you this, but Sandra has developed a crush on you. You seem to have become quite popular with both of my daughters."

"I'm really surprised," Doug replied, his face turning red. "Sandra's a pretty girl, and I'm sure she gets a lot of attention from the boys in the eighth grade."

Sensing acceptance by the women in the Vicelli family gave Doug a warm feeling. After losing his mother, he had lived in a men only world for four years, until Laura, Vickie, and her family had come into his life, and things were definitely better now. He was unaware of the growing self confidence showing in his demeanor, but Ingrid could see it, and she hid a smile when she glanced at him from time to time.

Throughout the morning, Doug waited for the sight of Vickie bouncing through the door, but his hopes were dashed when he later learned from Sandra that that she was visiting a cousin in Pearisburg for the weekend. It was the only downside to an upbeat day on the job.

At home, he caught up with JR in the back yard. The dog rolled about in canine ecstasy as Doug scratched his belly, barking in disappointment when he stopped. Moving into the house, he turned on the radio to his favorite music station and caught the last part of Rosemary Clooney's *Half As Much*, before going upstairs to shower.

Returning downstairs, Doug saw that his dad had dinner warming on the top of the stove. "Carolyn sent us over a chicken pot pie," Ed commented. "Better enjoy it, 'cause we don't get this kind of home cooking often."

"I definitely will. That was one of Mom's best dishes." Over dinner, Doug remarked, "I'm going to get Vickie a white gardenia corsage at the florist for the dance next Saturday. How much do you think that will that set me back?"

"Probably half of your wages for a Saturday's work. But flowers for a girlfriend are about the best investment you can make. You'll find out what I'm talking about when you go by her house to pick her up for the dance. The way to a man's heart may be through chicken pot pie, but flowers work a lot better with the ladies."

As they were busily scraping the last of morsels of food from their dinner plates, Ed mentioned, "I heard from a couple of people while you were at work today. Dr. Jannsen called to give me some good news. He said that Gideon Buchan's mind is a world clearer this week, and that he's hopeful that he'll soon be back to normal.

"And later I got a call from Sam Barry. He told me he's having trouble lining up chaperones for your school dance, and he's starting to get desperate. He asked if Laura and I would be willing to help out. I checked with Laura to get her OK, and called Sam back to tell him we'd both be willing to pitch in. Looks like we'll be there with you, and finally get to meet Miss Vicelli, whom you've told me so much about."

"I'm afraid you really got conned by Mr. Barry. None of the other parents want to be chaperones for school dances. You and Mrs. Jackson ought to get some kind of award. There are a few jerks that will be there, but I guess that isn't much different from when you were going to high school. But on the plus side, it'll give me a chance to introduce both of you to Vickie. I think you'll like her."

"What do boys and girls wear to school dances these days? I haven't heard you talk about renting a white dinner jacket or tux to go formal."

"The girls will all be wearing party dresses. The guys will wear suits or sport coats and slacks, but definitely no tuxes. None of the high schools go formal for their dances. The senior class planned everything. They've lined up Tommy Martin and his Mountaineer Band, who sound pretty good. Are you ready to take Mrs. Jackson out on the dance floor for a spin, without stepping all over her feet?"

"I'll never be confused with Fred Astaire, but I've had Laura on the dance floor before, and she didn't need steel-toe safety shoes. I'm actually looking forward to being there. Who knows, we just may have a better time next week than you kids."

"Don't have too good a time," Doug admonished him. "All my friends will be watching." Ed laughed, tossing a dish towel at his head.

"You worked today. Why don't you take the night off and do something you enjoy, while I clean up the dishes? What are your buddies up to tonight?"

"Mike and Ginny're going to the drive-in to see *Strangers On A Train*. It's an Alfred Hitchcock movie with a lot of suspense that played at the Lyric downtown last year. They invited me to go, but I found out Vickie's out of town for the weekend. Guess I'll take JR out for a run in the open field next to Wilson's Pond."

When Doug opened the door, JR bounded out, wagging his tail. He ran ahead with the energy of a dog that has been confined all day, but repeatedly trotted back to be sure Doug was still following behind him. Abandoned once, JR was determined not to let it happen again.

They walked to Wilson's Pond, idling away an hour near the water, Doug watching a heron stalking his dinner, and JR tearing around in circles, flushing frogs on the bank and leaping into the air after snake doctors. JR was panting heavily and his tongue was hanging out, as they made their way back to the house and went inside.

"I got the phone call I've been waiting for while you were

gone," Ed said. "Agnes didn't stay on the line long, but she managed to tell me that she's lined up a ride with a person she trusts who's coming through town next Sunday. She'll call back to let me know when she arrives, and where to meet her. That's about all of the information I could get out of her over the phone. I suppose a woman who thinks she's being stalked by someone out to hurt her can't be expected to say much more than that."

"Have you forgotten that next Saturday night you'll be out of the house, chaperoning the dance? If Agnes calls during that time to tell you she's changed her plans, how will she reach you? JR hasn't learned how to handle phone calls yet."

"That crossed my mind. I don't expect that Agnes will call while I'm out Saturday night, but to be safe, I've asked Carolyn if she'll come over to be close to the phone until I get home. Sam's OK with Laura and me leaving a little before the dance breaks up."

"Where in the world will Agnes stay out of sight after you meet with her, until you take her to the sheriff's department to turn herself in?"

"We already have that base covered. There's an out of the way motel on the edge of town that Laura has used for business clients. She'll help me get Agnes checked in there very discreetly."

"Sounds like y'all have a plan worked out. But one thing worries me. I'm afraid that something bad might happen to you. Why are you putting yourself right in the middle of all of this mess?"

"It's a calculated risk, son. If things go our way, we may be able to help solve some serious crimes, and at the same time possibly save the Buchanan farm, and preserve the valley. And if things go wrong, we'll have to deal with the consequences. There are times when you can't be certain you're doing the right thing, and you have to go with your gut instinct. Just hold the good thought that everything will turn out for the best."

"I've been holding that good thought for quite a while now, but I'm still worried about you, and want you to be careful." Doug wrapped his arms around his father, as he had not done since his mother's death. Ed held him close, inhaling the fresh air scent of his hair, and physically registering how his lanky arms and legs had stretched out over the past months. His gentle-hearted boy was becoming a compassionate man.

Later, Ed switched off the lights in the living room, and turned in for the night. He spent the next hour lying in bed, staring at the ceiling, deep in thought, before he finally dropped off to sleep. He did not stir until a beam of sunlight, sneaking past the edge of the window shade and touching his face, delivered him into Sunday morning.

By the time he had had eaten breakfast and scanned the newspaper, Ed decided that it was high time for everyone else to be up and around, and got Laura on the line. "This is your 8:00 AM wake-up call, m'am."

"Honey, you must be totally out of your mind to call this early on my day off," she replied, yawning. "Can't you find something in the morning paper to entertain yourself until a decent hour, before you start phoning a working girl trying to catch up on her sleep?"

"I was just giving you the courteous wake-up service of a five star hotel. The reason for my call is above reproach. I've decided it's high time that you experience one of Rev. Seymour's inspirational sermons, and I am hereby inviting you to attend the morning service with Doug and me."

Laura hesitated, and he knew she was desperately searching for a good excuse to decline. "You sure waited 'til the last minute to ask me, Houseman." Trying to suppress a laugh, she continued, "I happen to be a devout Presbyterian, and we tend to look upon some of your Methodist teachings with amazement and skepticism. Having said that, I can identify two other problems: I have to wash my hair and get dressed, and that will take me a while. Most importantly, if people in your congregation see us together in church, particularly when accompanied by your son, they may think you're getting serious about me, and I have no desire to mislead them."

"In my profession of legal mumbo jumbo, rebuttals are my forte. And in this matter, you must permit me to defend myself. You'll have more than enough time this morning to make yourself beautiful. As I recall, back in April, you cleaned up nice and quick in Bluestone Lake. And if people who see us together in church think that I have serious intentions toward you, they're only displaying normal common sense. If it's all right, Doug and I'll come by and pick you up at 10:00." Then he added. "The reason I'm coming by a few minutes early is to tell you about something that came up yesterday that I'd prefer not to discuss on the phone."

Hanging up, he called out to Doug. "We're going to give Rev. Seymour the chance to save another soul this morning. Laura's going to church with us."

Both got out of the car at Laura's apartment, with Ed heading to the front door, and Doug shifting to the back seat. Before he could ring the bell, Laura opened the door, wearing a fitted dark blue dress and matching blue hat and heels.

"You look incredible, Laura. Even more glamorous than when you waded out of the water and crawled up on the bank at Bluestone Lake. In fact, you look like you stepped out of the pages of Vogue. May I come in for a few minutes and talk with you? Doug is going to wait for us out in the car."

Ed quickly described Agnes' latest appeal, and Laura fell in with his plans, not hesitating to offer her help. Walking beside Ed to the car and waiting while he held the door open for her, Laura spoke to Doug.

"You look pretty this morning, Mrs. Jackson," he commented as she slipped into the front seat.

She replied with a smile, "Thanks for the nice compliment. But I'd prefer to have you call me Laura. I'm glad you'll be sitting beside me this morning, helping me stay on the right page in the hymn book."

After the service, Ed stopped to introduce Rev. Seymour to Laura. "Good to meet you, Mrs. Jackson," Rev. Seymour said. "I hope you'll be attending often."

"We'll both have to work on her to get her back here, Tom," Ed interjected. "John Wesley himself would have had a tough time saving these Presbyterians."

At the Eden Springs Resort, they found a table beside a window with a view of the mineral spring spa. Laura looked across the table at Doug, saying, "I understand you're taking a very nice young lady to the spring dance this coming Saturday night, and that your dad and I will get to meet her."

"Yes, m'am," Doug replied. "I told her Mr. Barry had twisted your arms and signed y'all up to be chaperones. She's looking forward to meeting you, too."

During lunch, Ed suggested, "If no one's in any hurry, let's go by and look at the mineral springs after we finish eating. I haven't been inside the spa for a long time."

Later, they walked over to the round brick and frame building enclosing the mineral springs pool with almost a full circle of long windows. Entering through a wide glass-paned door, they found the pool flooded with sunlight. A three-tiered white concrete bench for bathers ran its circumference. However, today there were no guests to be seen, and it only took a quick glance to understand why. Unlike the last time any of the three had been there, when the mineral spring water had been crystal clear, today the pool was a muddy clay color.

An elderly man walked through the door into the pool area and joined them. "My wife and I have been coming here for years. We arrived from Baltimore last week, and hadn't been around but two days before muddy water started showing up in the pool. I hear some mining company's been blasting along a creek, and they think that's what's causing the problem. Whatever's going on, we're checking out in the morning, and never coming back."

On the way home, Ed observed, "It's obvious that the resort is starting to feel the impact of Barker Mining coming into our area. That's why the battle for ownership of the Buchanan property is so critical. If we can stop Barker from mining those 2500 acres, he won't be able to get enough coal on the smaller tracts to cover his costs, and he'll have to pull out for economic reasons. But if he gets control of the Buchanan farm, he'll have a major strip mine operation by this time next year, and muddy mineral springs will just be one of the problems. The tourism business in Eden Springs will be history."

"I think we'd all be hurt if Barker takes over the valley," Laura concurred. 'The value of real estate in Eden Springs would take a big hit. I'd prefer not to even think what it would be like."

Back at Laura's apartment, Ed walked beside her up the steps to the porch. Standing at her front door, Ed leaned in for a kiss, then wrapped a glossy red curl around one finger to draw her closer for a longer, more satisfying one.

As he walked down the steps, Laura called out to him, "Ed, we can't afford to lose our confidence now. Some way or another, we're going save the Buchanan farm and keep Barker out.

Don't forget, there's a lot of us of us in this fight with you."

In the car, Doug spoke up, "I like Laura. Don't wait too long, Dad. I don't think you'll find another woman who can hold a candle to her."

"I know what you're telling me. The more I'm around her, the more I see a lot of the same wonderful qualities your mother had. You don't run into many people like that in a lifetime. Sometime soon I've got to find the right opportunity to have a very important talk with her."

Chapter 31

ED WAS engaged in a friendly conversation with the waitress at the drug store lunch counter on Friday when he felt a tap on his shoulder. Turning around, he watched as Dr. Jannsen took the stool beside him. "Good morning, Ed. Carolyn told me I'd find you here having lunch, so I decided to come over. There's a new development regarding the Buchanan family that I wanted to discuss with you. Do you mind if I join you? "

"Please do. It's good to see you again. What's going on at Roseanna? I've been so busy this past week that I've lost track of what's happening out there."

"I've received a report from Gertrude telling me that Julian Grant is helping Barker Mining evict the Buchanans from their home. This morning, Julian drove out to their house, and called Daniel and Jonah into Gideon's bedroom. Gertrude insisted on staying with them, knowing Julian can't be trusted. He announced that the farm, including the family home, had been sold, and that they would have to vacate the premises and move into town before the end of the month. The sons became extremely agitated, and a shouting match broke out.

"Their voices seemed to jolt Gideon back to his senses, and he joined his sons in taking on Julian, ordering him off the property. Julian must have realized that he was getting nowhere, and might have feared he could have his other arm broken if the sons got any angrier, so he left. The disappointing thing is that Gideon slumped back into confusion almost as soon as Julian was out of the house."

"What do we do now? We haven't gotten anywhere if he continues to come and go."

"I realize that. But Gertrude said she hasn't seen him as completely lucid in all the time she's been caring for him. She feels like he made a breakthrough, even if only for a brief time. To her, it was as if the emotional outburst by his sons triggered a boost of adrenalin that temporarily cleared his mind. She's going to have the boys continue talking to him, and see how he responds. I have a gut feeling that he's turned the corner. I've had more than one patient snap out of a coma, as if someone threw a switch."

"If you can bring him back to his senses, everything is all set for us to help him regain control. You and Gertrude are perfect witnesses. Laura is a licensed Notary of the Public, and she could validate the signatures on the new will and power of attorney. Both of those documents are in my glovebox, available at the drop of a hat. We'd have everything we need to petition that the farm sale contract be nullified."

As they left the lunch counter together, with no one standing nearby, Ed decided to lay all the cards on the table. "Something very important has come up that you need to know. Agnes Harper called and told me she's coming back to town this Sunday. She's been hiding out from both the police and a stalker. When she arrives, I told her I'd meet her, take her to the sheriff's office to turn herself in, and act as her lawyer."

Dr. Jannsen responded, "We seem to have reached a critical juncture in the battle over the Buchanan property. It's obvious that we're dealing with people who will go to any lengths to get that land. It would be wise for both of us not to let down our guard for a minute. Please call me right away if you learn anything new."

At the end of the day, Ed briefed Carolyn on how to reach him before leaving. At home, Doug was on the living room floor wrestling with JR, full of weekend high spirits.

"Did you have time to go by the cleaners and pick up my suit and your sport coat?" Ed called out to him.

"I sure did. And while I was downtown, I stopped by the

florist and got the gardenia corsage for Vickie. It set me back quite a bit of hard earned money, but you told me that buying it for her was a good idea. Would you like to see it?" Pushing JR away, he went to the fridge and took out a white box, handing it to his dad.

"The florist helped you make a nice selection," Ed remarked, picking up the unmistakeable floral fragrance coming from the box. "I believe Vickie will be very pleased to have you pin that gardenia on before you leave for the dance."

"I've never done anything like that before. I sure hope I don't get shaky hands, and stick her with that long pin. It's almost the size of a knitting needle."

"You'll do just fine," Ed reassured him, grinning. "We Housman men are noted for having steady hands when working to close tolerances on delicate projects."

"I hope you're right," Doug replied. "But I'll be a lot more relaxed when this project's complete."

Ed was just starting dinner, when he was interrupted by Laura, calling to tell him about her day. "I got a note in the mail today from Dan Wohlford. He apologized for what he called his 'earlier inappropriate persistence,' and he asked whether we could start off on a new foot."

"I hope you're not going to reopen that can of worms. And besides, you're 'spoken for' now, as the locals say. How do you plan to answer him?"

"I don't plan to respond to him at all. I just tore up the note. Has anything happened that will change our plans for the weekend?"

"No, everything seems to be going along just the way we expected." Then remembering that he had promised Doug the family car to drive Vickie, Mike, and Ginny, he inquired mischievously, "What time will you be by to pick me up for the dance?"

"I'll come by about 7:00. Are you expecting me to bring you a carnation boutonnière?"

"No, you can hold the flower this time. But I hope you'll come to the door to get me, and not sit out in the driveway and blow the horn like you usually do.

"Anyway, thanks for picking me up. It means a lot to Doug to be able to drive, and I couldn't let him have the Ford if you weren't such a good sport." Then, before he hung up, Ed added, "I think I'm looking forward to the dance tomorrow night as much as the kids, just being there with you."

"Me, too, honey," she agreed.

Seeing Doug through the window, tossing an old, bald tennis ball for JR to retrieve, Ed stepped to the door to ask, "You're working tomorrow, aren't you? If you'd like, I'll wash and simonize the car in the morning, so it'll look sharp when you go pick up your date."

"That would be nice, Dad," Doug called back. "I'm getting off at 3:00, but wouldn't have much time to clean the car up. I was just planning to take it the way it looks now."

A little later, Ed and Doug went upstairs for the night, and JR stretched out on a scatter rug beside Doug's bed. The town was quiet enough to be the setting for a Norman Rockwell cover on the weekly Post. As the courthouse clock chimed ten o'clock, the few remaining lights flickered out like fireflies. It seemed as if the sidewalks had been rolled up, and the world had shut down until sunrise would signal the start of another day.

Chapter 32

DOUG INHALED the familiar smell of freshly ground coffee inside the front door of the market on Saturday morning. He spotted Sandra busily stocking brown paper bags under the check out counter. "Vickie won't be in today," she said, smiling at him, her cheeks turning a light pink. "She has an appointment at the beauty parlor to get her hair done for the dance."

Doug had liked Sandra from the first day he had met her at the store. She was like the cute kid sister he had often imagined having. Sandra was even shyer than he, making her the perfect target for his good natured ribbing. "Do you think I need a permanent wave for tonight?" he said, holding up a handful of short red hair on top of his head. "I want to have a curly mop top just like you."

Sandra laughingly countered, "That hair's way too short for curlers or anything else. You'd better just leave it the way it is, straight as a stick. I'm araid that you'll never be able to have pretty curls like mine."

Doug spent most of the day bagging groceries for the steady stream of customers moving through the store. It was almost time for him to call it a day when he overheard a man talking to Tony.

"Sheriff Daniels and both of his deputies are out south of town right now," the man reported. "Someone's been setting brush fairs in that wooded area next to the furniture factory, and the wind's driving the flames toward the buildings."

Checking out with his boss, and happily tossing his apron into a box, Doug left the store and walked home. He could spot the maroon Ford sitting in the driveway as he approached the house, the sun reflecting off of the fresh coat of simonize wax. Seeing his father sprawled out on the couch with the sports page in his lap, he called out appreciatively, "You did a great job, Dad. The car looks like new."

"Glad you approve," Ed replied. "I didn't realize how dirty the car was until I got started, and then the job ended up taking me two hours. What time are you leaving to go pick up your friends?"

"I'll probably take off around 7:00. I think you told me that was the time Laura's coming by for you, so maybe I'll see her before I go." Then remembering the conversation at the market just before he left work, Doug added, "I think there's some excitement this afternoon, near one of the furniture factories. Some man came into the store and said there was a fire bug setting brush fires, and that the sheriff and his deputies were all out there investigating. That's about all I know about it."

When Doug glanced at the clock a short time later, he saw that the time had slipped up on him, and he hurried to put on his newly dry-cleaned sport coat and slacks, fresh white shirt, and best tie, run a comb through his hair, and splash a little Old Spice on his boyishly smooth face.

Ed had already dressed and gone downstairs. Looking out the front window, he saw Laura step out of the car, dressed in a pale yellow cocktail dress. As she came up to the front door, Ed called out, "Please come on in. I want you to meet my parents before I go out with you tonight."

"I'm not buying that," Laura replied, stepping inside. "You told me they've retired to Florida, so I'll have to get acquainted with them another time. Is Doug around?"

"He's still upstairs getting dressed, running late as usual. I think I detected a little of his Old Spice drifting down the steps a few minutes ago. You'll see him at the dance." Following Laura toward the door, Ed called out, "Doug, we're getting ready to leave now. Drive carefully tonight."

Ed walked toward Laura with his hand behind his back, and with a sudden flourish produced a white florist box, handing it to her.

"You didn't need to get this for me," Laura exclaimed, seeing the white orchid inside. "After all, I'm a chaperone tonight, not a high school date for the dance."

"I decided to get it for you this afternoon," Ed replied. "Chaperone or not, you're prettier than any high school girl who'll be there tonight. And after I heard Doug go on and on about the danger and excitement of pinning a corsage on a new girlfriend, I just didn't want to miss out. Can I do that now?"

"Ah, the Irish charm is definitely back," Laura replied. "Please pin it on. This goes a long way toward making amends for comparing me to your pet chicken when we were at Bluestone Lake. I think I'll even let you drive tonight."

"Couldn't we just go park somewhere out on Queen's Knob Road tonight and neck?" Ed grinned.

"Behave yourself, Housman, at least for the time being. Remember, tonight we're chaperones, in case you're starting to forget."

Doug caught a glimpse of his dad and Laura through the window as they drove away. Hurrying downstairs, he remembered to pick up the corsage from the refrigerator before dashing out the front door and slipping behind the wheel of the newly waxed car. Switching to a favorite song on the radio, he sang along with Joni James on the way across town to the Vicelli home, and for once, did not relive the encounter with Len Hacker as he turned into their driveway. Feeling like he was in the vicinity of cloud nine, Doug got out of the car, with the corsage in his hand, and walked to the porch.

Sandra appeared before he had time to ring the bell and led him into the living room. Tony and Ingrid glanced up as he entered. Both gave him a friendly hello, seeming to enjoy the timeless scene of a nervous young man appearing to escort their daughter to a high school dance.

When she entered, Doug caught his breath. Dressed in a powder blue sheath dress, powdered and lipsticked, with her long blonde hair swept up, Vickie looked like a model, far older than her sixteen years. And with high heels, she stood every bit as tall as Doug, despite his efforts to stretch his five foot nine inch frame as high as it would go. When he spoke, the best he could manage was, "Hi, Vickie. I brought you a corsage."

It was fortunate that Vickie had been out with other boys before, and was able to lead. Taking the box from Doug, and admiring the flower, she handed the gardenia back to him and asked, "Would you pin it on me?"

Under the steady gaze of both Vicelli parents, and younger sister Sandra, Doug took the corsage in one hand and the long, pearl tipped pin in the other, and successfully pinned the gardenia on the bodice of her dress in one easy motion. He knew that it was purely beginner's luck, but no one else seemed to catch on to that. His boss even commented, "Doug's got good dexterity with his hands, Ingrid. The first time I pinned a flower on you, I recall I stuck you pretty good."

Ingrid and Sandra followed them to the front door, watching as Doug helped Vickie into the car. On the way to Mike's house, he finally found his voice. "You sure look pretty tonight."

She smiled at him. "Thanks. And I think you look like a college boy in that coat and tie."

Mike was waiting outside when they drove up, and he slipped into the back seat. When they pulled up in front of the Johnson home, he jumped out with a corsage box in his hand and disappeared into the house. When he reappeared, Ginny was holding on to his arm, her mother following, snapping pictures of them with a flash camera. Ginny was wearing a bright red party dress and appeared to be in her usual high spirits. "I'm ready to get the party started now," she called out as Mike opened the car door for her.

"I still don't know what she sees in you, Mike," Doug cracked, glancing into the rear view mirror to see his reaction, and feeling an immediate light slap on the back of his head.

"Anybody have a tissue?" Ginny asked on the way across town. "Mike's got some red spots on his face again."

"I have a lot of trouble with that," Mike grinned. "It seems like a skin condition that pops up every time I get in the back seat with you."

"Vickie, check in the glove box," Doug suggested. "Dad usually keeps a box of Kleenex in there."

When Vickie opened the glove box, she discovered a manila envelope on top of the jumble of maps and papers inside. Taking it out, she found the box of tissues, and handed them across the back seat to Mike. Then, about to put the envelope back, she glanced at it and read aloud the three lines typed on the front: Gideon Buchanan, Last Will and Testament, Power of Attorney.

Doug exclaimed, "Holy cow! For weeks now, Dad's been carrying that envelope around with him everywhere he goes. He said he might need it at anytime, on short notice. I bet he forgot I'd be driving his car this evening. But it seems pretty unlikely anything will come up where he'll need it before tomorrow."

At the hotel, the parking lot had already started to fill. Looking down the row of automobiles closest to the building, Doug saw a white Olds wagon marked Jackson Realty and pulled in beside it. Vickie stepped out of the car, taking his arm, and walked carefully in her high heels across the uneven pavement, following Mike and Ginny to the front door. Inside, they were greeted by Patty Stanley, a member of the school dance committee and a senior cheerleader. "We have a souvenir dance card for you," she said. "Have a great time tonight."

Candles flickered on white linen covered tables spread about the room. An elegant crystal chandelier cast sparkling reflections across the shiny hardwood floor. Above the bandstand, a sign in silver glitter proclaimed the band to be Tommy Martin and the Mountaineers.

Spotting their friends, the two young couples made their way over to the far side of the room, where Ronnie, Barbara Ann, Wayne, Mary Pat, Freddie, and Shirley were holding four seats for them. "About time y'all got here," Freddie said, as they walked up. "We've had a lot of other people in our class asking if they could move over here to sit with us."

"Thanks for looking out for us," Doug replied. Catching Vickie's attention, he added, "Dad and his friend, Mrs. Jackson, are sitting at a table tonight with Mr. Barry and the new home ec teacher, Miss Allison. I promised them I'd bring you by so they could meet you. Can we go talk to them now?"

The two found his dad and Laura sitting alone at their table, talking over the background noise of the excited young people surrounding them.

"Vickie, I'd like for you to meet my dad and Mrs. Jackson. They're acting as chaperones, with Mr. Barry and some other teachers here tonight. Dad, Mrs. Jackson, this is my date, Vickie Vicelli."

Ed and Laura both pushed their chairs back and stood, smiling. Ed greeted her, "Miss Vicelli, I've been looking forward to meeting you. You look very lovely tonight."

Laura added, "I keep asking Doug to call me Laura, and you're welcome to do the same. May I call you Vickie? Why don't you two sit down and visit with us for a few minutes?"

"Thank you, Mrs. Jackson, I mean Laura" Vickie replied. "I'm glad to meet both of you." After the four sat, she inquired, "Does this seem like the dances you went to when you were going to high school?"

"I think Ed would agree that the clothing styles, dance steps, and music have definitely changed, but the sight of high school students having the time of their life is about the same," Laura replied, with a laugh. "Tell me, are you two in most of the same classes together?"

"Yes, m'am. Doug's a math whiz, and he's been giving me help with my geometry. Both of us do pretty well in English class, but neither of us seems to be much of a Latin scholar."

"But she made a higher grade on the last Latin test than I did," Doug interjected. "All in all, we both do OK in school, but neither of us is going to beat out Shirley Martin for class valedictorian."

Ed commented, "I understand that your mother is Dr. Jannsen's daughter. He's told me about his granddaughter who goes to Tyler High, and he's obviously very proud of you. He and I've become close friends in recent months."

"I know. He told Mom he has a lot of respect for you. He said you were doing everything you could to help two of his patients, Mr. and Mrs. Buchanan, keep from losing their home. My dad's been making special grocery deliveries to them for years, and Doug has started helping him on Saturdays."

As the band began to warm up, Doug stood to pull Vickie's chair back for her. "I guess we'd better get back to our friends before the music starts."

"I'm glad I got to meet both of you tonight," Vickie said,

smoothing down the front of her satin dress.

"We're glad we finally got to meet you," Laura replied, unconsciously speaking for Ed as well as herself. "Doug, you look quite handsome, and Vickie, you're definitely the prettiest girl here."

As Doug and Vickie walked away holding hands, Laura looked at Ed. "I don't think I've ever seen a boy and girl having a better time than they are tonight."

While the two teenagers wove their way through a sea of crinoline-puffed skirts and freshly pressed sport coats, Tommy Martin and his five piece band opened with their first set of the evening. As soon as Ed heard the first bars of *Deep Purple,* he stood and asked, "Mrs. Jackson, may I have this dance?"

"I'd be delighted, Mr. Housman," Laura replied, leading him out on the floor to join the high school couples. Feeling Ed pull her in tightly against him during the dance, pressing his face against her cheek, she laughed and said quietly, "Honey, remember that we're supposed to be here as chaperones, setting an example for the kids. You'd better save some of your dance moves until we're in a more private setting. It wouldn't be good if the chaperones had to be sent to the principal's office for inappropriate behavior."

For both Ed and Laura, the spring dance created a feeling of déjà vu. They could remember high school dances from the late twenties, with crepe paper decorations on the walls and streamers overhead, a live band playing the popular tunes of the day, and young people dancing the Charleston. The Tyler students in the ballroom seemed very similar to friends they had known growing up, likeable and well mannered teenagers enjoying their first boy-girl relationships.

"Do you get the same feeling that you've lived this evening before?" Ed asked.

"Yes, I do. And I'm reminded of the nice boy next door in Parkersburg who took me to my first school dance when I was the same age as Vickie. He ended up flying a B24 Liberator during the war."

Before the evening was over, two of the boys in the senior class, Willie Newman, and his accomplice, Harry Sutphin, demonstrated why they had been voted "class clown" and "teacher's poet" in the high school yearbook, Willie, tall and skinny, wearing his trademark baggy pleated pants, and Harry, with long black hair slicked straight back with Brylcream, had smuggled in a pint of gin that they had been saving since Willie's parents' New Year's Eve party. By the time Sam Barry caught sight of them, the bottle had been emptied into the ancient crystal bowl, mixing with several gallons of fruit punch. Sam quickly decided that the new blend would contain only a hint of hard liquor, and turned his back, trying to keep from laughing. Something like this had happened almost every year since he had joined the faculty and become the senior class sponsor. It was now as much of a Tyler school year end tradition as taking the wheels off Principal Norman Stoner's car, and leaving it in the parking lot up on cinder blocks.

When the band played *Tell Me Why*, Doug took Vickie out on the floor. At first, he felt much more self conscious with Vickie as his partner than he had when dancing with Ginny at the canteen. Ginny kidded around with him, making him feel relaxed. Holding the taller Vickie, who in high heels stood eye to eye with him, Doug had the uncomfortable sensation that he was a beginner in an advanced dance class. Sensing his nervousness, she laughed, telling him, "Relax, and enjoy the music. Don't you think the band sounds great?" At the same time, she moved in closer to him.

Her reassurance did wonders for his self confidence, and his tension evaporated. By the time the band was into their second set, and he and Vickie were dancing to *You Belong To Me*, Doug was holding her closely, feeling her blond hair against his cheek, oblivious to everything around him.

As the song ended, and he walked with Vickie back to their table, he saw his dad approaching. Taking Doug aside, Ed said quietly, "Something unexpected's come up, and I'm going to have to leave right away. Carolyn phoned from our house and said that I should get out to the Buchanans' as soon as possible. She got a call from a visitor we weren't expecting until tomorrow, saying she'd arrived early and is there now. Apparently Dr. Jannsen is also heading that way, too. I've already informed Sam Barry that Laura and I have an emergency and have to go."

"Do you need the car?" Doug asked. "We can find a ride home with our friends."

"No, we'll take Laura's station wagon. I'll call you at home later if we get tied up out there. I hope it won't be too late when I get in. Hang a lantern in the upstairs window for me."

Watching as his dad and Laura left the room, Doug took Vickie's arm and walked beside her back to their seats.

"I hope there's nothing wrong," she said, looking at him inquiringly.

"I don't think so. I'll tell you about it in a few minutes when it's not so noisy and we can talk without shouting."

The band took a break shortly afterwards, and the room became noticeably quieter. Doug leaned closer to Vickie, saying, "Dad said something unexpected had come up, and he and Laura were leaving to go out to the Buchanan's house. He mentioned that your grandfather was already on his way there. I'm not sure exactly what's going on, but it must be something pretty important for them to take off like they did."

"Doug, do you remember that brown envelope we found in the glove box of your dad's car? It held important papers for the Buchanans, like a will and something called 'a power of attorney.' If some emergency has just come up with that family, and Granddaddy has rushed out there, don't you think your dad may need that envelope tonight? Shouldn't we try to take it to him?"

"You may be right. I wish I'd thought about that envelope before Dad left, but it never crossed my mind. Would you be willing to stay here with Mike and Ginny until I get back? If something holds me up, y'all could ride home in the back seat of Freddie's car."

"I want to go with you," Vickie said. "Granddaddy's out there, too. I promise to take responsibility if Daddy finds out about this. I'll tell him you didn't want me to come along. But we should get back before the dance breaks up, if we leave right now."

After telling Mike and Ginny about their plans, Doug and Vickie walked unobtrusively to the door and out to the car. As they pulled out and headed north, she slipped over beside him and turned on the car radio, dialing in a music station. The song that was playing was the familiar theme from the movie they had seen together on their first date, *High Noon.* "I wonder if Dad and Laura have had time to get there yet," he wondered.

Five miles away, Ed and Laura approached Roseanna. They could make out Dr. Jannsen's Buick sedan parked in front of the house beside Gertrude Estep's old Plymouth coupe. A dim light filtered through the glass in the front door, and two windows near the back of the house, where Ed knew Gideon's bedroom was located.

Daniel and Jonah were standing beside the front door, as Ed carefully helped Laura up the porch steps in her high heels "Agnes is back here," Daniel said to Ed. "She says she won't talk to nobody but you."

Passing through the front door, Ed was startled to see Agnes standing just inside, looking like a woman on the verge of a nervous breakdown, with dark circles under her eyes, stringy hair, and seemingly twenty pounds lighter than he had last seen her. "Thank God you're here, Mr. Housman. Can we talk somewhere off to ourselves?" she implored.

"Would you please leave us here alone for a few minutes," Ed asked the two men. Hearing their heavy footsteps fading away, he said, "Agnes, this is Mrs. Jackson, who knows everything that's been going on. She's helped me find a safe place for you to stay until you're ready to go to the sheriff. You can trust her completely."

Speaking in a tear-choked voice, Agnes said, "Mr. Housman, whoever is trying to track me down found out I was staying at a hotel in Charleston. I had to get out right away, and I wouldn't have made it if a woman working there hadn't help me go down a fire escape. The woman got a truck driver to give me a ride this morning, and he dropped me off an hour ago on the highway down at the end of the road in front of the house. I'm afraid the woman who got me the lift will end up selling me out to the people who're hunting me."

"We're not going to stay here long, Agnes," Ed reassured her. "Mrs. Jackson and I will be driving you to a place where you'll be safe for a few days. I just need a little time to talk with Dr. Jannsen. He must be in Gideon's bedroom right now. Why don't both of you go back there with me."

Retracing the steps she had taken a hundred times before,

Agnes led the way down the dimly lit hall to Gideon's bed-room, where he was propped up in bed, Gertrude and Dr. Jannsen seated in chairs beside him. They both stood as Agnes, Laura, and Ed entered, but it was Gideon's response that caught Ed and Laura by surprise.

As they approached his bed, Gideon slowly lifted his head from the pillow, staring up at them, saying in a weak voice, "I was expecting you, Mr. Housman, and I've already seen Agnes, but I don't recognize the lady with you."

Dr. Jannsen rushed to speak, "Gideon's back with us now, Ed, and I hope the Lord's brought him back to stay. We've had a nice, normal conversation for the last half hour. He even asked me about the new will and power of attorney. I know you've been carrying both around with you for weeks, and I believe we may finally be able to get his signatures tonight."

Ed glanced at Laura with consternation. "There was so much going on tonight, I forgot to transfer them from my car to yours. The will and power of attorney are still in the glove box of my car. I don't know whether to drive back to town and get them now, or wait until morning. I don't want to call the Eden Springs Resort and have to ask Doug to bring them to me. And we have to get Agnes to safer quarters just as soon as possible."

At that moment, the sons entered the room, and Jonah inter-rupted them in a low voice, "A truck turned into our driveway down at the highway and stopped a little while ago. It don't have any headlights on." The words were hardly out of his mouth when every light in the house went out. Jonah muttered, across the pitch black room, "I'll go fetch the kerosene lanterns."

"Oh God!" Agnes whimpered. "Don't let them get me."

★

Running without headlights, Tolliver braked the truck to a stop on the gravel drive, between two power line poles. He and Hurd climbed out of the cab, leaving Grant behind, sitting si-lently, as he had throughout the ride.

Taking a long-handled razor-sharp pruning hook from the truck bed, Tolliver walked to the spot where the telephone wire drooped closest to the ground. Extending the pruning hook over the phone line, he gave a hard pull, watching the ends of the sheared wire separate and drop to the ground.

Meanwhile, Hurd had taken a length of chain from the truck and joined him. Coiling the chain like a lasso, he tossed it under-hand with a practiced spin, lofting it up and over the bare power lines. On the first try, the chain looped across the wires, causing a flashing arc and a sound like a pistol shot. As the power line went dead, Grant saw the lights in the house go black. Both men climbed back in the cab, and they continued on without lights up the unpaved road and in behind the darkened house, parking almost out of sight between two large shrubs.

Turning to face Grant, Tolliver asked in a terse voice, "You know what to do now?"

Julian voice cracked when he spoke. "I've got a can with ten gallons of gas, and buckets to carry it in. It won't take me but a few minutes to get a fire started in the back of the house. You have the sheriff and his two deputies still chasing their tails investigating the brush fires you started, so we won't have to worry about them showing up here. But don't forget, when we're through, this has got to look like an accidental house fire. There can't be a single survivor left to talk."

"You got the easy part, Grant," Tolliver replied contemptu-ously. "All you have to do is torch the house. We're the ones who have to make sure that no one in there comes back out."

"I may have the easy part now, but remember I was the one who spotted Agnes getting out of the truck here," Julian retorted. "I told you where she was hiding out in Charleston, but you still couldn't find her and take care of the problem."

Suddenly Tolliver exclaimed, "Shut up! There's a car turning in on the gravel road down at the highway, and it's coming up here to the house."

Watching the car slow to a stop, with headlights dying and both doors opening, Hurd whispered, "Would you look at who just got out and is walking up to the house carrying a flashlight. It looks like two high school kids going to a party. There's a good looking blonde girl, and I swear to God, she's wearing high heels."

The three men watched as the boy and girl paused at the door, then opened it and entered the pitch black house.

"I sure hate that," Jake said. "When we came out here, I

didn't count on having to kill a couple of kids. But we're in this way too deep now to get any seconds thoughts."

★

Chapter 33

"DAD, LAURA, Dr Jannsen!" Doug called into the darkness, with his voice echoing off of the walls. "Anybody here?"

At that moment, Doug saw a light coming toward him, and a deep voice boomed out, "Who's there?" Doug realized it was one of the sons walking toward them, carrying a lantern.

"It's Doug Housman, with Dr. Jannsen's granddaughter, Vickie," he called back. "Are my dad, Dr. Jannsen, and Mrs. Jackson here?"

"Just follow me," Daniel replied. "We don't have no electric lights, so watch your step." He led Doug and Vickie through the house to Gideon's bedroom, where a kerosene lamp with a sooty glass chimney was sitting on the bedside table, casting a dim light. Ed, Laura, Agnes, Dr. Jannsen, and Gertrude were gathered there, talking quietly.

Seeing the two teenagers in the doorway, Ed exclaimed in astonishment, "What in the world are you kids doing out here? I thought you were still at the dance."

Vickie held out the brown envelope to him. "Doug and I saw this in your glove box earlier, Mr. Housman, and we thought you probably needed it tonight, so we drove out here to bring it to you. We didn't know what to do when we reached the driveway and saw there were no lights on in the house, but since we'd already made it that far, we decided to come up here and see if we could find you."

"I think you two showed a lot of spunk driving out here at night, and coming inside this dark house," Laura commented. "Is that the will and power of attorney that you need, Ed?"

"You have those papers for me to sign here with you?" Gideon repeated weakly, fully comprehending what Laura had said. "I'll sign them right now. I've go a lot of trust in you, Mr. Housman."

"We've waited a long time for this, Ed," Dr. Jannsen said. "I think we'd better strike while the iron is hot and get Gideon's signatures on both documents. There are plenty of witnesses here, and you've told me Mrs. Jackson's a notary."

Ed began to read aloud to Gideon, fighting the urge to rush through the tedious legalese. Then handing a pen to Gideon, who with a surprisingly steady hand signed both documents, he watched as, there in the half-light of a kerosene lantern, the sun seemed to rise on Roseanna.

They had just executed the approvals when Jonah entered, excitedly whispering, "There's three men standing out back of the house. They've parked their truck between some shrubs where you almost can't see it. I think they mean to do mischief. If you come in the other room where it's dark, you can see them out through the window. I locked the front and back doors."

"We have no choice now but to call Sheriff Daniels and ask him to get out here right away," Ed said tersely, fully realizing there would be no time to wait for them to arrive.

"You can't call nobody," Jonah replied. "The phone's dead. I think whoever's out there cut the phone line and the power line both."

"Do you have any guns in the house?"

"The only thing we have on the place is a .22 rifle out in the barn for rats," Daniel replied. "Pa never let us keep guns here in the house."

Gertrude stood up. "I have a Colt .45 automatic pistol and a magazine holding seven rounds in my suitcase. I'll go get it."

Relieved, Ed said, "I'm glad we're not completely unarmed. Think carefully now, do either of you have anything else we can use to protect ourselves?"

Daniel left the room briefly and returned carrying an assortment of wooden pick and axe handles. "This is all I could find. I've got enough hickory tool handles here to go around. If you know how to use 'em, you can defend yourself against almost anything, even a bull."

Taking charge, Ed drew the others around him. "Here's what we're going to do: Every man take one of these clubs. Arnold and Doug, go get Hester. Roll her in here in her wheel chair, and then stand guard in here with her and the others. Use those clubs if you have to, and don't let anyone come through that door but us.

"Gertrude, Daniel, and Jonah, I want you three with me. Leave the lantern here. We'll split up, and each of us will take one side of the house. We'll try to see if we can spot anything through the windows. Gertrude, you take the back of the house, and I'll take the front. Daniel can cover the east wing, and Jonah, the west. We'll get back together here in fifteen minutes."

Glancing around the room, Ed called out, "Where's Agnes? She was standing here just a few minutes ago. I'm afraid we don't have time to look for her now."

Gertrude quietly slipped down the dark hallway into the un-lit kitchen. Kneeling beside an open window, she could not detect anything moving about outside in the faint light of a thin crescent moon. But she noticed something out of the ordinary, something terribly wrong. It was the pungent smell of gasoline, carried toward the kitchen window by the light spring breeze.

Focusing on a dark silhouette thirty yards away, she was able to identify what looked like the back of a pickup truck, parked between two boxwoods. As her pupils continued to adjust to the dim light, she thought she saw something move. A white object materialized in front of the truck, and seemed to be coming closer. It began to take shape, until she could finally discern what it was: a white cast on a man's arm. He was walking rapidly toward the house, carrying a metal pail by the handle with his good arm.

Hesitating only briefly, Gertrude operated the slide of the pistol to chamber a round and cock the hammer. However, in doing so, she inadvertently disclosed her position and intentions. Reacting to the unmistakable sound of the pistol being cocked, the man drew the bucket back, preparing to sling it through the window.

Using a two-handed shooter's grip she had learned from an army manual, Gertrude aimed the pistol at him, squeezing off two rounds. The first slug caught the man in the chest and knocked him backward, spilling the liquid from the bucket. The second slug clipped the rim of the metal pail, creating a spark that ignited the fumes from gasoline sloshing toward the ground. The resulting ball of fire caused Gertrude to quickly step back from the window, but not before the intense flash of light showed her who the man was. She now knew that she had just shot Julian Grant.

A flood of conflicting feelings engulfed her. Her quick response had undoubtedly saved Roseanna and the lives of everyone inside. Another few seconds, and the fireball would have exploded inside the kitchen, burning them alive. Still, she felt physically sick. Her shots had just taken the life of a man, something she would have never considered doing before that moment. Carefully putting the pistol back in the safe position, Gertrude walked back through the dark hallway toward Gideon's bedroom, feeling as if her legs were moving independently of her mind.

Crouching beside the window at the front of the house, Ed was unable to see anything outside, until an explosion and intense fire behind the house illuminated the entire property with a reddish glow. At that instant, he saw a heavy-set man climbing the steps, pointing a sawed-off pump shotgun in his direction. Glancing around, Ed quickly realized that the reflected light from the fire was streaming in through the windows, exposing him to anyone coming up on the front porch. He ducked his head below the window sash just before he heard the blast from the shotgun, and the quick reaction saved him.

The load of buckshot blew out the window just inches above Ed's head, peppering his face with shards of glass. Using the front of his shirt, he tried with little success to wipe away the blood trickling from gashes on his forehead down into his eyes. Pulling a handkerchief from his pocket, he wrapped it around his head bandana-style, slowing the blinding red stream.

With a crash that shook the house, the massive front door hit the crumbling plaster of the foyer wall. Ed knew that the gunman was now inside with him. Wiping the blood from his hands and taking a batter's grip on the pick handle, he moved into position beside the door and waited. A few minutes later, the creaking of floor boards told him that the intruder was moving slowly down the hallway toward him. When he sensed that the man was only a few feet away, Ed stepped into the hall and raised the pick handle to strike.

The blast from a shotgun muzzle only feet away deafened him, and a load of buckshot tore the club completely out of his grip. He heard the pump action quickly chamber a new shell, and he knew that the next load of buckshot would be in his chest at point blank range. Lunging forward, Ed's forearm struck the short barrel of the shotgun, and he grabbed it with both hands, desperately trying to push it away from his body. The butt of the gun swung around quickly, striking the side of his head with a stunning blow that knocked him to the ground. As he tried to stand, dazed, he heard the sounds of a struggle, and the thudding sound of the shotgun hitting the floor. Ed knew that an unknown force had shifted his attacker's focus.

A tree, smoldering from the heat of the gasoline fueled fire, suddenly burst into flames, dimly lighting the hallway. Ed could see two burly men standing chest to chest with their arms locked in a double bear hug, each trying to force his adversary over backward to the floor. One was wearing coveralls, and Ed instantly knew that it was one of the Buchanan twins.

For a minute, all he could hear was the grunting of two large men straining with all their might for an advantage, both gasping for breath. Then, slowly, the intruder seemed to tire and lose leverage. As he was bent over backwards, his hands unclasped, and Ed heard the unmistakable sounds of bones snapping. The other man released him, and the intruder dropped heavily to the floor, writhing on his back in pain, unable to get up.

"I saved your life, Mr. Housman," Jonah said, bending over him, chest heaving with each deep breath.

"I know that," Ed replied, trying to get to his feet. "He would have killed me if you hadn't stopped him."

Taking Jonah's hand for support, Ed stood. Studying the intruder's face in the dim light, he exclaimed, "That's William Hurd. He's one of the men who tried to wreck me earlier, and one of the two ex-cons wanted for Myrtle Spencer's murder. He's not much of a threat now, but his partner, Jake Tolliver, must still be around here somewhere. We need to get back to your pa's bedroom and make sure everyone's safe."

Picking up the shotgun, Ed led Jonah down the dark hallway. They hadn't gotten far when they were startled by the loud sound of a gunshot from the back of the house, followed by angry shouting.

As they approached Gideon's bedroom, Ed and Jonah noticed the beam of lantern light shining under the closed door. With the light of the burning tree outside reflecting through windows, they could see what had happened. Jake Tolliver had entered the house through the back door, surprising and overpowering Gertrude, and he was now holding her as a shield, with her own pistol pressed against her head. A large caliber revolver was tucked in his belt.

"I'm sorry," Gertrude whispered. "I didn't see him come up behind me until it was too late."

"I want that shotgun now," Jake demanded. "Otherwise this woman's dead. Then I want you to tell me what's happened to my partner."

"Don't worry about me, Mr. Housman. Do what you have to for you and the others. But if he shoots me, use that shotgun on him. Don't let him walk out of here."

"There's no need for anyone else to die or get hurt tonight," Ed said to Tolliver. "Your partner's in a room up front with some serious injuries. Let's work out a deal. We'll both put our guns down, and then we'll help you get your partner out to your truck. We'll give you a long head start before we notify the sheriff and the state police."

Jake didn't bother to respond. Keeping Gertrude in front of him, with the muzzle of the gun pressed against the side of her head, he moved with her toward the beam of light shining under Gideon's doorway, and kicked the door open. Doug was standing just inside, holding a pick handle with both hands. Dr. Jannsen stood in front of Gideon's bed, with Laura and Vickie to one side, in front of Hester's wheelchair.

"Here's what we're going to do," Jake shouted. "I'm swapping this old bird for those two pretty ones in there. You help me get my partner out in the bed of the truck, and I'll drive out of here without anyone getting hurt. I'll let the two women out when I get to the next town. I'm going to trust you not to get the law involved 'til daylight, and you're going to trust me to let them go like I said."

"No," Ed replied firmly. "I've already made you my offer."

Laura answered in a clear voice that carried from the bedroom into the hallway, "I'll go with you as a hostage, but the girl has to stay here."

"That's not going to happen," Ed interrupted her. "Jake, you're in this game by yourself now, and you're not holding a very strong hand. You can walk away and take Hurd with you, but you're not taking any hostages along. In an hour or two, people are going to wonder where we are, and someone's going to start checking up on us. When they call out here and find a dead phone line, they're going to have the sheriff come out to see what's going on. The clock is running out on you, and if you want to get a start out of town ahead of the law, you need to leave right now."

"You can go straight to hell," Jake spit out, turning toward Ed. "We're going to do it my way. If those two ladies aren't out here in the hall ready to go with me by the time I count to five, I swear, I'm going to shoot this woman in the head."

Stepping from the shadows, Agnes brought Gideon's cane down on Tolliver's arm with the full strength of her 100 pound frame. Spinning quickly toward her, Jake whipped the pistol against her forehead, knocking her backward. Just as Agnes crumpled to the ground, Daniel's axe handle struck Jake squarely in the side of the head with a sickening thud, knocking him senseless. Jake's finger convulsively squeezed the trigger of the pistol as he crashed to the floor, sending a .45 caliber slug through the plaster ceiling and into the rafters above.

Hester began to cry, an eerie, high pitched wail that did not stop until Laura bent over the wheelchair, putting her arms around her and pulling her close, as she would a terrified child.

Daniel exclaimed, "I been standing here out of sight waiting for a chance to club him, but he had that gun so tight against Gertrude's head, I didn't dare. If Agnes hadn't hit him on the arm with the cane and made him pull the gun away, I couldn't have done nothing."

Gertrude awkwardly embraced Agnes, then Daniel, saying with emotion she couldn't conceal, "Thank you. He would have killed me."

Then, turning to face the others, she told them, "Julian Grant's body is out in the backyard. He was trying to set the house on fire, and I shot him. I saw him burn up in his own gasoline. Someone ought to go outside and be sure he's beyond helping."

Using rawhide shoelaces, Daniel and Jonah tied up Jake Tolliver, hand and foot. Drifting back to consciousness, he began to spit out a string of profanity, until Jonah stuffed a rag in his mouth, leaving him lying on the floor, unable to move or speak.

"I almost don't know where to start," Dr. Jannsen said quietly, as he cleaned and dressed the cut on Agne's forehead, covering it with a gauze bandage from his medical bag. Turning next to Ed, he gently removed the bloody handkerchief Ed still had tied around his head. He then removed bits of glass, disinfected the cuts with alcohol, and after giving Ed a shot of Novacaine, sutured several of the deeper gashes.

Drawing closer to Ed, hopeful that she could distract him from the doctor's needle, Laura said, "You keep telling me that I look like your pet chicken, Lucille, and now you're starting to look like my old torn-up rag doll, Barney. We make a fine pair, don't we?"

When Dr. Jannsen finished attending to Ed, they both followed Daniel and Jonah to the front of the house where William Hurd was still lying on the floor, struggling to breathe. Working by lantern light, it took Dr. Jannsen only a few minutes to determine that Hurd's broken ribs had punctured one of his lungs. "I need an ambulance to move him back to the hospital in town," Dr. Jannsen said. "If we're not careful, he could puncture the other lung, and that would be bad. He's no threat to escape, so it's better if we just leave him lying here, and don't try to move him for now."

"We need one thing from him before we take him to the hospital," Ed insisted. "And we'll get him there a lot sooner if he cooperates." Staring at Hurd, he demanded, "I want to hear a confession that you and Jake Tolliver are the ones who killed Myrtle Spencer."

William refused to say a word. Ed, Dr. Jannsen, and the two sons stood by in silence, watching him struggle to hold in the truth. Finally, the constant pain became more than he could stand, and he gave up, saying weakly, "Myrtle wanted more money to keep doping up the old man, and she was threatening to go to the law if she didn't get it. Grant had us run her down with a truck. It was his idea to throw her in the field with the bull to make it look like an accident. She was dead a long time before the bull went to work on her."

"That's what we needed to hear from you, in front of witnesses," Ed replied, unable to keep the disgust from his voice. "Now we'll keep our part of the deal and get you to the hospital."

Returning to Gideon's bedroom, Ed spoke to the others. "Doug, take Vickie home, and then call Carolyn and tell her we're safe. Laura and I will follow you back to town, and get Agnes to the motel as quickly as possible. I'll contact the sheriff from town and tell him what's happened out here tonight, and that Agnes will turn herself in to him Monday morning.

"I'll be here with Hurd until the ambulance arrives," Dr Jannsen insisted. "I don't mind staying. I've had to take care of some mighty sorry people before."

"I'm planning to come back out here to be with Earl and his deputies," Ed replied. "I'll see you then."

By flashlight, Doug and Vickie found their way back through the dark house to the car. As they drove off, he said, "It's almost 12:45, and your family must be frantic, wondering what's happened to you. I don't know what your dad will say to me when we drive up, but it won't be good. This was supposed to be a date for the dance, and it's turned into a life or death experience."

"Dad's going to be awfully upset until we explain what happened," Vickie replied. "I thought you showed a lot of courage, waiting by the door with nothing but a club. You didn't know it, but Laura found some old scissors in Gideon's dresser, and we had them hidden on us. We agreed that if someone forced their way into that bedroom, we weren't going to just stand back and watch."

Turning into the Vicelli driveway, Doug noticed that every

light in the house was on, including the front porch light. He quickly helped Vickie out, and together they walked toward the house. Doug saw Tony coming toward them, and there was no misunderstanding the look on his face. "What the hell do you have to say for yourself, young man?" he shouted angrily. "You were supposed to have Vickie home two hours ago."

He would have continued his tirade, if Vickie hadn't stepped in. "Daddy, please stop! It's not Doug's or my fault that we're late. Give us chance to tell you what happened tonight. We're lucky to be here now, safe."

Their words tumbling out, interrupting one another as they shared their story of all that had happened, Vickie and Doug watched her parents' anger turn to shock, and then relief. But Tony was still not ready to let Doug off the hook. He lectured him, saying, "I'm sure you meant no harm, son, but you should never have allowed my daughter to go out to the Buchanan house with you tonight. You know that, don't you? But you did get her home safely, and that's the important thing. You all have had a hell of an experience tonight."

As he left the house, Vickie followed Doug out to the driveway. "You're forgetting something, Doug," she called out to him, causing him to wheel around and walk back to her. Wrapping both arms around his neck, Vickie pulled his face toward hers and kissed him. "Forget what Daddy said when we drove up," she whispered. "I know he likes you." Then she spun on her high heel, her skirt flaring, catching the envious gaze of her little sister watching from the familiar security of the front porch.

Chapter 34

Ed and Laura drove Agnes back to town, continuing on to the Homeplace Motel. Laura helped her check in, and Ed handed her enough money to cover expenses. "I'll come back to take you for arraignment on Monday morning," he promised.

As the two were leaving her room, Agnes spoke to Ed. "I want you to know that when I slipped out of Gideon's bedroom tonight, I was only trying to get away and save myself. I knew those men would kill me if they found me. But when I started to run again, I realized you're the only friend I have, and the only person who's ever offered to stand up for me. That's when I picked up the cane and came back to try and help."

"We're both your friends now, Agnes. What you did tonight will go a long way toward getting you more lenient treatment from the court when you go to trial."

After Agnes shut her door, Ed and Laura went to a pay phone in the lobby, where he called Sheriff Daniels at home. The sheriff picked up on the first ring, and asked impatiently, "Who's calling, and what do you want?"

Ed identified himself, then begin to relate what had taken place at the Buchanan home only a short time earlier. "We tried to get in touch with from the house, but the phone lines had been cut. I'm calling you from town now, and want you to know what you'll run into when you get there.

"You can go out there now and pick up Hurd and Tolliver. Tolliver's tied up hand and foot, so he won't be any problem to handle. Hurd has serious chest injuries, and could die if he's not handled carefully. Dr. Jannsen wants to see him moved to the hospital in town for emergency treatment. Julian Grant's body's still lying out in the back yard, burned beyond recognition."

"Good Lord Almighty!" Sheriff Daniels exclaimed. "It looks like all hell broke loose around Eden Springs today. I thought I had enough trouble on my hands when my boys and I were chasing an arsonist, but it sounds like you just went through World War Three out at Roseanna. I'll call my deputies back in, and we'll get over there right now."

"We lived through a nightmare in that old house tonight. It's a miracle that Roseanna didn't burn to the ground with all of us trapped inside. If Grant, Hurd, and Tolliver had been able to pull it off, they might have committed the perfect crime."

"One other thing I need to tell you," Ed added. "Agnes Harper has come back to town, and she's retained me as her defense attorney. She'll turn herself in to you the first thing on Monday morning."

Ed hung up the phone and walked Laura to her station wagon, saying, "If you'll just drive me home, I'll pick up my car, and get back out to Roseanna to check on everyone. Most importantly, I need to pick up the papers I left behind."

"You sure you won't need me?" Laura inquired, slipping behind the wheel. "You're going to be in a lot of pain from all those cuts and that blow to your head when the Novocain starts to wear off."

Ed shook his head, "Truthfully, it's already worn off, but I'll be fine."

When they reached his house, Ed saw that Doug had already made it home. He stepped out of the station wagon and came around to her side, saying quietly, "I won't forget how you volunteered to go with Jake Tolliver, to protect Gertrude and Vickie. I saw you take the scissors out of your dress after Daniel had knocked him cold. You're one brave person."

"That goes both ways. You took charge at the Buchanans' trying to keep the intruders out, and almost got killed trying to stop them after they broke in. Waiting in the bedroom wondering what was happening to you and the others was the most nerve wracking experience of my life."

Ed dropped down and rested his knee on the floorboard of the car. "You mean the world to me. I wish we could stay here together a little longer, but right now, I need to get back out to Roseanna."

"I know," Laura said softly. Drawing him toward her, without thinking about his sutured cuts and bruised cheek, she kissed him gently. Then, realizing her fingers were resting directly on the wounds, she pulled her hands away. "I hope that didn't hurt."

"Not even possible." Pulling her close to him, they shared a long kiss. As she drove away, Ed watched the taillights on her car slowly disappear in the distance.

As soon as she was out of sight, Ed went inside to check on Doug, who was sleeping soundly in his bedroom, then drove back to Roseanna. Inside the lantern-lit house, he found that Sheriff Daniels was alone on the job, still looking over the crime scene. Both of his deputies were gone, and so were Hurd, Tolliver, and Julian Grant's remains.

Ed soon located the brown envelope containing Gideon's new will in the dimly lit bedroom. The road was deserted on the return to town, with nothing to be seen outside the reach of his headlights. The stations he tried to tune in on the car radio had all gone off the air, leaving nothing but the sound of static. At home, Ed went straight upstairs to his room and kicked off his shoes. Sprawling across the bed on his back, he closed his eyes, and was immediately asleep. He did not stir again until the sun was high overhead, and the room was flooded with light.

When Doug woke at sunrise, he could hear his dad snoring down the hall. JR noticed him stir, jumping off the rug onto the bed, and licking his face. "OK, I'm up now, boy," Doug exclaimed, pushing JR back down to the floor. "You may want to try a little Listerine in the mornings."

Dressing and quietly slipping downstairs and out on the porch, he retrieved the Sunday Post. Settling down in the living room over a bowl of cornflakes, he started to read the newspaper, and by the time he finished, much of the morning was gone. It was past noon when the phone rang, and he found

Mike on the line.

"Dawg, I went to church this morning with Ginny, and the Vicelli family was sitting in the pew in front of us. Word's spreading fast about all the action last night after you and Vickie left us and drove out to meet your dad and her grandfather. Tell me everything about what went on out there."

Doug recounted to Mike the chain of events from the time he and Vickie had left the dance to the time he had brought her home. "That's pretty much the whole story," he concluded. "It seems unreal now, talking about it with you in broad daylight. But last night, we had some scary moments that will stick with me for the rest of my life."

"The things y'all went through would have scared the hell out of anyone," Mike said "Mr. Barry was at church this morning, and when he saw Vickie talking with Ginny and me, he came over to find out what had happened. He had no idea where your dad and Mrs. Jackson were headed when they left the dance, or what happened after that. He never even saw you and Vickie sneak out."

"I'll bet he was as amazed as everyone else by what took place. When we were at the farm with him, everything was so peaceful and quiet that you couldn't imagine people trying to kill each other there. Did anyone say anything about Mr. Vicelli's reaction when we go back to their house?"

"No, that never came up. But here's one thing you'll really like to hear, Dawg, before I hang up. I can tell you that the entire Vicelli family, including her old man, has a very high opinion of your dad and you right now."

"That's good to hear. He jumped on me with both feet when I finally got her home last night, and I'm glad to hear that he's not still holding it against me."

"You probably owe a lot to Dr. Jannsen. Vickie told us her grandfather bragged about the way your dad and you stepped up when things started happening."

As soon as he put down the phone, Doug heard his dad in the shower. When Ed came down the steps, the dark bruise, swollen cheek, and sutures on his face showed what he had been through the previous night.

"You look pretty beat up, Dad," Doug said sympathetically.

"How do you feel?"

"Physically or emotionally?" Ed asked. "My head feels like it's been through a rock crusher. But I still feel incredibly well, knowing so many of the threats we've been dealing with are gone now. There's still some hard work ahead, but I feel more optimistic than I have for a long time."

"What did you and Laura talk about when you took her home last night, or early this morning, after everything that went on?"

"We didn't say that much, but I know that she has the same feelings for me that I do for her. You told me earlier you thought I shouldn't keep waiting around. I decided before we split up last night that I'm not going to put it off any longer; I'm going to ask her to marry me."

"That's the best news I've heard in a long time, Dad," Doug answered. "There'll be some big changes to life around here with a woman in the house again, but I know everything will work out fine. Our home lost its heart when Mom died. I believe Laura may be the one who can bring it back."

That afternoon, Ed made two phone calls. The first was to Agnes, checking to see that she was still holding up emotionally. "I'll come by the motel and pick you up for breakfast, and then we'll go over to the sheriff's department together. I'm going to stand by you all the way, and you're going to get through this fine."

"Do you think I'm going to go to jail?" Agnes inquired apprehensively.

"I can't make any promises, but the court is usually lenient with someone like you who has no previous criminal record, particularly when they can see remorse and a change of heart like you've shown. If you want my opinion, no, I don't think you'll have to serve time."

Afterward, he called Laura, inviting her out to dinner on Tuesday evening. "You pick the place to go, and be sure it's somewhere really special."

"That's an easy call, Barney. The Eden Springs Resort is still my favorite place. It's not just the food. A lot of it for me is the setting."

"Then that's where we'll go, Lucille. I'll come by and pick you up around 7:00." Ed was humming to himself when he set down the phone, and his high spirits stayed with him throughout the day.

When Ed knocked on Agnes's door the next morning, he heard the rattle of the safety chain, then saw a suspicious bloodshot eye peering at him through the crack that opened. "I just wanted to be sure it was you, Mr. Houseman, before I let anyone in. I still get scared when I hear someone lurking outside." When the door opened, Ed saw that she was still wearing the same wrinkled clothes that she had on Saturday night when he had first seen her at the Buchanans'.

"We'll eat breakfast here, before we go over to the sheriff's department," he reminded her. "Mrs. Jackson will bring some things you need over to your room later this morning."

In the motel coffee shop, they slid into a vacant booth. Looking across the table, Ed couldn't help feeling sorry for her. With her disheveled appearance and fearful expression, Agnes was pathetic. As soon as the waitress left, Ed outlined the best legal option. "I strongly recommend that you agree to a plea-bargain, making a full confession before the court and offering to testify against the ring leaders, in exchange for leniency. The fact that you risked your life to save Gertrude Estep should make a big difference in the outcome."

"I'll take your advice, Mr. Housman," she replied. "Is there anything else I need to do to keep from going to jail?"

"When we meet with the sheriff this morning, let me do the talking for you, and check with me before you make any statements or answer any questions."

Agnes was arrested and booked at the sheriff's department. Afterward, Ed told the sheriff that he planned to meet with the district attorney to work out a plea-bargain.

"Agnes is prepared to go cooperate with the DA and tell him everything she knows, including her role in giving drugs to Gideon and Hester under the direction of Julian Grant and his handlers. There'll be witnesses including me to testify that she stuck her neck out to save Gertrude Estep's life."

He added, "Although Julian's dead, he must have left tracks leading to the person he was taking orders from. I can't say much without the risk of libel, but I believe your investigation should cover possible involvement by the owner of Copperfield Enterprises and Barker Mining."

After arranging for Agnes to post bail through a local bondsman and securing her release, Ed took her back to the motel. As he left, he told her, "I promise I'll do everything I can to see you're treated fairly at the time of your hearing. Keep your chin up."

Back at his office, Ed dug out a phone number and made a phone call to his retired friend, John Crawford. "John, I'm glad you've kept your license to practice law in West Virginia, because I may have to call on you for help. I'm representing two clients, and there could be a problem with conflict of interests. If that's the case, I'm going to ask you to represent a woman named Agnes Harper in a plea-bargain. She's a deserving person trying to start a new life. I promise, it won't be a difficult case."

"Good to hear from you again, Ed," John's friendly voice replied. "I'm always ready to do a favor for you. Let me know if you need me."

After the call, Ed worked with Carolyn on papers starting the legal process to supersede Gideon Buchanan's existing power of attorney and will with the new documents recently signed, and to void the sale of the Buchanan farm by Julian Grant to Copperfield Enterprises.

That afternoon, Ed drove to the court house, where he encountered Shirley Baker in the clerk's office. She took him aside, saying in a whisper, "I have some news I think you'll be pleased to hear. Judge Kirk has just announced that he's taking an extended leave of absence, and the rumor mill is at work speculating why. Anyway, that means Judge Wine will be handling all of the court cases for the indefinite future."

"I'm definitely pleased about that," Ed replied with a faint smile. "The timing for Judge Kirk to take a long vacation seems curious, doesn't it? I hope he decides to stay away permanently. The reason I'm here now is to file this new will and power of attorney for Gideon Buchanan, and to initiate a suit to void the sale of his farm due to criminal conspiracy and fraud."

"I've heard stories about what happened out at Roseanna," Shirley said. "I expect it will all be on the front page of the newspaper any time now. You look like you've been through the mill. I'm glad you're OK."

Carolyn was eagerly waiting with news, when he returned to the office. "Laura called while you were out. She wanted to pass on the word from her sales agent that Barker Mining has taken their work crew away from the site on the former Simpson property. There hasn't been any blasting or excavating going on out there since last Friday. On a hunch, I called the owner of the Eden Springs Resort, and he told me the mineral springs started running clear again today. He said he's decided to pump the mud out of the spa pool, and hope for the best. I told him how pleased you'd be to hear that."

In the afternoon, Ed walked across town to the courthouse at a leisurely pace, enjoying the late May weather. Climbing the worn marble steps to the district attorney's office on the second floor, he went inside, seeing a young, athletic-looking man coming toward him. "I appreciate your dropping by to meet with me on such short notice," Jack Bradford, the new DA, said as the two shook hands. "Come on in my office and have a seat." The two men hit it off from the start, and were soon talking together like old friends.

"I'm trying to hit the ground running in building a case for the state against the conspirators in this crime," Jack explained, "and I'm approaching it from the bottom up. I've been going over everything I can find to learn more about the people involved.

"Myrtle Spencer and Agnes Harper are obviously small fry. They both committed serious crimes against the Buchanans, but Myrtle didn't deserve to be murdered. I'm still trying to decide what I want to do about Agnes."

"Agnes has changed," Ed said. "Obviously I'm biased, since I'm her attorney. But she put her life on the line to save Gertrude Estep, and I think she deserves a break. She's willing to plea-bargain. I hope the court will take her actions into account when she's prosecuted."

"I'll be willing to go along on the plea-bargain for Agnes. I'm going to come down hard on Hurd and Tolliver. Those two ex-cons provided the muscle and took care of the hands-on dirty work, and they're about as bad as they come. They've spent their entire adult lives in and out of prison for crimes that just seem to keep getting worse and worse. This time they committed premeditated murder, and I'm going to see that they're put away for life.

"From what I've learned about Julian Grant, it looks like he was the middle man in the whole affair, a devious, greedy punk who waded in way over his head, and paid with his life. If he were still alive, I'd be building a case against him for arson and murder. It's a pity he didn't live, so that I could make him testify against his handlers. Not having him around to turn state's evidence will make my job more difficult in prosecuting the ring leaders.

"I believe that the masterminds behind this whole conspiracy are Barker and Thorpe, and they're the two I'd like to throw the book at. Barker has done more harm to the state of West Virginia and its people than anyone I know. We may not be able to pin enough on him to send him to prison, but I'm determined not to let him get off with just a slap on the wrist. I'm confident we can drive him back into his cave to lick some serious wounds. Going after big time criminals like Barker is the reason I took this job."

"I hope that you can get a conviction against Barker, but I don't need to tell you that no one has ever been able to make any criminal charges against him stick up 'til now," Ed remarked, as their conversation ended.

At home, Ed found Doug putting the plates on the table for dinner. "What all went on today?" Doug asked.

Ed pulled up a kitchen chair and shared the encouraging news from his busy day. When he was finished, he added, "I saved the most important thing for the last." Pulling a box containing a diamond engagement ring from his pocket, he handed it to Doug for inspection. "What do you think of this? I picked this out today at Epsteins' Jewelry Store."

Doug held the ring up carefully, admiring the way the large stone refracted and flared the bright kitchen light into a rainbow of color. "I'd like to see the look on her face when you give it to her. I think she's going to be very surprised, in a good way."

"I hope you're right. By the way, I'm taking Laura to dinner tomorrow evening. You may want to go by Gil's and get a hamburger."

"Thanks, but I've already gotten a better offer. The Vicellis are having a dinner party for Vickie's grandfather, and she's invited me to come. They're celebrating his seventieth birthday."

"Then we should both have some exciting stories to swap when we get home tomorrow night. I can drive you to the Vicellis' before I go to pick up Laura, and maybe someone there will be willing to give you a ride home later."

"That sounds fine, Dad. I don't mind walking home if I can't get a ride. I'll be thinking about you, and waiting to hear what Laura says. Tell her if she takes you, she gets JR and me thrown in as part of a package deal. On second thought, you might want to hold that news, until you're absolutely sure she's going to accept the ring."

Chapter 35

JUMPING OUT of the car in front of the Vicellis', Doug called to his dad, "I really hope that everything between you and Laura goes the way we want it to. If she says yes, JR and I are going throw a big party to welcome her to the family."

"Thanks, son. I think she knows how you feel. Say hello to Vickie and her family for me, and tell Dr. Jannsen I said happy birthday."

Vickie met Doug at the front door in a pretty red print dress. "Hi, Doug," she said, taking his hand. "I'm glad you came. Come on in the living room with me. Everyone's here."

Following her inside to join her family, Doug felt a sense of nervous anticipation, almost like he had the first day he had walked into the building at Tyler High.

Her dad and mom, and both grandparents, were seated around the coffee table, glasses of Chianti in hand, with Sandra and Tony, Jr., standing to one side. Vickie's mother handled the one introduction required. "Doug, I believe you know everyone here but my mother, Mrs. Jannsen. Mother, I'd like you to meet Douglas Housman. His father is an attorney and a good friend of Daddy's."

Mrs Jannsen extended her hand, with a smile that reminded Doug of her granddaughter, saying, "It's nice to meet you, Douglas. I've heard that you were with Vickie and my husband during some exciting times Saturday night at the old Buchanan mansion."

"It's nice to meet you, ma'am. I was there with Vickie, but we were mostly spectators. Fortunately, everything seemed to come out all right."

"I think the boy is being a little modest, Greta," Dr. Jannsen entered the conversation. "His father and he are a big part of the reason things turned out the way they did. Young Douglas acquitted himself quite well."

Doug could feel his anxiety drain away, including the nervous feeling of being in the room with an occasionally no-nonsense boss. "Good to have you here tonight with us, son," Tony said at one point, draping his arm across Doug's shoulder.

After dinner, Vickie led Doug out onto the wide porch behind the house, clutching something in a small paper bag. And they sat down side by side in the yellow metal glider, Doug slipped his arm around her and pulled her closer. "I have something for you," she said, handing him the bag.

Opening it, he discovered a cardboard framed glossy black and white picture of Vickie, suntanned and wearing a white one-piece swim suit, sitting in a calendar pose on the low diving board of the town swimming pool. "It's for you," she said softly. "Take it out of the frame, and look on the back."

He had received gifts before, and would get many more later, but none would mean as much to him as the one she gave him on May 21, 1952. Written on the back of the photograph in her round, girlish cursive was the message, "Doug, All my love! Vickie."

He knew that the moment was too good to last, and he was right. As if on cue, little Tony came outside to join them, taking a seat on the other end of the glider, wanting to know more about the ex-cons they had encountered Saturday night.

Vickie saved the day when she spoke up. "Tony, you always like to use a camera. Why don't you go in the house and get my Brownie Hawkeye, and take some pictures of Grandaddy and Grandmother?" Immediately, Tony was off, the porch screen door slamming behind him.

"I really like this picture of you," Doug said, when little Tony out of earshot. "I'll tell you something you probably don't know. I've had a crush on you since the first day I saw you at Tyler High."

"I could see you staring at me when you didn't think I was

looking," Vickie said with a mischievous grin, "but I wasn't really sure how you felt until I found that the Valentine in my locker with the mushy message."

"You knew I didn't put it there," Doug replied defensively. "The two class clowns, Mike and Freddie, pulled that stunt. They wouldn't even tell me what they wrote on the Valentine. All Mike would say later was something about how you would know I was a member of your fan club."

"Oh, the Valentine had that on it and a whole lot more," she continued, watching his face turn red. "Don't you want to know when I first started to like you?" Doug nodded.

"It was the night you gave me a ride home from the canteen. Len was drunk, and he'd just pushed me out of his car. When I saw you getting ready to drive off, I was desperate. I knocked on your window, and you let me in and drove me home without asking me to explain anything. I never meant to get you involved in a fight that night. But even after the fight with Len and the chewing out Daddy gave you because of me, you never told anybody at school what Len had pulled on me. You kept it all to yourself, along with Ginny and Mike. That's when I first started to think about you in a whole new way.

"Ginny tried to tell me that she thought you were similar to Mike in a lot of ways, but I couldn't see it before then. After that night, when she asked if I'd go out with you on a double date, I told her yes. You know the rest."

The screen door opened and the pesty kid brother reappeared, returning to sit beside them in the glider. "I just ran out of film," he said. Little Tony stuck to them like glue for the rest of the evening.

Making the best of things, the two played Parcheesi and Rummy on the porch with Tony and Sandra, to background music on the radio provided by a popular disc jockey. From time to time, Doug stopped to think about his dad and Laura, and wonder how she had responded when he gave her the ring. He had a quiet confidence that things would go well, and that made the birthday party at the Vicelli home even more fun.

After dropping Doug off, Ed drove to Laura's apartment, climbing the steps two at a time. He heard her voice through the screen door saying, "Come on in and have a seat in the living room. I'll be out in a minute." Actually, it was a quarter hour before Laura appeared, but to Ed it was worth the wait. Laura was dressed in a pale yellow fitted summer dress and high heels, her pretty face glowing.

"Excuse me," Ed said. "I didn't realize I had wandered onto a movie set."

Laura giggled like a young girl. "Heathcliff, don't break my heart." She offered her hand, and together they walked down the steps to the car, Ed's mind turning, trying to recall the old movie where he had heard that line before.

"I want to try something different tonight," Ed proposed. "No business talk, no discussion of problems, just the fun stuff." Laura nodded enthusiastically.

In the dining room at the resort, they saw that there were still a few decorations left from the Tyler High spring dance. "I'm getting a feeling of déjà vu," Ed commented. "Haven't we been here before?"

"Yes, I believe we have. But this time we aren't designated chaperones for a room full of impressionable high school students. You can loosen up this evening and show me a really good time."

The hostess seated them, and when the waiter approached, Ed ordered a bottle of champagne.

"You're off to a very good start with the wine selection, Mr. Housman. I can hardly wait to see what comes next. Will there be a floor show?"

When the waiter returned, Ed ordered for both from the top of the menu, filet mignon. The meal was delicious, and afterward Laura said, "You're on the way to winning my heart with the wine and dinner."

When the pretty young lady at the grand piano began to play *Unforgettable*, Ed led Laura out on the dance floor. He held her closely, whispering the lyrics into her ear while they danced. "You're putting on a terrific act three," she said, playing along. "I just hate to see the show end. I'd like for there to be a grand finale."

"Oh, there's more," Ed replied.

When the song ended, he slipped his arm around her waist and walked with her across the room toward their table. But instead of stopping, he continued to lead her through the door, until they were standing alone on the terrace. The sun was just disappearing below the horizon, leaving a spectacular red sky in the west. Ed gently turned Laura until they were standing face to face. Reaching into his vest pocket, he withdrew the ring, held it up for her to see, and asked, "Laura, will you marry me?"

For the first time that evening, Laura seemed to be at a loss for words. Looking into Ed's eyes, she replied, "Yes. I was just...." She was unable to say more as he kissed her.

Moving slowly to the muted strains of the piano, he slipped the ring onto her finger. They held one another, until two older couples came onto the terrace. For the rest of the evening, they danced to their favorite songs, lost in their own private world.

On the way home, Laura slipped over toward Ed, and they sat as close as any high school girl and boy. As they approached her neighborhood, she leaned in toward him, and kissed him on the cheek, murmuring, "When I told you earlier I wanted a grand finale, I had no idea what was about to happen. I wish I had asked for a command performance months ago."

"Can we go ahead now and set a date?" Ed asked. "I don't see any reason for a long engagement. I'd like to marry you as soon as you're ready."

"If you'd like to move quickly, so would I. We could set the date for Sunday, the first of June, and it would allow time for your parents, and my folks and my brother, to get here. I don't think either of us is looking for a big second wedding. I'd be happy with a small ceremony at your church. The important thing is for you to make Doug feel he's being brought in on the planning. I want to get off to a great start with my future son."

"We have a lot of time to make other decisions, like where we'll want to live," Ed said. "You could move into the house with Doug and me, just for a few months, while we plan to buy or build a bigger house."

"We can work all of that out later," Laura replied. "I own a ten acre tract on the edge of town, with a creek and a beautiful hilltop site for a home. I believe a boy like Doug would be happy living there."

Ed walked her to her door, and they stood face to face. "What an incredible evening we've had tonight," she said, as they kissed.

"I love you," Laura called out to him, as he reluctantly walked away.

Doug met him at the front door, JR at his side. "Well, what did she say?" he asked anxiously.

"She said she'll marry me, and she wants to be sure you're included in all the plans. I don't think she had any idea I was going to propose tonight. Everything just seemed to turn out perfectly."

Doug took his dog's head in his hands, saying, "See, JR, I told you so. If she had turned him down, he wouldn't have lipstick all over his face again." Releasing JR, he asked, "May I call Laura now, before she goes to bed?" Ed smiled in assent.

Picking up the phone, Laura heard a young voice say, "I just called to tell you how glad I am to hear that you and Dad are going to get married."

"Doug, you're so sweet to call. I told your dad that I wanted to get off to a great start with my new son, and your phone call is the perfect way. Did he tell you how surprised I was when he gave me the ring?"

"He said you were surprised, but he told me everything went exactly the way he hoped it would. It went the way I hoped, too. Dad's tried to cover it up, but his life hasn't been the same since Mother died, and neither has mine. It's been pretty quiet at times, just two men living here alone. He's been so much happier since he met you."

"I've had some lonely times myself, since I lost my husband, so I can understand what both of you have been through. I never expected to meet another man who could fill that void in my life, until I met your father. Having you come into my life as the son I never had makes me feel incredibly blessed." Laura had tears in her eyes when she hung up.

Chapter 36

E D AND Laura had to move quickly getting ready for the June wedding. She booked rooms at the Eden Springs Resort for her parents and her brother, who were coming down from Parkersburg for the big event. Robert remarked to her on the phone, "After hearing about what happened to you and your friends a couple of weeks ago, I think you ought to change the name of your town from Eden Springs to Dodge City. Should those of us coming to the wedding plan to wear guns?" Laura finally convinced him that guns were not part of the wedding plans.

Ed helped his parents make plans for their first trip up from St. Pete in several years, and cleared out the spare bedroom downstairs for them. "How about marking up an Esso road map for us showing the best route to take," Ed's dad requested. "We don't do much traveling these days."

When Ed approached Rev. Seymour, the minister willingly changed his plans for a week of vacation at Mountain Lake, in order to stay in town and conduct the wedding. He commented to Ed, with his usual dry sense of humor, "I hope you'll be able to stay awake while I'm performing the ceremony."

After both families arrived, a dinner was held at the Stafford Steakhouse. Ed and Doug quickly came to like Laura's parents and her brother. It was obvious that Laura had inherited much of her good nature and quick wit from her father. When she introduced him to Ed, the first thing he said after shaking hands was, "Well, I guess it isn't necessary for me to ask about your intentions toward my daughter, is it?"

Ed didn't miss a beat, replying, "No sir, I intend to marry her, and make her an honest woman." His future father-in-law broke into a wide grin of approval, and gave him a friendly pat on the shoulder.

Ed's folks were overjoyed at being reunited with their son and grandson. When they were introduced to Laura, both gave her a warm welcome to the family. "I've been hoping for years that Ed would find a lovely girl just like you," his mother confided. His dad could not take his eyes off Laura, clearly pleased with the new addition to the family.

The wedding took place in the sanctuary of the Eden Springs Methodist Church on Sunday afternoon, the first day of June. Laura's mother commented on the way to the church, "I think this beautiful weather on your wedding day is an omen of what a wonderful marriage you and Ed will have. Your dad and I were married on a sunny summer day just like this, and I wouldn't change a minute of the life we've had together."

Among those in attendance at the ceremony besides the immediate families, were Carolyn, Dr. Jannsen and his wife, the Vicelli family, Sam Barry, Doug's friends Mike, Ronnie, Freddie, and Wayne, and a few other close friends of the new bride and groom. Doug was best man, and Vickie was one of the bridesmaids. Laura was given in marriage by her father.

Waiting at the altar, Ed watched Laura come toward him, smiling, as the organist played the traditional wedding march. Dressed in an off-white suit, carrying a wedding bouquet, she looked lovlier than he had ever seen her before. When he took her hand, he could feel it tremble a bit in her mother's ivory lace glove.

The service went smoothly, with only one slight hitch, when Doug fumbled trying to retrieve the ring. When his fingers finally found it, those standing close by could hear him say with relief, "There it is."

When Rev. Seymour concluded the ceremony with, "I now pronounce you man and wife. You may kiss the bride," Ed embraced Laura, momentarily oblivious to the small circle of family and friends surrounding them.

A small reception was held on the lawn behind the church following the wedding ceremony. The guests settled into folding chairs under a shade tree, making it easy for Doug and his friends to sneak off and decorate Ed's freshly waxed Ford. They tied strings of tin cans and old shoes to the rear bumper of the car, and marked up the windows with white shoe polish.

When the reception ended, Ed and Laura ran hand in hand to the car through a shower of rice, waving goodbye. Cans and shoes clattered and thumped behind the car against the pavement as they went up the street, driving off together for a honeymoon at Myrtle Beach. "Just Married," could be seen printed on the windows in bold letters. Near the bottom of the rear window was the message, "Happy Motoring."

For a blissful week, the newlyweds stayed at the Sea Mist Motel, spending long hours swimming and walking the beach hand in hand, looking for shells and sharks teeth. In the evenings, they went out for seafood dinners, and downtown to the Pavilion and amusement park. By the time they were ready to leave, Laura's creamy complexion was sunburned a vivid red. "Coppertone just doesn't keep me from burning in this South Carolina sun. I guess it's the price you pay for being a gorgeous redhead," she joked.

"Lucille never seemed to have that trouble," Ed replied.

"Oh, Lord," Laura said, with a resigned sigh. "I'm going to spend the rest of my life competing with the ghost of a chicken."

The two drove back to West Virginia in high spirits at the end of the week, with the radio turned up loud, the windows cranked down, and the hot summer air blowing across their damp faces all the way.

Doug was playing with JR in the front yard, on the lookout for his dad's car, when they pulled into the driveway. He ran out to welcome them home, while JR bounded around in circles, barking to celebrate, as dogs do when they have absolutely no idea what's going on.

'I'm really glad to see y'all," Doug said, greeting them with big hugs. "It's been pretty quiet around here the past week with just the two of us. JR doesn't carry on a very good conversation, and I've finally gotten enough of the hamburgers at Gil's. Let me help carry your bags upstairs."

Watching Doug disappear in the house with her bag, and a having JR jump up on her with tail wagging, gave Laura a warm feeling that now she was part of the family. Looking at a house that she had never stayed in before, it suddenly seemed as though she had just come home. That feeling of belonging only increased in the days ahead.

Two weeks later, Ed and Dr. Jannsen brought Gideon Buchanan to court in a wheelchair for a mental competency hearing before Judge Wine. Gideon answered all of the questions put to him without difficulty and was ruled to be of sound mind, clearing the last obstacle for approval of his revised will and power of attorney.

During the following weeks, Ed continued to spend time supporting the DA in building a case against those who had conspired to harm the Buchanans. Agnes Harper became a star witness for the prosecution as part of the plea bargain. Hurd and Tolliver, acting upon the advice of appointed legal counsel, offered written confessions. Julian Grant was implicated for his role by sworn statements from the two accomplices, and by physical evidence.

But neither of the two ex-cons could be made to testify against Robert Barker or William Thorpe for their involvement in the conspiracy. Reluctantly, Jack Bradford dropped his attempts to indict both men.

After a short trial, the sale of the Buchanan farm by Julian Grant to Copperfield Enterprises was declared illegal, and the contract was declared void, restoring ownership of the 2500 acre farm to the Buchanan family.

Ed asked Dr. Jannsen to join him when he visited Roseanna to deliver the news to the Buchanans. Gathered in Gideon's bedroom, with both he and his wife seated in wheel chairs, and Daniel and Jonah standing beside them, Ed handed the deed for the farm to Gideon. "The last time we were in this room together was not a happy occasion," Ed began. "But today we can celebrate together, because this home and this land are yours again." He stopped, as Gideon and Hester both broke into tears of exhausted relief and gratitude. While the sons remained behind, comforting their parents, Ed and Dr. Jannsen quietly slipped away

Groundbreaking for the new Housman home took place near the end of August, just before Doug and his friends returned to Tyler High for their junior year. Ed, Laura, and Doug gathered between two widely spaced oak trees on top of the hill, looking across the valley toward Chestnut Ridge. "Your turn now," Laura said, handing the spade to Doug. Together the three dug a hole in the dark soil where the foundation would lie. A crew of builders started the next day, finishing just in time for Christmas.

After the movers unloaded the truck, Ed went back to town. Feeling more than a little nostalgic, he closed and locked the door of the old home for the last time. When he returned, Laura and Doug were waiting for him on the front porch in the crisp December air. Doug held the door, and Ed swept Laura up and carried her across the threshold into their sparkling new house, immersed in the smell of fresh paint and new carpeting.

That evening, the Housmans gathered among the sea of boxes and bags left behind by the movers and toasted their new home with wine of no particular vintage, in a collection of mismatched glasses. Soon, in Laura's grandmother's china cabinet, Louise's dogwood patterned china would mix with Laura's gold-rimmed service, in perfect harmony, as three lives would come together.

A week later, the family invited Vickie, Carolyn, and a few close friends for a party to decorate the Christmas tree, a tall white pine stretching all the way to the ceiling, in front of the picture window. Vickie was wearing Doug's red and white Tyler letter sweater that he had given her the week before, when they had decided to go steady.

A cold front had moved through the area earlier that day, leaving the air crystal clear. As the revelers stood at the window holding cups of eggnog, and peering across the valley in the direction of Chimney Rock, they could just make out in the distance the faint lights of the old mansion, Roseanna.

Epilogue

"You can feel the January chill in the air," Sam Barry exclaimed, turning toward Jack Barnes and Henry Claffey, as the three stopped to catch their breath under a massive red oak. "These gusts are blowing hard enough to make the mistletoe up at the top hang on with both hands.

"I'm glad the Buchanans left this lone tree standing on top of the hill to shelter us from the wind today. It must have been growing here since the Revolution, and somehow it managed to make it through the Civil War. I can picture Eleazar Buchanan standing under it on a hot summer day a hundred year ago, looking out over his land."

"I think that Daniel and Jonah did a remarkable job laying out their graveyard," Jack commented, looking about. "Grading this site with horse drawn equipment, and digging the graves with picks and shovels, was a mighty big job."

"Everything's pretty rustic, but that seems fitting for the victims of a Civil War battle," Henry added. "The chestnut rail fence and gate they built will still be here long after we're all gone. I think the marble headstones donated by the United Daughters of the Confederacy were a nice addition. After all, there are twelve Yanks buried here and only ten Rebs."

"This hill would be part of a strip mine if it weren't for the work of Ed Housman and Arnold Jannsen," Sam observed. "The two unsung heroes who saved this place will never get the recognition they deserve."

"There's been a lot written in the papers, but the Housman and Jannsen names don't seem to come up much," Jack agreed. "They're the two who stuck their necks out, and stopped Barker from taking over this entire valley. If they hadn't, we'd be looking at an entirely different scene, and it wouldn't be pretty."

"It's interesting how it all played out," he continued, moving so that his back was turned against the wind. "Myrtle Spencer's greed got her tangled up with two killers, and she paid with her life. Then Agnes Harper got involved the same way, but turned her life around, and came away with a suspended sentence."

"Grant paid the same price as Myrtle, but he deserved it more," Henry added. "And Hurd and Tolliver got what they had coming. With first degree murder convictions, they'll never see the light of day outside of Moundsville. But the really sad thing about this debacle is that the masterminds behind the conspiracy, Barker and Thorpe, walked away scott-free."

"I don't think they got away free," Sam interjected. "Barker lost a bundle of money, buying up all the land around here for far more than it's worth, and then getting checkmated by Housman and Jannsen on his plans for a strip mine. To a power-obsessed person like Barker, losing the fight over the land's a lot worse than dropping all that money. He's never had his butt whipped before, and he's going to have a lot of trouble living with it.

"The big winners are the Buchanans. Ed helped the family sell part of their stand of walnut and oak timber, which brought them a considerable amount of money. Some of it's already being used to restore Roseanna. And Ed's begun work on Gideon's dream of conserving the farm as a Civil War park after the family's gone."

"Something that's really bothered me," Jack remarked. "Why wasn't the district attorney able to pin any crimes on Barker and Thorpe while he was building his case against Hurd and Tolliver? Why couldn't he squeeze the truth out of those two ex-cons?"

"I can answer that one," Henry replied. "Hurd and Tolliver know that if they ever testify against Barker, they'll be found dead in their cells before the week is out. Barker's money gives him a very long reach, even inside the walls of Moundsville State Pen."

"I'm starting to get a little cold standing up here on top of this hill in the wind," Sam said, rubbing his hands together briskly. "Let's go back into town for lunch where it's warm."

"Sounds like a good idea to me," Jack replied, watching the chill air turn each breath into a brief wisp of fog.

"I like the idea of going somewhere warmer, myself," Henry said, zipping his jacket up tighter around his neck. "We've got a lot of planning to do for our new book."

As the three started to make their way down the wind-scoured slope, lost in their own thoughts, it seemed that the faint thread of a bugle call drifted through the restless branches of the old oak on the hill. But none of them felt sure enough to comment, and by the time they were sipping hot coffee in the café, the moment was quite forgotten.